MERRY
Mysteries

THE LOST NOEL

JO ANN BROWN

Guideposts

New York

Merry Mysteries is a trademark of Guideposts.

Published by Guideposts
110 William Street
New York, NY 10038
Guideposts.org

Cover and interior design by Müllerhaus
Cover illustration by Gail W. Guth at Guth Illustration & Design
Typeset by Aptara, Inc.

Printed and bound in the United States of America
10 9 8 7 6 5 4 3 2 1

✳ Chapter One

"Ivy Bay really knows how to do Christmas," Mary Fisher said as she drove with her sister, Betty Emerson, along Ivy Bay's Main Street. The windows of each shop were brightly lit and filled with seasonal scenes and speciality items.

Bright lights in the shape of snowmen and bells were draped in garlands across the street. Plastic candy canes hung from telephone poles over the sidewalks. These decorations had been stored away by thrifty town leaders and forgotten for almost fifty years before being rediscovered weeks ago at the back of the Department of Public Works barn. Now the retro decorations were back, front and center. During the day, the plastic looked a bit faded, but now after dark, they glowed as brightly as when they were first hung in the 1960s.

"It looks better this year than ever," Betty said.

"All we need is snow, and the town would look like a Christmas card." Mary braked as a mother and two young children stepped out from between the cars and hurried across the street. Their arms were filled with packages and bags from the shops. The mother gave a harried wave, then herded her kids onto the opposite sidewalk.

"Our children and the grandkids would like that," Betty said.

Mary stole a glance at her older sister. "I'm glad we're going to be together for Christmas this year."

"It's something we should have done years ago."

Mary laughed. "It hasn't been for a lack of trying. I'm glad that this year everyone's schedules have meshed." She put her hand gently on the sleeve of Betty's bright red cashmere sweater. "The house is going to be crowded and busy for the holidays. I hope it's not too much."

"Don't be silly." Betty's smile grew even wider. "I can't wait to have everyone there."

Mary knew that was true, but her sister hadn't been sleeping well and had stayed in bed very late this morning, a sure sign that Betty's rheumatoid arthritis was flaring up again. She sent up a quick prayer that Betty's chronic pain would ease enough to let her enjoy the holiday.

Betty had been busy with Grace Church's big Christmas project. For the first time, the church was presenting a living Nativity. Members of the church had been chosen for the various roles, and a bevy of talented seamstresses had been hard at work on the costumes. The living Nativity would begin tomorrow night and run until Christmas Eve.

Betty had been overseeing the project's details, and, while she loved every minute of it, the long hours were exacting a

toll on her. That was why Mary had offered to take her into
Hyannis earlier this afternoon to finish up her Christmas shopping. The shops along Main Street in Hyannis offered a variety
of unique gifts, and it had been fun to look at the Christmas
decorations there. They'd shopped a little bit, then stopped for
lunch at a pizzeria before heading back to Ivy Bay.

As they passed her bookstore, called Mary's Mystery
Bookshop, Mary glanced in the windows and saw several
customers inside along with Rebecca Mason, who stood by
the cash register. Once Mary dropped off Betty at church,
she would head back to the shop and help Rebecca close
up. The shop didn't usually stay open late, but in the week
before Christmas, the shops in Ivy Bay were keeping
longer hours. In addition, she and Rebecca with help from
Ashley, Rebecca's young daughter, were planning an event
for the afternoon of Christmas Eve. The centerpiece would
be a reading of *A Visit from St. Nicholas* in the children's section of the bookshop.

Mary had moved to Ivy Bay and opened the bookshop
after retiring from her job as a librarian in Boston. It was
a dream she'd had her entire life, and sometimes she still
couldn't believe the store was *hers.*

Mary slowed, then turned onto Water Street. On their
right, the church was brightly illuminated inside and out.
Now that the leaves had fallen from the trees, the stained-
glass windows shone even more brilliantly. The vane at the
top of the spire was silhouetted against the full moon. Every
line was crisp and clear on the cold night.

She smiled when she thought about how her late husband, John, had called nights like this "an extra-log-on-the-fire night." When their children, Jack and Lizzie, were small, they had started a fire on the hearth and sipped hot chocolate after turning off the lamps, so the only lights in the room came from the Christmas tree and Jack and Lizzie's wide eyes. Those precious memories seemed even sweeter now that John was gone.

As they passed the church to pull into the parking lot, Mary caught sight of the stable backdrop being built by Kip Hastings. The handyman had been working on it for the past week whenever he could find time.

"Looks like it's almost done," Betty said as Mary flipped the turn signal and eased into the parking lot. "I wonder what Kip decided to do about hanging a star over the stable."

"I'm sure he's got some good ideas." Mary pulled into a parking spot and turned off the car. "He often does."

Betty opened her door. As she climbed out, she pulled on her coat. The chilly, damp air made the breeze off the bay slice through to the bone. "If it's going to be this cold, it might as well snow."

"I agree." Mary closed her door and shrugged on her own heavy coat. "Let's get inside."

"I want to check how far along Kip's gotten." Betty took a step toward the front of the church, then paused and bent down to pick up a crumpled page. "What's this?"

"I guess litterbugs don't worry about the cold. Do you want me to take that and throw it out for you?"

Betty didn't answer. Her forehead furrowed as she smoothed open the page. She tilted it to allow light from the church to wash over the lettering on it. "This is one of the posters announcing the living Nativity. Look! It's been torn down."

Mary took it. Her sister was right. The top of the page had been ripped.

"There hasn't been much wind today," Mary said. "Nothing strong enough to tear this off a telephone pole."

"Then someone must have done it. Why would anyone want to tear down posters for the living Nativity?"

Mary shook her head. "Let's not jump to conclusions. Just because it's torn on the top doesn't mean anyone pulled it down. All we can be sure of is that it was torn off the pole."

"Must you always sound like Sherlock Holmes?" Betty's good humor returned as she laughed. "Or should I say your favorite, Miss Marple?"

"She's one of my favorites, for sure, but right now I'm enjoying Agatha Christie's *The Adventure of the Christmas Pudding*. That's a Hercule Poirot story."

"Does Dame Agatha have a story for every season?" asked Betty as she folded the page and stuffed it in her pocket.

"It seems so. Let's go and see the stable, so we can get inside and warm up."

Mary zipped her coat and pulled her gloves out of her pockets as she went with Betty around the church toward the front lawn. Her sister's motions were stiff, but Mary knew Betty wouldn't give in to her pain when anyone might see.

A hammer rapped sharply several times as they walked to the simple open-sided building that would serve as the stable. It was big enough to allow several people to stand inside, and the sides were splayed outward to allow a better view from the sidewalk. Something moved in the darkness closer to the driveway, catching Mary's eye.

"Look! It's a real sheep." She paused by the simple slatted pen and looked at the horns that curled on both sides of the sheep's head. They seemed pretty sharp on the ends, so she didn't reach over and pat the sheep's wooly back.

"Isn't that great?" her sister asked. "When we put word out that we'd like real animals as part of the living Nativity, we got several calls. In addition to this sheep, we have chickens being delivered tomorrow afternoon. Maybe even a cow." Betty chuckled. "A fully outfitted stable."

"That's wonderful."

The sheep continued eating the hay spread out on the ground, paying them no attention. Its wool, which was thick with the onset of winter, seemed bright white in the light from the church. Someone must have cleaned it up in preparation for its role in the living Nativity, because not a single burr clung to it.

"Hi!" called Kip from where he was squatting down, putting the finishing touches on the simple manger. He had the fuzzy flaps of his cap down over his ears, and a single brown curl of hair popped out on one side of his cap. He pushed himself to his feet as they approached. "What do you think?"

"It looks perfect, Kip," Mary said.

"Perfect?" He laughed. "I wouldn't go that far, but the roof won't fall in on our church members, and the manger is strong enough to support a real baby if it's not too cold on Christmas Eve. As long we don't get a strong nor'easter, the stable should hold up fine. Once I get the donation box done, we'll be good to go." He pointed to another man who was leaning over something on the ground. "Have you met Luis Alvarez? He's helping me get the lighting wired right."

Luis raised his head and smiled when Kip introduced them. Straight black hair fell into his eyes, and he shoved it aside with a quick motion. He wore a dark parka over jeans. He stood and pulled off soiled work gloves, sticking them in his back pocket.

"Hi, ladies. Nice to meet you," he said as they shook hands. "We should be ready for the first full test of the lights in about ten minutes."

"Is it that complicated?" Mary asked.

"Mrs. Johnson wants to be able to highlight various parts of the scene at different times."

Mary exchanged a glance with her sister. Dorothy Johnson refused to be left out of any project at the church. Some members found that annoying, but Betty had mentioned several times in the past week what good ideas Dorothy had for the living Nativity.

"I hope it hasn't been too much extra work," Betty said.

Luis chuckled. "At least Mrs. Johnson knows what she wants right from the get-go, so we haven't had to make many changes. It's made the work easier in the long run."

Kip clapped Luis on the shoulder. "It helps that we've got the best electrician on the Cape for this project. We're lucky you could take some time away from your neighborhood's lighting contest to help here, Luis. I don't think our Bethlehem star would have shone very brightly if I was doing this by myself."

"Glad to help," Luis said as he knelt back down to continue working.

As Mary was turning to go to the back of the church and the fellowship hall in the cellar, she paused and looked back at Kip. "You haven't forgotten that I need you to come over to the bookshop to fix that drip in the bathroom sink, have you?" She laughed. "A couple of my customers have complained that the sound intrudes on their riffling through the books while they figure out which ones they want to read."

He grinned. "I thought Henry was going to handle that for you."

Mary shook her head. Henry Woodrow was a dear friend, and he often handled small fixes at the bookshop. She could always depend on him, but sometimes he took on more than he could manage by saying yes to too many people, so she tried not to ask too often.

"He's got an unexpected charter this week," she said. "Must be someone home for the holidays. No local would want to go out on the Bay when it's this cold."

"True." Kip rubbed his chin with the back of his fingers. "I may not be able to get over before Christmas. We're going out of town to visit friends for a few days. Can it wait until after Christmas?"

"Yes. With last-minute shoppers, this week nobody could describe the shop as being so quiet that you can hear dripping water."

He gave her a slow grin. "Sounds doable, then."

"Great. Now I'm getting out of the cold." She put her arms around herself and gave an exaggerated shudder.

"I'm set here, Kip," Luis said, standing again. "It's secured down so nobody should trip over the wires."

Mary saw that Luis had placed wide strips of rubber over the wires, holding them together and making the location easy to see even in the dark. "That's a good idea."

"Kip's actually." Luis pulled a packet of wet wipes out of his other back pocket. He gestured with it toward Kip. "Want one?"

"Naw," Kip replied. "I'll go in and wash up in the church."

"All right. You go ahead. You know I'm set here." He started to clean his hands with the moist towelette.

Betty gave him a curious glance. Mary saw it, and Luis must have, too, because he gulped and wadded the towelette in his hand.

"It's nothing against your church, ladies," he said quickly. "I can't use unfamiliar soap. A lot of soaps have lanolin in them, and I'm allergic to lanolin."

"Then you'd better avoid the sheep over there." Kip's eyes twinkled with merriment.

Betty nodded. "Back in the old days, ladies used to rub their hands on the back of sheep to make their skin soft."

"Good thing I'm not a lady." When Luis laughed, Mary and Betty joined in with him and Kip.

Wishing them a good night, Mary and Betty went back around the church. The sliding doors to the cellar were closed but opened easily when Mary pushed on them. She let her sister precede her, then slid the doors closed again.

She was struck by both heat and noise. As she slipped off her coat and folded it over her arm, she frowned. "What's going on?"

"It sounds like there's a debate being held in the fellowship hall," Betty said. "I wonder what's up."

Instead of answering, Mary hurried toward the fellowship hall. The voices rose to a higher pitch as she paused in the doorway.

The room was crowded with everyone who had worked on the living Nativity during the past two weeks. Pastor Frank Miles and church member Dorothy Johnson stood by the tables that had been pushed into a long line in the center of the room.

To the right, the "actors" were gathered. Many of them were high school students who'd volunteered for the various roles because they seemed less bothered by the cold than their elders. Most would be out only one or two evenings, but some had signed up to participate more often. Brian Flanagan, who would be their Joseph, stood with his back against the wall and his arms folded in front of him. He was more than six feet tall and so skinny he looked like he could slip through a straw. His face was as white as the sheep, but color returned to it slightly when his mother, Mavis, came over and patted his shoulder. He nodded and shifted his backpack to his other side.

Seeing Mary and Betty, Mavis started toward them. She was the opposite of her son: short, quite pudgy, and her hair was a pale blonde. Mary had heard that she had studied at the Crane School of Music, the prestigious program in northern New York. Grace Church was lucky to have her skills with music and people, and she had been the choir director since she moved to Ivy Bay twenty years ago. She had been pleased when Brian was selected to play Joseph.

Mavis halted in mid-step when someone called out, "Attention, people! Attention!" The voice belonged to Hannah Titus, who'd overseen the seamstresses making the living Nativity's costumes. A brash, round woman with her dark brown hair twisted in wild corkscrews, she wore a collection of bracelets that jangled with every motion, making Mary wonder what it sounded like when she was sewing.

The ladies around the table quieted down, but nobody else did until Pastor Miles spoke to the people gathered close to him. Slowly silence trickled through the room.

"There has to be an answer to this," Pastor Miles said once the room was quiet.

Mary wanted to ask what he was talking about, but pushed down her impatience. If she spoke, others might jump in, too, with their questions. She saw many puzzled faces in the room. The high school kids looked as distressed as their parents.

Pastor Miles went on, "Before we jump to any conclusions–"

"Too late for that," muttered someone to Mary's left. She didn't see who it was because several others quickly hushed the speaker.

"We need to make an organized search," the pastor said as if nobody had interrupted.

Mary's impatience couldn't be held back any longer. "Search for what?"

Hannah Titus put her hands on her full hips as she whirled to face Mary and Betty. "The living Nativity costumes. They've vanished."

✳ Chapter Two

Betty gasped. "Vanished? What do you mean?"

Hannah swept a bangled arm toward the tables. "They were right here. Now they're gone. We're going to have to cancel the living Nativity if we don't find the costumes."

Mary was tempted to roll her eyes like one of the kids. Hannah didn't need to be so melodramatic. Even if there were no costumes, anyone who came to the church and saw the volunteers by the makeshift stable would understand the meaning and joy of the season.

Then sympathy rushed through her. Hannah and the other seamstresses had worked hard, and they probably couldn't imagine the show going on without the costumes.

"How could they vanish?" Betty asked into the silence that followed Hannah's pronouncement.

Instantly more than a dozen people began talking as they tried to answer Betty's question. It took Mary several seconds to sort out the story.

The finished costumes had been laid out on the tables in the center of the fellowship hall. The various church members playing the roles were supposed to try them on one more time tonight to make sure everything was right. Then the seamstresses under Hannah's watch would give the costumes any final adjustments and iron them and hang them up so they'd be ready for tomorrow evening. Everything had been exactly as it should be...until they discovered the costumes were gone.

"When is the last time anyone saw the costumes?" Pastor Miles asked. Waving his hands to halt the explosion of answers, he said, "One at a time, please." He turned to the head seamstress. "Hannah, when did you last see them?"

"About 4:30 this afternoon."

"That's close to two hours ago," Mary said to her sister as Pastor Miles asked if anyone had seen them after Hannah did.

Nobody answered for a moment, then Felicity Andrews, the teenager who was scheduled to play Mary tomorrow night, said, "I stopped by about fifteen minutes to five. I'd promised to bring in the hand-warmers we use when we go to New England Patriots home games." She looked around, suddenly abashed that everyone was watching her. Her voice took on a defensive tone. "I had to pick up some of the other kids, and I didn't want to have someone sit on them."

"It's okay," Mary said. "Nobody's accusing anyone of anything."

"That's right," Pastor Miles said. "We're just trying to get our facts straight. Felicity was here at 4:45. Anyone after that?"

Heads swiveled back and forth to see if anyone would answer, but no one did.

"So we know the costumes vanished sometime between 4:45 and when people returned here at…" She looked at Hannah.

"About six o'clock," the seamstress said.

Mary did a quick calculation. In an hour and a quarter, there would have been plenty of time for someone to move all the costumes. She looked around the room. Could the person who moved them be here right now? Why? And with all the drama, would that person dare to admit what he or she had done?

"All right, people!" Clapping her hands, Dorothy Johnson stepped forward. Even though she wasn't tall, she commanded everyone's attention. Probably because each person in the room had worked with her on one project or another at the church, and they knew she was good in a crisis.

"We need to find the costumes. Now," Dorothy announced. "You and you." She pointed to two of the teenagers. "You can start searching in the closets near the furnace room." As they dropped their backpacks on a nearby table and hurried out the door, she began to divide everyone else up in groups. She told each group where to look in the church.

Mary didn't wait for Dorothy to get to her. Instead, she took her sister gently by the arm and steered Betty to a chair near the tables where scraps of fabric and bits of thread were the only sign that the costumes ever existed.

Mary noticed that many of the threads ran off the table in the same direction. The rest were curled up as if they'd been caught in a whirlpool. At first glance, that seemed to suggest that someone must have scooped the dozen costumes up and carried them out in one large armful. But she knew better than to trust something at first glance.

"How could this happen?" Betty asked, shocked.

"Maybe the costumes were moved by mistake," Mary said, though she wondered how that could be true.

"If someone moved the costumes, why doesn't that person speak up?" asked Betty as Mary eased her down on the folding chair.

Mary didn't reply. All she could offer were platitudes, and they were useless now. But she was as perplexed as her sister. Who would have moved the costumes?

Everyone involved with the living Nativity had been in the fellowship hall. Even Kip and Luis had come in to see what the hubbub was about. They stood to one side of the door, looking as if they wished they were back outside working. They hurried out when Dorothy shooed them from the room and urged them to finish the scenery and lights.

"Mrs. Fisher!" Ashley Mason ran to where Mary stood. The little girl was the daughter of Mary's assistant at the bookshop and had become a regular fixture there and in Mary's heart.

Now Ashley's eyes were bright with tears, and Mary put her arm around the little girl.

"My angel costume was so very, very pretty," Ashley said, her voice breaking on each word. "It had big white wings that sparkled. Now all I have is this." She held up a halo covered with glitter. "Mom made it for me. Without wings, will I ever get to be an angel?"

"Let's hope so." Mary didn't want to make a promise to the little girl that couldn't be kept. She felt bad, because she'd asked Rebecca if Ashley could be one of the angels, even though the Masons weren't members of Grace Church. She'd thought Ashley would enjoy dressing up, but now...As she bent to give Ashley a hug, her eyes were caught by something under the table. "What's that?"

Ashley looked to where Mary was pointing. She handed the halo to Betty in a shower of glitter, then dropped to her hands and knees. Crawling under the table between two chairs, she came back out and held up her hand.

Two things sat on her palm. Mary took them and examined both. One was a spool with a small length of purple thread, and the other was a thimble. The thimble was a dull gray, and Mary guessed that any shine had been worn away by long use. Tipping the thimble over, she saw a couple of scratches inside. She wasn't sure if they were supposed to mean something or were left from the thimble being taken on and off a lot.

"People! People! Work with me here!" called Dorothy. She was having a tougher time getting the attention of the adults. When she selected teams to search together, several people disagreed. Voices popped up quickly and were talked

MERRY MYSTERIES * 18

over by so many other voices that Mary couldn't identify all
of them.

But she recognized Hannah Titus's voice when it rose
over the others. Hannah wrung her hands in despair. "Why
are you standing here? We should call the police right away."
She swept her purse off the table and onto a chair. She pulled
it open. Groping inside, she frowned. "I must have left my
phone at home. Can I use someone else's? Or will someone
go across the street and get a cop to come over here?"

Mary said, "I don't think calling the police now will do
anything to help. The first question they're going to ask is if
we checked to make sure that the costumes weren't moved
somewhere else in the church." She looked at Pastor Miles
for his help in calming Hannah's near-panic.

"Mary's right," he said walking over to the seamstresses.
"Once we've searched, we'll know better what to do. Let's
look in every nook and cranny of this old church."

"But, Pastor, my team worked hard on those costumes!"
Hannah hid her face in her hands, and her voice began to
crack. "They are just so beautiful."

He put his hands on Hannah's shoulders. When she looked
up, he gazed straight into her eyes. His voice was gentle and
compassionate as he said, "Anyone who's seen the work you
ladies have put into these costumes knows it's been a labor of
love and faith. Now have a bit more faith that we can find them."

For a long moment, Mary thought Hannah wouldn't listen to common sense. Then Hannah nodded. "You're right,
Pastor Miles."

"Good." He smiled, then held out his hands. "Shall we ask for God's guidance in our search?"

Mary bent her head with others and, after setting the thimble and spool on the nearest table, took both Ashley and Betty by the hand.

"Lord," Pastor Miles said, "You see all, and You know why the costumes have disappeared. If it is Your will, lead us to the missing costumes. Reach into the heart of the person responsible for their disappearance so that person knows we always forgive a mistake."

After she said, "Amen" along with the others, Mary looked back at Betty, who was rising from the chair. "Why don't you stay here, Betty? You can be our coordinator."

Dorothy opened her mouth to protest.

Mary smiled at her. "With Betty sitting here, each group can come back and tell her where they've searched. If there are any places we've missed, then she can send them out. Once the costumes are found…" She made sure neither her face nor her voice suggested that wouldn't happen. And if the person who'd moved them was present, maybe once Pastor Miles's prayer settled into that person's heart, he or she would come forward and be honest. She looked back at Dorothy. "Then Betty can send out the word to everyone. That way, nobody wastes time looking where someone else has or after the costumes are found."

"An excellent idea," Pastor Miles said, then went to speak to Hannah.

Betty gave him a weak smile, and Mary knew her sister was feeling even worse than she'd let on. Dear Betty!

She'd put in long hours on the living Nativity, and now her gift to the church might be for naught. Tears pricked Mary's eyes. She was going to do whatever she could to try to keep the living Nativity from being canceled. She resisted her urge to give Betty a hug. Doing that could cause her sister more pain.

Bending toward Betty, she whispered, "Just keep an eye on that thimble on the table. It was underneath the table, and it may have fallen there unnoticed when the costumes were moved. If someone comes to claim it, let me know."

"You think it's a clue?" Betty asked as quietly.

"Dame Agatha's sleuth always considers everything a clue until it's proved not to be. How can we do otherwise?"

That brought a brighter smile to her sister's face.

When Dorothy asked Mary to look in the storage rooms behind the organ and the baptismal font, Mary turned to Ashley, who stood to one side, holding her halo tight to her heart.

"Will you be on my team, Ashley?" Mary asked. "We're going to need to look high and low."

"I'll do the low while you do the high!" The little girl bounced from one foot to the other in excitement.

"I'm not sure how high I can reach. I'm not very tall."

"You're taller than I am. How about I do the low and you do the higher?"

Mary smiled. "Sounds like a plan. We're going to be a perfect team."

"Can I bring my halo?"

Mary put her arm around Ashley's shoulders and gave them a gentle squeeze. "Of course!"

As they went out of the fellowship hall and climbed the stairs to the church's main floor, voices came from every direction. The sound was distorted because people were inside small spaces or looking in closets. Dorothy really must know each inch of the church, because she'd sent people everywhere.

Mary and Ashley walked through the choir room where Felicity and Brian were searching. When Mary asked if they'd found any sign of the costumes, Felicity said, "No." Brian shook his head and repeated her short answer before continuing to search the room. Unlike the other teens, he still toted his backpack easily over one shoulder.

"Maybe you'll find them in this room," Mary said.

"And if we don't?" Felicity asked.

"We're supposed to head back down to the fellowship hall and see if Dorothy has another place for us to look."

"Okay," Felicity said.

Brian nodded as he shifted the choir robes and peered behind them.

Mary opened the door to the storage room at the back of the sanctuary. She switched on the light. The room was lined on both sides with white cupboards.

"Why don't you try that side?" Mary asked, pointing to the left. "I'll look on this side."

Ashley opened a door and quickly began removing stacks of hymnals. Standing on tiptoe, she looked over the rest of the books.

"Nothing back here," she said.

Mary turned from opening the upper doors and peering into the cupboards that were only deep enough for a single stack of books. "You don't need to take out everything. Remember how big that pile of costumes was? They can't be squashed into a teeny space."

"That's right!" Ashley grinned. She put the books back and looked into other storage spaces.

Dust sprayed into Mary's face when she shoved aside some choir robes that weren't used any longer. She sneezed, then kept searching.

When Ashley met her at the back of the room, the little girl frowned. "Nothing."

"Don't get discouraged," Mary said, though she understood the feeling all too well. "We still have the other room to check once I look in a few more of these cupboards."

"I'm done with the low part. Can I go to the other room now?"

"It's right across the hall."

"See ya." With a wave of her fingers, the little girl was gone.

Within a couple of minutes, Mary closed the last upper door and went to the door. She turned off the light. No sign of the costumes here. She headed toward the room across the hall. Already she could hear Ashley opening and closing cupboard drawers.

She paused for a moment to admire the dimly lit sanctuary. It looked beautiful in preparation for Christmas.

Battery-operated candles were set on the windowsills in circles of holly and ivy. Greens hung from the pews and draped over the pulpit. Poinsettias were a bright splash of red near the organ and altar. She wondered if Dorothy had sent anyone to search the sanctuary. If she and Ashley didn't have any luck, she'd check with Betty and Dorothy and suggest coming back here.

She walked past the exquisite Nativity set on top of the baptismal font. Betty had told her that it had been made in Germany many years ago. The tallest porcelain figures were almost a foot high. Painted by an expert, each face had a unique expression and skin tones. The Virgin Mary's face was softened with love and awe for the miracle she was a part of. Joseph's expression was one of quiet determination to take care of the precious responsibility entrusted to him by God. The shepherds either stood with a lamb hoisted over their shoulders or knelt before the manger. Most of the figures wore simple clothing, but the Magi's robes glowed with jewel tones to match the gold of the halo around the baby's head.

Whoever had designed it spent as much time on the individual animals as the people. The cow and the donkey were focused on the Holy Child. Each of the three camels that brought the Wise Men to Bethlehem looked in a different direction. She saw one of the Wise Men in the stable. Another figure was on its side behind the manger. She picked it up and saw it was a wingless angel. She put the misplaced Wise Man with his camel and set the angel on the roof of the stable where it could gaze directly at the altar.

She scanned the floor but didn't see its wings. She'd mention it to Pastor Miles when she got back to the fellowship hall.

"Mrs. Fisher?" Ashley called from the other storage room.

"Coming." With a last glance at the stable roof to make sure the angel was secure, Mary went to where Ashley stood in the doorway. "Did you find something?"

"A *lot* of boxes!"

Mary looked past the little girl and saw the reason for Ashley's frustrated tone. In a large closet at the back of the room, packing boxes were stacked almost to the ceiling. On the side of each one was a label listing the sheet music stored inside it.

"We don't have to move all those, do we?" Ashley asked.

"If someone did hide the costumes, there wasn't enough time to move the boxes and put them back between when Felicity was here and Hannah returned. I think we're safe to leave them be."

"Good." She hurried over and closed the double doors, then continued to look under tables and behind stacks of folded tablecloths.

Mary peeked into the top drawers of a pair of dressers that had been pushed beneath two small windows. More sheet music and tablecloths filled both of them.

A strange rumble filled the air. Mary looked over her shoulder.

"It sounds like a vacuum," Ashley said.

"That's what I thought, but who...?" Instead of finishing her question, Mary walked out in the sanctuary.

In the center aisle, Dorothy was furiously cleaning the carpet.

Mary, with Ashley following, went to where Dorothy worked without noticing them. The upright vacuum slid over the floor, picking up streaks of dirt and sparkling glitter. Mary waited until the other woman looked up, then made a motion for Dorothy to turn off the vacuum cleaner.

"Find anything?" asked Dorothy.

"Some dust bunnies," Mary said, and Ashley giggled. "Why are you vacuuming *now*?"

"I was searching in the prayer chapel, and I noticed the mess over here. I wanted to get it cleaned up before the dried mud got ground into the carpet or tracked up onto the altar." She leaned one hand on the top of the vacuum and shook her head. "I wonder if either Kip or Luis thought about wiping their feet before they tramped through here to get to the electrical box." Looking at Ashley, she added, "Why don't you take that halo back to the fellowship hall? We don't need more glitter on the floor."

Ashley nodded. "Is that okay, Mrs. Fisher?"

"Go ahead. I bet your mother will be looking for you down there soon."

"Uh-oh!" Ashley took off at a run, more glitter falling off the halo as she hurried back up the aisle toward the Christmas tree that was bedecked with mittens and socks.

Every year Grace Church had a gift tree. Requests for help were written on a slip of white paper and hung from the branches, and the parishioners could select one and make that dream come true. When a wish was taken, a pair of mittens or brightly colored socks were put on the branch to show how many dreams were being fulfilled. Last Sunday, Mary had noticed there wasn't a single white paper left. Today, she was relieved to see that none of the mittens and socks seemed to be missing.

"Has anyone found the costumes or any hint of what might have happened to them?" Mary asked.

"Not that I've heard of." Dorothy reached for the switch on the vacuum. "Let me get this finished up. We're supposed to be meeting back in the fellowship hall soon, and I want to make sure this is cleaned up. Men! They never seem to think about little things like dirt on their shoes."

The vacuum's rumble halted Mary's answer. As she went up the aisle, she was amazed anew at how Dorothy's kind heart was hidden too often behind a prickly exterior. Even in the midst of the uproar over missing costumes, Dorothy thought about small details that others might have overlooked.

Ten minutes later, everyone, including Kip, had gathered again in the fellowship hall. The dejected faces told Mary that the search had been futile.

Even so, Pastor Miles asked, "Betty, what can you tell us?"

"No one found the costumes," Betty said, blinking back tears.

Hannah let out a groan, and the seamstresses sank onto chairs around the table. Mary saw that the thimble remained exactly where she'd left it. Either nobody had noticed it, or it didn't belong to anyone in the room. She'd check with Betty to see if anyone had stopped to look at it or comment on it.

"Someone must have stolen them," Hannah said, waving her arms around to the jangle of silver and beaded bracelets.

"Do you think they were taken by the person who let the sheep out?" asked Felicity from among the teenagers.

Everyone whirled to face her, and her face turned a bright red.

"The sheep is gone?" Kip asked into the shocked silence.

"But it was in its pen when I helped Luis load his tools into his truck. And it was there when I came back around to the stable to make sure I got all of *my* tools."

"It may have found a way to get out and wandered away," Pastor Miles said. "Will some of you kids go out and see if you can find it before it gets hit by a car?"

Several boys ran out along with three girls.

"But what if someone let it out?" asked Hannah, her hands clasped tightly on the table. "Maybe it was the same person who's torn down all our living Nativity posters."

"*All* our posters?" Betty pulled the wrinkled one out of her pocket. "You mean this isn't the only one that's been torn down?"

Dorothy came into the fellowship hall. "They're missing all over Ivy Bay."

Mary shared a glance with her sister as everyone again began talking at once. When they'd found the torn poster in the parking lot, she hadn't wanted to believe that it'd been ripped down intentionally. Who would want to sabotage the living Nativity? And why? The living Nativity was a gift to the community, and Kip was building a donations box to collect money for two Cape Cod homeless shelters.

Missing costumes, a sheep that had disappeared, and their posters being torn down…Three separate incidents that all connected back to the living Nativity. Had someone done this solely to halt the living Nativity, or for another reason?

One of the teen boys came back in to report that there was a small gap between the boards on the pen. The sheep must have gotten out that way, but it was so small a cat would have trouble squeezing through.

"Isn't it time to call the cops *now*?" Hannah came to her feet and slammed her fist on the table.

The thimble bounced and rolled to the edge of the table. Carla Donahue, one of the seamstresses, caught it. She didn't even glance at it as she set it in the middle of the table again.

Walking over to where Hannah sat, Mary said, "If we call the police, they're only going to tell us to do what we're already doing."

"We're not doing anything."

"Yes, we're looking for the costumes, and we're trying to get the sheep back in its pen."

"And," said Mavis, "we'll plaster the town with more posters. We'll put up so many that they'll give up trying to get them down."

Laughter met her words.

But Hannah wasn't laughing. "Posters for what?" she moaned. "Without costumes, we can't have a living Nativity."

Pastor Miles sighed, then said, "We still have almost twenty-four hours before the living Nativity is supposed to start. Let's not throw in the towel yet."

Hannah turned away to talk to her seamstresses, as Dorothy walked over to Mary.

"It looks like we've got a real mystery," Dorothy said.

"One without a lot of clues."

Dorothy waved her hand. "Don't worry about it, Mary. I know you've got your children and grandchildren coming in for Christmas. Leave it to me. Perhaps this is one mystery that *I* can solve." Her smile was cool.

"I hope one of us does. If we share any information we discover–"

"Of course, I'll share everything I discover."

"As will I. It's always good to have another perspective on the clues, and I appreciate your offering to help figure out what happened to the costumes. You're right. With my family coming in, I'm not going to have a lot of extra time to chase down clues." Mary honestly was glad to have Dorothy's help, especially when it wasn't that long until Christmas.

Pastor Miles called them all together to pray for God to reach into the hearts of those who took the items and bring them peace. When Dorothy added a prayer for God to guide them to an answer, Mary smiled and silently said, "Amen."

✳ Chapter Three

T he next morning, Mary came down the stairs of the house
she shared with Betty. It was Betty's house, really, where
she had lived with her late husband and raised her son, Evan,
but she had been generous enough to open her home to Mary
when Mary decided to move to Ivy Bay. Mary loved living with
her sister again and getting to spend precious time with her.
They had fun together, but they also took care of each other.

Mary entered the kitchen, relieved to see Betty awake
and making breakfast early. Her sister still moved tentatively
but was determined to be up and around to greet Mary's children and grandchildren when they arrived that afternoon.
Wisely, Mary's cat, Gus, avoided the kitchen. Somehow, he
sensed when Betty was hurting and made himself scarce.
Having Mary's family here would make it up to him, if he
would deign to let them pet him.

"Could you pick up some milk and more coffee while
you're out this morning?" Betty asked. "We're getting low on
both."

"Be glad to."

Betty chuckled. "You've got three mysterious events, and nothing will keep you from trying to figure out the answer before Dorothy does."

"If she finds the answer first, it won't matter."

Again Betty laughed. "You can say that because she's never really tried to solve a mystery with you before."

"There's always a first time."

"I'll believe that when I see it."

Mary enjoyed her sister's better spirits while they ate breakfast. She added a few items to the shopping list and headed out to her bookshop.

As soon as she unlocked the door and walked inside to the tinkle of the chime that sounded whenever the door was opened or shut, Mary savored the scents of books and ink and old wood that had been polished by many different hands through the years. The familiar creak of the wide pine boards matched her steps as she walked around the specials table that was now topped with a variety of Christmas-themed mysteries. She had also added some cookbooks and decorating books that featured both Christmas and mystery writers. A tree waited to be lit in the children's section, each of the ornaments created by local children to celebrate some of their favorite stories.

She could imagine a large gathering of kids listening to the reading of *A Visit from St. Nicholas*. Those wide eyes filled with wonder and anticipation that maybe, just maybe, this year they would awake and find Santa Claus filling the stockings at their house.

She switched on the lights and picked up a feather duster. Running it along the books and shelves, she'd just reached the back of the shop when the door opened. She looked around the shelf and smiled when she heard, "It's just me, Mary."

Rebecca Mason shrugged off her coat and draped it over her arm. She had one of those faces that made everyone an instant friend, and her heart was just as warm. Mary thanked God for bringing this young woman and her family into her life.

Taking off her knit cap, Rebecca laughed and tried to smooth down her static-filled hair. "Bad hair day," she said as she put her coat away and booted up the computer. "Cold and dry is the best recipe for a bad hair day."

Mary walked back to the counter. "How's Ashley doing? She was pretty upset last night."

"She was." Rebecca pulled up a stool and sat. "Were the costumes ever found?"

"No, or not the last I heard."

"That's really bizarre." Rebecca tapped a couple of keys, then shook her head. "Those books we ordered last month are still listed as on back order."

"If they don't get here by tomorrow, we might as well cancel the order. Christmas books don't sell the day after Christmas." Mary smiled before putting away the feather duster. "Did you have a chance to go into Sweet Susan's and drop off the order for refreshments for the Christmas reading?"

"Took care of it yesterday, and my Mrs. Claus costume is almost finished."

"Great. Why don't you put the *Open* sign up? Maybe we'll get a few early morning shoppers."

But the morning was so quiet that, while she unpacked a box of books that had arrived the previous afternoon, Mary's thoughts turned again to the puzzles that she couldn't get out of her mind. She didn't realize how obvious her distraction was until Rebecca laughed.

"You've told me the title of that book three times now," her assistant said. "I'd ask if something's on your mind, but I don't have to."

"You know how I am with a mystery. I can't let it go until I can figure out what's going on."

"Anything I can do to help?"

Mary was about to shake her head, then said, "If you don't mind finishing unpacking and shelving these books, I think I'll go run some errands."

"And chase down some clues."

"Or find some to begin with."

"Go ahead. I'm glad for the overtime now."

Mary guessed that Rebecca had asked for the extra work hours because she hoped to buy Ashley something special for Christmas. Mary had seen a couple of catalogs showing Victorian-style dollhouses that Rebecca had hurriedly stashed away. Mary hadn't asked any questions. Secrets were part of the fun of the holidays.

But not secrets like who had taken the costumes or what had happened to the sheep or why someone was tearing down posters for the living Nativity. Who would want to halt the living Nativity? And why? The latter question was more puzzling than the first. She couldn't imagine why anyone would be upset enough at the living Nativity to try to keep it from going on.

Going out to her car, Mary drove to Luis Alvarez's neighborhood. Maybe he had seen something odd that could give her a hint to at least one of the puzzles. Last night, after she'd said her prayers, sleep eluded her. She kept hearing Kip saying how the sheep had been there when he helped Luis pack up his tools and Dorothy mentioning how the men must have tracked dirt into the church. Nobody among the living Nativity participants admitted to being down in the fellowship hall for the hour between when Felicity stopped by and the costumes were discovered to be missing. That meant Luis could have had access to both the costumes and to the sheep when nobody else was around. Yes, the sheep had been there when Kip returned to get his tools, but the two men had worked together long enough so they'd know each other's habits. Luis could have waited for Kip to finish and gone back into the church before he released the sheep. He had been wearing work gloves that would protect him from the lanolin.

But, of course, the sheep could have wandered off on its own. She was sure of one thing. She was glad she had persuaded Hannah Titus not to call the police. She could imagine how hard Chief McArthur would laugh at the idea of "sheep rustling." Then he'd suggest they contact the township's animal-control officer.

That was an idea. Mary made a mental note to find out who that was and give that person a call…in case someone brought a vagrant sheep to the animal shelter. But that would mean the sheep had wandered off on its own and nobody had taken it. Yet costumes couldn't wander away on their own. And why was someone tearing down the posters for the living Nativity? And if Luis was involved, why?

When her mind went round and round in circles like this, it was frustrating. She needed to get some facts. Right now all she had was conjecture. The church had been open, and anyone could have walked in. With Kip and Luis working in the front, someone could have gone in and out of the cellar's sliding doors without being seen. So she couldn't assume that *nobody* had been in the fellowship hall during the time between when Felicity had been there and the rest of the cast arrived. Obviously someone had, but who? And why?

Facts. She needed facts.

The neighborhood where Luis Alvarez lived was farther inland and down a road edged by two stone pillars. *Sea Breezes* was spelled out in large brass letters on a colonial-style white sign next to the column on the right. At first, she saw no houses, because trees and artfully arranged boulders edged the street. She drove into an open area. Filled with new custom homes, the curved streets were edged with a mixture of scrub pine and maples. Lawns had turned brown-gray with the coming of winter. Many of the houses had Christmas decorations out front, and she saw several lit trees through windows, even though it was still quite early in the morning.

Mary smiled as she remembered how Lizzie had pleaded every morning to have the tree's lights turned on, even if she was heading out to school. Did her grandchildren, Luke, or Emma, beg Lizzie now to plug in the lights as soon as they rolled out of bed in the morning?

She couldn't wait for them to arrive later today. On their way down from Melrose, Lizzie and her husband, Chad, and the kids were stopping at Logan Airport. Jack, Mary's son, his wife, Christa, and their daughter, Daisy, were flying in from Chicago. Lizzie and Chad assured Mary that they'd squeeze safely into the minivan. It was sure to be an interesting ride.

As she turned onto the correct street, Mary drove more slowly as she looked for the house number Kip had given her. She didn't want to drive by. Then she realized she didn't need to worry. Luis stood by his truck, which was parked in front of a pale green house. He was reaching into the truck and pulling out what looked like a sign that could be set up on a lawn. He had a hammer and a pair of working gloves stuck in the back pocket of his jeans. Even though it was chilly, he didn't wear a coat over his plaid flannel shirt.

Mary braked and rolled down the window. Cold wind pushed its way into the car, and she shivered. "Do you have a minute?"

"Mrs. Fisher!" Luis flinched, then put the sign into the back of the truck. His face brightened with a smile as he walked over to her car. "How are you doing today?"

"I'm doing well. Busy."

"Me too." He glanced back at the house, then grinned. "What can I do for you?"

"Well, I was wondering if you noticed, before you left the church last night, if the sheep was still in the pen?" If Luis had seen someone else loitering around the church or the sheep's pen, he might be able to point her toward the person who was causing so much trouble for the living Nativity.

He leaned his hands on the open window. "Why are you asking? Did it get out?"

"Yes."

"It was there when Kip and I packed up my tools. I remember because he kept joking with me about avoiding it so I didn't end up with hives." He chuckled.

"Any chance you noticed something or someone out of the ordinary hanging around?"

He shook his head. "I can't say that I did. Then again, I wasn't looking for that. Like I said, the sheep was there when we packed up. Any idea where it wandered off to?"

"Not yet." She hid her disappointment, reminding herself that no mystery was ever solved that easily. "I hope we can find it before it gets hurt."

He pushed back from the car door, pulled on his work gloves, and smiled. "Me too."

Mary closed her window and continued along the street. She wasn't even sure if someone *had* taken the sheep. Dorothy could be right that the sheep had wandered off on its own. If so, she should focus on two incidents instead of three. But she didn't know enough about sheep to know if she or Dorothy was right. As she stopped at a corner and waited for several cars to pass, she knew she should learn more about sheep. Her knowledge was pretty much at the level of Little Bo Peep.

She needed a sheep expert, and the obvious one was the owner of the missing sheep. A quick call to Betty got her the name she needed, because one of her sister's tasks had been to arrange the live animals for the living Nativity. She was relieved to hear how chipper her sister sounded. *Thank You, Father, for easing her pain.* So many times she'd prayed that, but her gratitude never lessened.

And she was grateful, too, that Betty could tell her the name of the farmer–or should she say shepherd?–who'd lent the sheep to Grace Church's living Nativity. Ken Gomes had a small farm on the southern side of the Cape in Centerville. It'd take her about twenty minutes to get there at this time of year.

Route 6 was busy. Some drivers were in a big hurry. Fortunately, Mary only had to drive about five miles before she could leave the four-lane for a secondary road that led her past neat houses and into Centerville. She turned at a light by a shopping plaza filled with seafood restaurants and continued east.

Ahead of her, the sky was a deep gray with low clouds that looked like they would snow at any moment. The sea was the same color. She hoped she'd get back to Ivy Bay before it stormed.

Mary turned her car onto a dirt road that led through scrub pine. It twisted and turned so she couldn't see more than a few yards in front of her. She pulled into a clearing about a quarter of a mile from the blacktop road.

The two-story house in front of her was, like most on the Cape, covered with shingles that had weathered to a lovely silver-gray. The barn just beyond it could have been picked up out of Vermont and set down behind the cozy house. It was bright red with white criss-cross boards on the double doors. Simple, flat-railed white fences created a large pen on its right side. Two large meadows were separated by stone walls that had been topped by barbed wire.

A pair of black-and-white dogs came rushing toward the car, barking as their tails wagged into a blur. They raced around the car until a tall man with closely cropped brown hair appeared from the barn and called to them. He motioned for Mary to get out of the car.

"Don't worry," he said as she did. "They like to herd everything that moves, even a car." He wore a dark brown barn coat over bib overalls and a flannel shirt. "I'm Ken. You are…?"

"Mary Fisher. I'm a member of Grace Church in Ivy Bay."

His mouth hardened. "Have you found Peep?"

"Peep?" she repeated, astonished. "You named a ram 'Peep'?"

"She's a ewe."

"But the sheep has horns."

"Horned Dorset ewes have horns exactly like the rams. We usually dehorn the ewes, but I always keep a couple with horns around because the kids get a big kick out of them when they visit the farm." He paused, then said, "I guess you didn't come out here to tell me that Peep's been found."

She shook her head. "I wish I had, but we've got people on the lookout for her. There can't be that many sheep wandering around Cape Cod."

"You'd be surprised. Stupid sheep."

Mary was taken aback by Ken's vehemence. "I don't understand. If this is a bad time…"

He ran his hand over the stubble on his head, then pulled a cap out of his coat pocket and put it on. "Sorry, Mrs. Fisher. It's been a tough day." He shot a scowl in the direction of the sheep. "My herd gets out far too regularly, and I know it's a common complaint among sheep farmers. Today they escaped from their field, and I chased them halfway to the main road before Jip, Mac, and I found them and brought them back here." He patted both black-and-white dogs on their heads. "I don't know what I'd do without these guys."

"They're border collies, aren't they?"

"Partly, but they've both got a hundred percent of a border collie's herding instincts. Good thing, too, because those sheep like to lead us for a chase whenever they get a chance."

Mary looked at the herd clustered close together near a pile of dried grass. "I thought sheep were like birds, flocking together."

He laughed, his mood lightening. "That's true, and when one finds a weak spot in the fence and pushes through, the rest of them follow like a stream bursting out of its banks. They don't know where they're going, but they're sure the grass is greener on the other side of road. Sheep may be the dumbest creatures on four hooves that God ever created. They make cows look like Rhodes scholars."

Laughing, Mary said, "It sounds like you don't have any suggestions of where to find Peep."

"Most likely someone's yard or someone's field. Sheep will push into a field like they'll push out of one if they think there's something to eat in it."

"When Peep got out of her pen, would there be any signs to point us in the right direction?"

He waved his hand. "C'mon. I'll show you where my herd went on the lam this morning."

"Lam, or lamb with a *b* at the end?" She laughed.

He groaned. "That pun was purely accidental, I promise you." He chuckled as he led the way through the dried grass to a section of the fence. He pointed to where the barbed wire had been shoved apart enough to let a sheep squeeze through and escape. "Right there is where they got out of the field."

"Is that wool on the barbed wire?" She pulled off-white wisps from the barbs and rubbed it between her fingers.

"Yes. They often lose bits of wool while wedging themselves through the fence."

"Peep should have left some behind, too, then?"

"Unless there's a big gap in the pen. How big was the space where Peep got out?"

Mary didn't answer right away. She hadn't even thought about going to look at the opening in the pen herself last night. Not that she would have known what to look for before now, so she was glad she had come to talk with Ken before examining the pen.

"I'm not exactly sure how big the opening is," she said. "Do you have time to drive into Ivy Bay? I'd like to have you look at the enclosure we had for Peep."

"I saw the pen after it was built. The carpenter did a good job following my specifications."

"But the sheep got out somehow. Maybe on its own. Maybe with help."

Ken's brows lowered. "Are you saying that you think someone *stole* my sheep? That's a whole different matter, Mrs. Fisher."

"I don't know what happened. All I know is that it's missing, and we haven't found it. Maybe if you look at the pen, you'll be able to tell which."

He nodded. "Let me get my truck, and I'll follow you back. It's one thing for a sheep to stray. But to steal it…" His hands clenched at his sides, then he walked away. He whistled to his dogs. They ran after him and leaped up into the cab of his dark red truck as soon as he opened the door.

Mary went to her own car. Backing around, she drove out of the barnyard. She kept checking her rearview mirror. Ken's truck followed her onto Route 6 and off the exit that led to Ivy Bay.

As they reached the white sign with "Est. 1685" on either side of the town's name, Mary kept an even closer watch that Ken was following. A school bus pulled out in front of her at a four-way stop, and she smiled. With its frequent stops to drop off kindergartners from their half-day session, she didn't have to worry about getting ahead of Ken.

She watched the youngsters jump down from the bus steps and run up to their houses where someone welcomed them home. It seemed like such a short time ago that she'd been the one waiting for Jack and Lizzie to return from school.

The bus pulled out from its third stop. As it passed a nearby telephone pole, it set a bright green poster on the pole flapping. As Mary followed the bus, she noticed the posters hanging from about half the poles. Mavis had been as good as her word about getting up even more posters than had been hung before.

A *beep* jerked her out of her thoughts. She looked in her mirror to see Ken motioning for her to go around the bus which had pulled over to the side of the road to let them pass.

"Focus on what you're doing," she said to herself.

Mary drove only a short distance, then slowed to a stop again. A large garbage truck was half in her lane. She started to edge around it, then saw Jason Fernandes lifting a can and tossing its contents in the back. He picked up the trash from Betty's house, too, and she'd said hi to him a few times when she was out early. He was a handsome young man, probably not yet thirty. His black hair glistened, and his olive complexion was darkened by spending time outdoors year-round.

Outdoors...He might be the ally she needed.

She lowered the window on the passenger side. "Jason?"

"Mrs. Fisher?" He dropped the can he had been hefting. Fortunately it fell into the back of the truck, so the garbage didn't scatter across the ground. Color rose up his face, and he hastily pulled it out and set it back on the curb. "You startled me."

"Sorry about that. Could you do me a favor while you're collecting garbage and keep an eye out for a sheep wandering around town? We've had one escape its pen."

"Of course." He chuckled, the bright flush fading from his face, though his ears were still red. "A full-grown sheep roaming through Ivy Bay won't be hard to miss."

"Thanks!"

She raised her window and waved to him as she checked for oncoming traffic. Seeing none, she passed the truck. She looked back to check on Ken. He was right behind her, but she also noticed that Jason was standing motionless, watching her as she drove away. He probably thought she had lost her mind as well as a sheep. She chuckled as she drove north along Main Street.

When the beautiful Chadwick Inn came into view, she turned left toward the church. She parked and waited while Ken pulled in beside her.

"This way," she said when he got out.

They walked around the church. Ken looked back along Main Street and gave a low whistle.

She thought he might be calling Peep, but then he said, "Wow, I haven't been up to Ivy Bay at Christmastime in a few years. You go all out, don't you? Decorations and a living Nativity." He paused and looked at a poster hanging on a telephone pole. "And a lighting contest. Something for everyone, it sounds like."

Mary looked more closely at the poster, which was printed on plain white paper. She remembered Kip saying something about Luis being busy with a lighting contest. Sure enough, the lighting contest was being held in the Sea Breezes community. It was scheduled for Sunday evening, and the public was invited to vote for their favorite house by putting a donation in the boxes set in front of each house.

On the other side of the pole was a bright lime-green poster like the others she'd seen while driving into town. She was surprised when she saw it wasn't for the living Nativity.

The posters announced that a group called Pets Aren't Props were calling for a boycott of the living Nativity because Grace Church intended to use live animals as part of the presentation. Her eyes widened as she saw how many of the bright posters hung along Main Street. There must be at least two dozen. The group clearly was determined to get their message across to everyone.

Could this group be the one trying to sabotage the living Nativity? She needed to find out a lot more about them. And fast.

✳ Chapter Four

A s Mary and Ken walked around the church, Mary saw two familiar women, bundled up against the cold, on the far side of the stable. Dorothy gestured emphatically. She was talking with Hannah Titus, the head seamstress. Was Dorothy excited because she'd found the costumes?

Mary hoped so, but as she walked nearer, she heard tension in both women's voices.

Ken shot one glance in the women's direction, then mumbled about going to check the pen.

"I'll be there in a minute," Mary said before continuing toward Dorothy and Hannah.

They turned as she approached. Her hopes that the costumes had been found fell when she saw Hannah's distraught expression. The young woman kneaded her hands together, running them along the side of her jeans, then rubbing them together again.

"Who is that, Mary?" Dorothy asked.

"Ken Gomes. He owns the sheep that's missing."

"Why is he looking for it here?"

Mary ignored the annoyance in Dorothy's voice. Everyone had been on edge since the costumes went missing.

"I went out to his farm to talk to him," she said, "and he generously agreed to come here to check the pen to see what he might be able to tell us."

"It's a waste of time," Dorothy said. "His and yours. We need to be looking for the costumes, not a sheep that's wandered off to look for greener pastures."

Instead of answering, Mary turned to Hannah. "I take it there's been no sign of any of the costumes?"

"We've looked high and low. We haven't even found a loose thread in the church." Hannah blinked back tears. "After all our hard work, we got the costumes done just in time. For what? So we could cancel the living Nativity?"

"Don't give up hope," Mary said. "We may still find them."

"And Pastor Miles told me," Dorothy said, "that the living Nativity isn't canceled. It's been postponed, and no final decision needs to be made right up until Christmas Eve."

That was good news, Mary thought. "And can't we put together enough costumes to have a smaller version of the living Nativity?"

Hannah didn't want to be consoled. "You don't understand. My volunteers put in many hours on those costumes. To make some quickie costumes would be disgraceful. We toiled over those costumes. Now they're gone. We're crushed."

Mary thought of Betty, who was disappointed too. And sweet Ashley had been heartbroken that she wouldn't get to be one of the angels.

"I'm sure everyone is upset," she said.

"Everyone but Abbie Lindstrom. She quit on us." Hannah's mouth became a straight line. "Not that I should have been surprised. That girl has never finished a single thing she's started in her whole life."

Dorothy frowned. "You knew that before you let her be part of your team."

"With so many costumes to make," Hannah said, "I needed every pair of hands I could get. I hoped that—this once—she would stick with something until the end. But no, she flits from one thing to the next. How many different jobs has she had since she dropped out of college?"

Mary wanted to shift the conversation back to the costumes. "But the costumes getting finished isn't the issue. They—"

Hannah didn't want to hear anything Mary had to say. She just railed against Abbie. The seamstress was furious at her most skilled seamstress quitting and made no secret of it.

"We need to focus," Mary said. "You got the costumes done, even without Abbie. But our problem is that they're missing."

"And do you have any idea how to find them?" Hannah asked. "I don't. Dorothy is trying, but she doesn't have any real answers. What suggestions do you have?"

"I thought if we could discover who took the sheep, that might give us a clue."

Dorothy sniffed. "Like I said, you're wasting your time, Mary Fisher, by worrying about the wrong thing. What could a wandering sheep have to do with our stolen costumes?"

"It's important to examine every possibility. Otherwise, we may miss a clue."

"You solve the mystery in your way, and I'll do it in mine."

Mary decided not answering was the best choice. Dorothy refused to consider that the sheep hadn't wandered off on its own. Hannah was upset and wasn't going to listen to anyone else. Mary could understand why Hannah was angry about the costumes, but why was she furious about Abbie quitting? Volunteers often had to quit because other obligations, like family or a job, had to take precedence. Anyone who worked with volunteers had to learn to accept that.

Ken came over to where they stood, wiping his hands on a kerchief. "I'm sorry, Mrs. Fisher. I don't see any sign of where or how Peep got out." He motioned for her to come over to the pen. She went, with Dorothy following. He pointed to the spot where the boards had been pushed apart. "As small as that space is, if she squeezed out, she would have left wool along these two boards."

"Then how did she get out?" asked Dorothy.

"Either someone let her out or"—he grinned—"she flew away."

Dorothy stared at him until Mary chuckled and said, "I think we can safely say she didn't sprout wings and fly."

"But that means," Dorothy hurried to say, "that someone let the sheep out."

"That's my guess."

"Oh." Dorothy blinked hard a couple of times, but didn't say anything else.

Ken stuffed his kerchief into a back pocket and leaned his hand on the upper slat of the pen. "That's actually good news."

"Why?" asked Mary.

"If someone let her out, that means there's a better than even chance that person took her somewhere. She's not out wandering around where she could get hurt."

"That *is* a blessing," Mary said.

"A blessing in disguise." Dorothy's tone was so grim that Mary hid her smile.

But Dorothy was right. That the sheep wasn't out on its own was a relief. On the other hand, Ken believed that someone *had* stolen the sheep. Who would want a sheep and costumes for a living Nativity? And what did the vandalized posters have to do with either?

"You can't tell us anything else?" Mary asked.

"Not really," Ken said. "The ground is too hard for any hoofprints to show, so I can't guess in which direction they led Peep away." He gave her a crooked grin. "I'll put out a few feelers at the feed store and other places. If someone comes in to get feed for a sheep, they'll let me know. But if you hear, let me know right away, okay?"

"And please let me know if, like Bo Peep's sheep, she comes home, wagging her tail behind her."

He chuckled as Mary gave him her cell number and keyed his into her phone. Waving good-bye and wishing them a merry Christmas, he walked to his truck in the parking lot.

"Well, that's that," Dorothy said. She strode back to where Hannah still stood on the other side of the stable, looking like a lost lamb herself.

Mary followed, then glanced over her shoulder at the pen. Something niggled in her brain. Something she was overlooking. Something that was right in front of her, but she wasn't seeing it.

Lord, open my eyes, if it is Your will. Help me to see the truth.

Dorothy put her arm around Hannah's shoulders. "Don't give up. I'm going to find out what happened to those costumes for you." She glanced at Mary and added, "We both are."

"That's right," Mary said. "Do you have any scraps of the fabric you used, Hannah?"

"Yes," Hannah said, wiping away tears. "There should be some in with the thread and pins and needles."

"Maybe if you show us those scraps, we'll be able to recognize the fabrics if we see them again."

Hannah sighed. "It seems like a waste of time."

"Nonsense," Dorothy said in her best no-nonsense voice. "Even though I've seen the costumes many times, I have to say I wasn't paying attention to the specific fabrics. I doubt Mary even knows what she's looking for."

Dorothy didn't mean for her words to be insulting. Mary knew that, but still she prickled at Dorothy's tone. On the other hand, Dorothy was correct. Other than Betty's enthusiastic description of the work being done by Hannah's seamstresses, Mary had only the most general idea of the colors and fabrics.

In the fellowship hall, Hannah sorted through the supplies her volunteers had used. She pulled out fabric. Some pieces weren't much bigger than Mary's longest finger, but others were several inches on each side. She identified each one as she placed it on the table. Red worsted for Joseph and a pale blue satin for the Virgin Mary. The kings' costumes had been made of brilliant shades of green, gold, and white satin. The robes for the angels were the same white as the third king's. For the shepherds, simple ecru linen had been chosen.

Hannah also spread out pieces of gold fringe used for the Magi's costumes and white lace edging for the angels' wings. When Mary picked up one strip to examine it, glitter fell onto the table.

"We planned to use this," Hannah said, "so the costumes would shimmer in the light."

"Did you use a lot?"

"Some of the gals were more enthusiastic about applying the glitter than others." She gathered up the fabrics and trim and tossed them back into a basket. "And, of course, the little angels had glitter on their halos and wings." She bent over the baskets. "I'm sure there's one around here for you to see."

"I saw Ashley's halo, so I'm set on that." Mary put her hand on Hannah's arm and wasn't surprised to feel it tremble.

The poor young woman was frantic. "Thank you for showing us this. I know both Dorothy and I appreciate it."

Sorrow clamped around Mary's heart as she saw the dejected set of Hannah's shoulders while they went back outside. They bent as if Hannah carried the whole weight of the church building on them.

Mary glanced toward the abandoned sheep pen. The feeling that something else was wrong washed over her. She looked around, and her gaze fell on a bale of hay by the wires that Luis had been stringing last night.

"Dorothy, that bale of hay was in the pen before," Mary said.

"Was it?"

"Yes."

"Someone moved it out." Dorothy shrugged. "Anyone could have done that at any time."

Mary shook her head. "It was in the pen when Betty and I arrived last night. Now it's been moved. My guess is that it was taken out of the pen when the sheep was led away. Whoever took Peep might have wanted to take the hay to have something to feed her."

"But," Dorothy said, jumping on the idea, "they didn't have a chance before the kids came out here to look for the sheep."

"That's what I think." She smiled. "Dorothy, you're really getting the hang of this."

"Thanks." Honest pleasure warmed Dorothy's face. "If you need me, Hannah and I are going to talk to Pastor Miles to get his advice on what to do next." She hesitated, then asked, "Do you want to come along?"

Mary shook her head. "I need to puzzle out a couple of other things here. Will you let me know what he says?"

"I will. He always has good advice. I can't wait to share the progress we've made."

When they'd left, Mary sat on the bale and stared at the pen. Yes, they were making progress, but progress only brought more questions. Who could have taken the sheep?

The answer was simple. Anyone. Everyone involved with the living Nativity had been busy scurrying through the church while they searched for the missing costumes. Even Kip had been inside, which meant a passerby could have stolen the sheep.

But no passerby would even know the costumes were in the church. Only the volunteers and Pastor Miles had known that. A passerby might let the sheep out, but sneaking it away and then taking care of it was a big task. It couldn't have been a spur-of-the-moment snatch. She thought about the posters put up by that animal rights group. Could they be involved? But would they have had the opportunity to take the costumes and halt the living Nativity? Again, she couldn't make all three incidents come together to focus on a single culprit.

If stopping the living Nativity was the reason, it hadn't been a very good one. The living Nativity was postponed, but not canceled.

But whoever had taken the costumes and Peep wouldn't have known that. Someone had wanted to keep the living Nativity from happening. Why?

It would have competed against the basketball game at the high school on Saturday night and against the lighting contest that started on Sunday and ran until Christmas Eve. Her stomach clenched as she looked at the wires running across the ground.

Luis Alvarez was in charge of the lighting contest at the Sea Breezes subdivision. It was running concurrently with the living Nativity. It would reach its finale on Christmas Eve just as the living Nativity would, when the choir would come out from the candlelight service to sing around the stable.

But would Luis sabotage the living Nativity in order to turn more attention to his lighting contest? He had the opportunity to take the sheep, but would he risk brushing up against Peep when he was allergic to lanolin? And why would he agree to help Kip with the lighting if he intended to sabotage the living Nativity? He could have done it to give himself a chance to get into the church, but there must be easier ways for him to do that unnoticed.

She needed more information. Pushing herself up, Mary wiped bits of hay from her slacks. She glanced at her watch. Jack and Lizzie and their families should be arriving soon. Happiness rippled through her. She didn't get to see Jack and Christa and their daughter, Daisy, as often as she liked. Now that Daisy was a teenager, her schedule was as packed as Jack's with his pediatric practice. Mary wasn't going to miss a moment of their visit.

✳   ✳   ✳

Gus was walking down the stairs when Mary entered the home she shared with Betty. He glanced at her, then raced toward the back of the house. She knew what that meant. He was hoping that she'd forgotten that she'd fed him this morning and he could persuade her to give him another can of cat food.

After she'd hung up her coat, she went into the kitchen where her sister was pouring a cup of coffee. Betty asked if she'd like one.

"Love it," Mary said.

They fixed their cups and sat at the kitchen table. As soon as Mary drew in her chair, her sister asked, "What have you found out about the missing sheep?"

"It didn't get out on its own."

"I hoped you wouldn't say that. Now we've got a stolen sheep and missing costumes."

"And don't forget the ruined posters." Mary stirred sugar into her coffee as she went on, "I did get a chance to see samples of the fabric, so maybe I can recognize it if I see it again. Hannah mentioned Abbie Lindstrom a couple of times."

"Yes, Abbie was working on the costumes. She's a tremendously skilled seamstress."

"Then it's a shame that she quit."

Betty looked up from her cup. "Quit? Hannah said Abbie quit?"

"Yes, and Hannah was furious that Abbie walked out on the other volunteers when they had so much work to do."

"Abbie didn't quit."

"What?" Mary set her own cup on the table.

"Hannah fired her."

"Are you sure? Hannah was very definite that Abbie quit."

Betty's mouth tightened into a straight line. "I don't know why Hannah would say such a thing. There were several people who witnessed the argument that ended with Hannah telling Abbie to leave."

"But why would Hannah fire Abbie? Even Hannah admits that she is the best seamstress of the group."

"I was told that it was something about making the costumes too complicated."

"Too much decoration?"

Betty shook her head. "That's what I assumed at first, too, but one of the other gals explained to me that Abbie wanted to make sure each of the costumes would fit each volunteer who would be wearing it. For example, we planned to have four different girls playing Mary. The shortest is at least six inches shorter than the tallest, and one is as skinny as a rail while another is very round."

"That sounds a little complicated."

"There are easier ways. When Evan was young, there were annual programs every year at school. Even the mothers who were good with a needle didn't have the time to take up or let down the hems or pick apart the seams so the costumes fit each child. Someone suggested we use tape." Betty chuckled. "That worked just fine, but then someone else suggested velcro. It was even simpler. Cut two pieces to size, peel off the backs, and stick them to the fabric to let the costumes in or out."

"That makes more sense."

"It does, and that's what Hannah wanted to do, but Abbie had the idea that the costumes should be color-coded with embroidered dots, and the volunteers should each be told which color was theirs."

"That sounds complicated."

"On one hand, it would have made everything simpler, because each volunteer would be able to find his or her costume easily. In the long run, it would actually have been a very good system." Betty picked up her cup and leaned back in her chair. "But it added a lot of work to making the costumes, and Hannah decided it wasn't worth the time. Abbie didn't like that, and they began arguing. It ended with Hannah firing Abbie."

"I'm sorry to hear that. I wonder why Hannah didn't tell me the truth."

"Probably because she's still upset over the whole argument."

The doorbell rang.

Mary's heartbeat doubled. That must be the kids and their children. She jumped to her feet so fast, her chair almost careered into the wall.

"They'll wait," Betty said, standing more slowly, "for you to answer the door." She chuckled as they headed to the front door. Suddenly Betty stopped. "Oh, I just thought of one other thing about that argument. From what I heard from the women who saw the whole thing, Abbie told Hannah that she'd be sorry for kicking her off the team of volunteers."

Mary arched her brows at her sister as they walked to the door.

They opened it to find a box delivered by UPS. After a moment to recover from her disappointment, Mary carried the box inside and glanced at the return address label. It should be the soccer pads she'd ordered for her grandson Luke. Carrying it upstairs to her closet, she didn't bother to open the box. She'd check it later.

She sat on her bed and picked up the phone book on the stand beside it. She looked up Abbie's phone number, then called it. Abbie's phone rang until the answering machine picked up. Mary drew in a breath to leave a message, but clicked the phone off when she heard the door open downstairs. The jumbled voices announced that her children and grandchildren had arrived.

The mystery would have to wait until after she gave each of them a big hug…or two or three.

✳ Chapter Five

It was Evan's family at the door instead of Mary's children and grandkids. Betty's son and his family came in, hugs were exchanged, and their two girls chattered as if they hadn't seen their grandmother and Mary in a year instead of just the past week. Meanwhile, Mary couldn't stop thinking about Betty's explanation of the argument between Hannah and Abbie.

Mary offered to take everyone's coats while Betty led them into the living room. Betty's older granddaughter stayed behind to help Mary hang them up.

"When are my cousins getting here?" ten-year-old Betsy asked.

"Should be any time now," Mary answered as they went into the comfortable living room.

"Do you think Daisy will braid my hair like she did last time?" Betsy's eyes glinted in eager anticipation. "It was pretty, and I'd like to wear my hair to school like that."

Mary smiled. "If it's okay with your parents, why don't you stay over one night this week so you and Daisy can have some time together?"

Evan and his wife, Mindy, quickly agreed to both girls having a sleepover, but told them that they must wait until their cousins got settled in. Betsy and her younger sister, Allison, began making plans for what they would bring and where they would sleep and what they would do.

Just as Mindy reminded them that they should wait until the other kids arrived before mapping out every detail of their visit, the doorbell rang again. The girls jumped up and ran to the door.

Mary glanced out the window and saw the bright red minivan that belonged to her daughter and son-in-law. She wanted to rush out into the hall, too, because she couldn't wait to see her family.

The door opened, and her son and daughter and their spouses and children poured in to be greeted with another round of hugs. Daisy, Mary's oldest grandchild at sixteen, was instantly flanked by Betty's granddaughters.

Greeting her son, Jack, and his wife, Christa, Mary smiled and asked about their trip from Chicago while Daisy waved in her direction. She waved back, then was enveloped with hugs from her younger grandchildren, Emma and Luke. Even though she saw them more often than Jack and his family because they lived just outside Boston, she loved every moment she was able to spend with them.

Somehow, everyone fit into the suddenly cramped hall. As luggage was sorted out and coats and mittens shed, the bustle was fun, and soon everyone was laughing as they figured out who was sleeping where. The stairs rang with footsteps hurrying up and down.

Mary went to the kitchen to help Betty prepare and serve lunch. They were having tomato soup and tuna sandwiches. The children ate in the kitchen while the adults gathered around the dining room table. Even though it seemed as if everyone talked at once, the conversation flowed brightly.

After getting her son and daughter and their families settled in the house and leaving them to unpack in the bedrooms and makeshift bedrooms, Mary needed to return to the bookshop. She had left Rebecca on her own too much in the past week.

"I'll be back in time for dinner," Mary said as she carried the last of the dirty dishes into the kitchen. "Is there anything I can pick up while I'm out, Bets?"

"I think we're set," Betty replied. "We have the casseroles I made, and I iced the two cakes you took out of the freezer, so we should be fine."

"Great."

Out in the hallway, Gus was peeking from the living room. He'd made himself scarce amid the hubbub. He gave her a mournful *mew*.

"You'd like to come, wouldn't you?" She bent to pat the gray cat between the ears. "All right."

She got his carrying cage and set it on the floor. He scampered in without a backward glance when loud giggles came from upstairs. He wasn't used to this many people in his house at one time.

But Mary couldn't imagine anything that made her happier than to have her family with her for Christmas.

✳   ✳   ✳

The shop was so busy when Mary walked in, she could barely hear the door chime. She wouldn't give in to her temptation to stop next door at Sweet Susan's Bakery. She wasn't hungry, but the luscious scents always teased her. To avoid being tempted by the delicious goodies was one of the reasons she'd asked Rebecca to take the order over for the Christmas reading refreshments.

Several adults were looking at books on the shelves and in the Christmas display. In the center of the children's section, Ashley was talking with a dark-haired girl her own age. Large glasses perched on the little girl's nose, and they slipped down each time she pushed them up. Mary recognized the other little girl as Courtney Flanagan, the daughter of the Grace Church organist, Mavis. The girls sat in the bathtub in the center of the children's section, their backs propped on piles of pillows and their legs draped over the sides.

Mary smiled as she saw the little girls enjoying the white footed bathtub that had been a gift from her sister. Having the children enjoy the tub, which was lined with blue carpet, was just what she and Betty had imagined when her sister purchased the tub at the flea market.

Ashley looked up and waved. Mary waved back, then set the carrying case on the floor and opened it.

Gus leaped out and onto his favorite spot by the front window. Drawing his paws up beneath him, he looked over the shop with an expression that told everyone that it was *his* domain.

By the time she had put the carrying case and her coat away, Mary found Ashley and Courtney waiting by the counter.

"Hi!" both girls said at the same time before Ashley added, "Did they find our costumes yet?" She pointed to her sparkling hair. "See? We're all ready for the play."

From the question, Mary guessed Courtney must also have been chosen to be an angel for the living Nativity. With her older brother slated to play Joseph, it made sense for Mavis to have them both involved. Besides, Mary had rarely met a little girl who didn't enjoy dressing up in something shiny and covered with glitter.

"Not that I've heard of," Mary said.

"Oh." Ashley's smile vanished.

Courtney looked directly at Mary. "My mommy says that maybe someone who didn't have any clothes took them so they'd have something to wear to stay warm. But I don't believe that could be true. I was supposed to wear my winter coat under my costume."

Mary tried not to smile at the little girl's logic. "I'm sure the costumes are going to turn up soon."

"We still have our halos," Ashley reminded her friend. "We can always wear those."

"That's right." Courtney's blue eyes began to sparkle. "Cool. We'll be the best angels ever."

Ashley nodded. "The very best." She looked at Mary. "Courtney likes being best, but I like it when we both can be best."

"I like how you think, Ashley." She knew she couldn't talk with the girls for long. Several customers were gathered by the table with the Christmas book specials, and at least one looked as if she might need some help soon.

"But Mom says I have to try to be my best," Courtney said, "if I want to be first-chair violin in the Cape Cod Youth Orchestra."

"Don't you have to be in middle school before you audition?" Mary searched her memory, and she couldn't recall any children as young as Courtney in the youth orchestra when it presented an open-air concert in Ivy Bay last summer.

"Yes, but I have to practice now if I want to be good enough then."

"You must really enjoy playing the violin."

"It's my favorite instrument." She giggled. "Don't tell my mom that. She wants me to love playing the organ as much as she does, but I like my violin a lot better."

"Your secret is safe with me." Mary pretended to put a key to her lips and turn it.

Both girls giggled again. They skipped back to the bathing tub, crawled in, and began whispering together.

Rebecca walked over to the counter, pausing only long enough to greet Gus.

"I'm back for the afternoon," Mary said when Rebecca greeted her.

"With answers to your puzzles?"

"If only it were that easy..."

"A mystery wouldn't be as much fun if it was easy to solve," Rebecca said.

Mary smiled and went to help the uncertain customer who was having trouble choosing whether to buy an Agatha Christie or an Ellery Queen mystery. With a few quick questions, Mary helped the woman decide which book the recipient would prefer, and the woman left with Mary's recommendation of Christie's *Hercule Poirot's Christmas*.

When Rebecca came out of the back room with her coat and hat and purse, she motioned to the girls to get their coats on too. "No dawdling," she said as they walked past her. To Mary, she added, "I'm dropping them off over at the Flanagans'. Mavis and I switched off today."

"So you could both finish up your Christmas shopping?"

"I'd better finish up. Only six more shopping days." She swung the bright red and gold scarf around her neck and let the ends run down her back. "Thanks for being extra-flexible with my time this week."

"Not a problem. You've been flexible for me enough times when I'm on the trail of a mystery."

Rebecca grew suddenly serious. "Speaking of mysteries, when Mavis dropped off Courtney, she was pretty upset. It seems that Dorothy Johnson has been asking people if they know anything about where the costumes are."

"Dorothy has decided this is one mystery she intends to solve."

"I figured that, and it's nice of her to try to find the costumes." Rebecca took a deep breath and released it. "But it's the way that Dorothy's asking that had Mavis upset. And apparently she's not the only one bothered by it."

Mary motioned for Rebecca to come behind the counter, so their conversation wouldn't be overheard by the customers. "What do you mean?"

"It's like she's accusing each person of being the one who took the costumes. Mavis was so offended that she considered taking her kids out of the living Nativity, and that's huge because she's been proud of them being in it, especially of Brian portraying Joseph. Any chance you could say something to Dorothy? You guys have a better relationship than she and I do."

"I don't know if I would go that far."

Rebecca gave Mary a sidelong look. "Oh, come on. You guys have your disputes, but I've seen the way you two banter. Could you please talk to her? I just don't want Dorothy grilling Ashley."

"Sure, I'll talk to Dorothy. I know her intentions are good."

"Nobody questions that. It's her methods."

Mary smiled, though she knew she shouldn't. Dorothy was single-minded, and once she got a bee in her bonnet, it wasn't easy to stop her.

"I'll do my best," Mary said.

"That's more than good enough for me."

"Maybe I'll offer her a few tips on refining her sleuthing technique."

Rebecca laughed and went to hurry Ashley and Courtney. Once the girls had their coats on, they left with cheery waves.

Others must have had the same idea about finishing up their Christmas shopping, because a steady stream of customers came into the bookshop all afternoon. Mary enjoyed helping them find specific books. When asked for suggestions, she asked a few questions about other favorite authors, then steered customers to a specific book.

"Can I leave these on the counter?" asked a woman who looked to be in her early thirties. She was slender, and her dark hair was cut in a pageboy that swung on her shoulders. She set a large stack of books on the counter.

"Of course," Mary said, wondering who the woman was. She seemed familiar, so she must live in Ivy Bay.

"I shouldn't leave them here," the woman said with a chuckle. "With my hands free, I'll only get more. I love Christmas shopping."

"I'll keep them here on the counter. Let me know when you're ready to check out, and if you decide not to buy these books, just let me know that too."

"Oh, I'm going to get all those books. You have a wonderful selection here."

Another customer asked Mary about a title that was part of a currently popular mystery series. He wanted to know which number it was in the series since it wasn't stated in the book. Quickly she found the information on the internet and then rang up the book and two more that he wanted to buy.

Mary looked around the busy shop and couldn't help smiling. It was lovely to be surrounded by people who loved mysteries as much as she did. A family gathered by one set of shelves and another in the children's section.

She was certain the dark-haired woman who now stood by the holiday specials table must have been in the shop before because she looked familiar. She wore a bright red coat, and her scarf was decorated with wreaths and Christmas trees. She picked up another book to add to the new stack in her arms.

Mary placed the woman when Jason Fernandes entered the store and walked over to stand beside her. She must be the garbageman's wife. It seemed odd to see Jason wearing a light yellow knit shirt beneath his dark overcoat and a pair of khakis. When he was working, he wore denim overalls with the company's name on the back. That made him look like all the other garbagemen, and Mary had never noticed he had a dimple when he smiled as he did when he stood beside his wife.

"Look, honey!" She showed him one of the Christmas books she had picked up. "I didn't even realize that this author had written a book set at Christmastime."

"Uh-huh."

"Oh, Jason, look at it!" She held the book up to his eye level. "I can't wait to read it. And look here! Another one I haven't read. This is a real treasure trove."

"Patti, you've got a ton of things planned for this week. How are you going to find time to read?"

She laughed. "If I don't get them read before Christmas, I'll read them after. I'm such a sucker for holiday stories, so I don't mind if it's August when I'm reading them."

Before he could answer, a little boy, who looked to be around five, rushed over with a picture book in his hands. "Daddy, can we get this book?"

"And this one?" asked a girl who looked only a year or two older. She was a miniature of her mother, right down to the red coat and holiday scarf.

Jason hesitated, but his wife quickly motioned for the children to add their books to her pile. They scurried back to look at the others in the children's section.

"No more," he called after them. "You've got a bunch at home you haven't read yet."

"We'll need to have a lot on hand for Christmas vacation." Patti Fernandes smiled. "Unless it snows, of course, and then they can play outside." She put a loving hand on her husband's arm. "But you don't like snow."

"Only because it makes every trash can weigh about twice what it should."

They walked to a different section of the shop, and Gus jumped up onto the counter. Mary was about to pick him up and put him on the floor when a teenager walked over. The girl wore her black hair in a sassy ponytail. It sparkled when she moved as if she'd put glitter in it. She was dressed in a brightly colored sweater with a big reindeer head on the front. Mary had seen other teenagers in campy sweaters, so she guessed it must be the latest fad. The girl set a well-worn backpack beside her on the floor and began petting Gus, who accepted it and her coos as his due.

Mary smiled when Gus sidled away and returned to his favorite spot to curl up and take a nap.

"He's a nice cat," the girl said. "Some cats are too shy or frightened to let strangers pet them."

"Gus has his moods." Mary chuckled. "I've learned to pay attention to them since he came to live with me."

"Was he a rescue cat?"

"A stray. He picked our home and decided we would suit *him.*"

The girl's eyes twinkled. "Cats can be that way, but it's good of you to take him into your home and your heart."

Mary smiled in agreement. "Can I help you?" She asked.

"I hope so." The girl smiled as she picked up her backpack and set it on the counter. "I'm Shelby Ellis. I'm a senior at Ivy Bay High and the president of PAP, an animal rights group. I was wondering if you'd hang one of our flyers in your window and if you'd let us leave some here for your customers?"

"May I see one?"

"Sure." She pulled out a folder. Setting her backpack on the floor again, she placed the folder on the counter. She flipped it open and pulled out a bright green page.

Mary bit her lip to keep a gasp of surprise from popping out. The page was the exact same color as the posters she'd seen around town denouncing the living Nativity, so when she saw the flyer belonged to Pets Aren't Props, she realized what PAP stood for.

"If you'd be willing to display this," Shelby said, barely able to contain her excitement at having what she believed was a sympathetic ear, "it would be wonderful. PAP believes that animals deserve dignity exactly as humans do. That doesn't include parading them around. Animals should be left to do what animals do in a proper farm and natural setting."

"You have these all over Ivy Bay."

"Yes." Her smile faded. "We need to make sure people who share our beliefs step forward now."

"Now? Why?" she asked, though she suspected she already knew.

"Grace Church is having a living Nativity. That's wonderful, but they shouldn't leave a sheep in such a small pen. They are accustomed to having a field to wander around in while they graze."

"Did you know the sheep was taken by someone?"

Shelby clamped her lips closed, then said, "I hope it was the farmer who owns the sheep."

"It wasn't."

She opened her mouth to answer, then seemed to think better of it. When she smiled, it looked forced. "I hope the sheep is all right. I know it'll be happier out of that small pen."

Had the kids, in their zeal, taken down the posters for the living Nativity and then put up their own? Maybe she should read the information on the poster more closely.

"All right," Mary said. "I'll take one."

"To hang up in your window?"

She glanced at the window where she had taped up a poster of her own with information about the Christmas Eve afternoon reading. "I'll think about it."

"Good. Animals can't speak for themselves, so it's important that those who love animals do." She glanced at where Gus was washing himself. "As I know you do."

Mary nodded, unwilling to commit herself to hanging the poster until she learned more about the group. When Shelby thanked her, flung her backpack over her shoulder again, and left, sparkles of glitter lingered on the counter.

Wiping them off into her hand and tossing them into the wastebasket before Gus decided to taste them, Mary brushed the lingering glitter off her hands. It was the same gold that she'd seen in the sanctuary, but she couldn't jump to conclusions. Both Ashley and Courtney had glitter in their hair too. It might be a new fad or simply a holiday one, but she needed to keep an eye on who was using glitter. The gold specks in the sanctuary had to come from something or someone, and someone who was as interested in protecting animals as Shelby Ellis might resort to doing whatever was necessary to keep the living Nativity from going on. She might see this as justifiable means to keep Peep from being, in her opinion, exploited.

But would Shelby or another member of her group actually have snuck into the church and taken the costumes? That was a big conclusion to leap to when Mary had no other information than the fact that Shelby wore glitter in her hair and wanted to protect Peep.

She slid the brochure and poster into a drawer under the counter just as Jason and his wife approached. She smiled and greeted them.

Instead of answering, Jason asked, "Are you getting *all* of those books, Patti?" He must have realized how strained his voice sounded, because he added, "Don't you want to leave a few for other people?"

"Oh, Jason." She slapped his arm playfully as she opened her wallet. "Christmas comes but once a year."

"Good thing," he mumbled under his breath.

"I look forward to Christmas all year long," Patti said. "I think I get more excited about it than the kids do."

"There's nothing wrong with that," Mary said.

"Tell him." Patti hooked a thumb at Jason. "Sometimes, he can be a real Scrooge." She turned back to Mary. "You don't have any books about decorating for Christmas, do you?"

"No. I'm sorry."

"Oh..." She looked disappointed. "All the books on decorating for Christmas at the library have been checked out already. The kids are hoping to make a wreath for the front door, and I don't know where to begin."

"I can give you the name of a shop in Hyannis that sells more general titles. Here, we're pretty much just mystery titles, children's books, and a few local interest titles."

"I should have guessed that." She dimpled and put the rest of the books on the counter. "Will you write down the name of that bookshop in Hyannis? Maybe I can get over there later to see what they've got in stock."

"Certainly—" Mary began.

Jason interrupted, "Patti, don't forget that we're going over to my folks' house for dinner tonight."

"We can squeeze in a quick trip to Hyannis." She pulled out her wallet and looked around the stacks of books to Mary.

"I promised my father I would help him with–"

"Go ahead over there," Patti said with a smile for her husband. "I'll take the kids with me. That way, they won't be pestering you while you work with your dad." Her smile became teasing. "And we can play Christmas carols in the car and sing really loud without you giving me *that* look."

"I like hearing you sing."

She patted his arm. "I know you do. Oh," she continued, pointing to a book displayed on the other side of the cash register, "I didn't see that book. Do you have any other copies?"

"All the books are shelved alphabetically by author."

"C'mon, kids…" She motioned for the children to follow her as she went over to the proper section.

Jason didn't move. "She was honest when she said she looks forward to Christmas all year." He chuckled wryly. "She starts playing Christmas music before Labor Day. If I hear 'The Twelve Days of Christmas' one more time, I may scream."

"Lots of people love this time of year. So much so that they start celebrating earlier and earlier every year." Mary gave him a commiserating shrug. "The first time I saw Christmas ornaments for sale right after the kids went back to school, I feared that the next year, they'd be in stores right after the Fourth of July."

"Let's hope not." He grinned and then glanced at the stacks of books his wife had already collected. "Sometimes she gets a little carried away. She makes too many plans, and then when I don't have time to help her with everything, she gets really disappointed. I hate when that happens, but reality isn't always like the happily-ever-after ending to a Christmas movie. And then there's the cost of everything. Sometimes I can't wait for the holiday season to be over so I don't have to deal with the hassles of bills and the time crunch. I don't understand why Christmas can't be simple like it used to be. And now this lighting contest is going on..." Color rose up his face, and she guessed he hadn't intended to say that much.

Mary gave him a sympathetic smile. She remembered how she and her husband, John, had struggled to balance the many events surrounding the holiday and still savor the joy of the season with their children, family, and friends. It had often been a balancing act, especially when the kids were the same age as Jason's.

When Patti came back with two more books to add to the pile, Jason didn't say anything. He waited while she paid, then picked up the bulging bags of books. His wife and children walked out of the shop with an excited bounce in their steps. His footfalls were heavy as he followed.

Sympathy rushed through Mary. Even without the bags, it was clear that Jason felt burdened by the holidays though his family was enjoying it to the fullest. She'd keep him and his family in her prayers. She'd pray that Patti really heard what Jason was saying about Christmas, how he wanted to keep it simple because her enthusiasm was overwhelming him. She prayed as well that Jason would learn to discover the joy that Christmas could bring.

✳ Chapter Six

....

Mittens?" asked Mary as she pulled on her own. Everyone had gathered in the front hallway. Evan's family had come to join Jack and Lizzie's families, and each face glowed with happiness.

"Got 'em!" shouted everyone.

"Hats?"

"Got 'em!" The children laughed at their parents and grandmothers acting silly.

"Voices?" asked Betty. "We need strong and happy voices for the caroling."

"Got 'em!"

"I can't hear you!" Jack called.

"Got 'em!" The shouts rang through the hallway.

Mary put her hands over her ears and said, "I definitely heard you that time."

That brought more laughter.

Tonight was a carol sing in the park. Mavis Flanagan had volunteered to lead it, and everyone in town was invited. The original plan had been to have the singing and then light up the living Nativity. They'd hoped that one event would draw people for the other.

Now...

No, Mary told herself. She wasn't going to think grim thoughts. Her family and Betty's were here, and she was going to enjoy the time they had together.

They had just crossed Route 6A where the local police were directing traffic to give pedestrians plenty of time to cross when Mary heard an annoyed voice behind her. She turned, surprised to see her grandson and Betty's granddaughter scowling at each other.

"We always make the sugar cookies first," said Luke with the certainty of a seven-year-old.

"We always make gingerbread men first." Allison crossed her arms in front of her.

Luke turned to Mary. "Grandma, will you explain to her that making sugar cookies first is the right way to make Christmas cookies?"

Mary smiled at the youngest grandchildren. "I think both ways are perfectly fine." She glanced at her sister. "Isn't that right, Betty?"

"That's true," Betty said from where she walked with her hand on her son Evan's arm. "And you know what? Our kitchen is big enough for *lots* of cookie making."

Luke and Allison both opened their mouths to respond, but both were halted when their mothers called for them to come and walk with them. With a glance at each other that suggested the matter wasn't settled yet, they hurried to obey.

Mary held back her laughter until they were out of earshot along the street. Betty dropped back to join her as the rest of the family continued toward the park.

"I guess this isn't going to be a silent night," Betty said.

"Apparently not. Did you and Evan make gingerbread men first?"

She shook her head. "Not that I remember. That must be a tradition from Mindy's family."

"Remember when we were little? We didn't make either sugar cookies or gingerbread men first."

"We made Russian teacakes." Betty laughed along with her. "They were small, so we could sample a few without anyone noticing."

"But now our children and their children have traditions of their own."

"I know." Betty smiled. "This year will be a good chance for each of them to get to know everyone else's traditions."

"And for us to learn them too." Mary gently looped her arm around her sister's as they joined the jovial crowd entering the park.

The park was beautiful with several trees lit with colorful Christmas lights and strung with garland. Other trees wore white blinking lights. People filled the open area, greeting neighbors and chatting with friends. No one seemed to notice the chilly wind coming off Cape Cod Bay.

Seeing some bright red posters flapping on telephone poles, Mary stopped to read one. It was for the living Nativity, and it listed the days the program had been scheduled but urged the public to check the church's Web site for the most up-to-date information.

As she saw the number of posters hung around the park, she whispered to Betty, "Mavis sure has been busy."

"She and the members of her prayer circle." Betty chuckled. "All of them have children in the living Nativity, and they're determined that, as soon as the costumes are found, the show will go on." She paused by a bright green poster that had just been stapled up by a group of teens. The kids moved on to the next tree. "What is this? It's not for the living Nativity."

In the dim light, Mary couldn't see if Shelby was one of the kids hanging the posters. "Those posters belong to a group over at the high school. They call themselves PAP, and they're all about animal rights. The president stopped by the bookshop today to ask me to display one of their posters in the window."

"Isn't it nice that they care about animals?" Betty smiled. "I'm not surprised they stopped in to see you. They must have noticed Gus at the bookshop."

"They're protesting the use of live animals at the living Nativity."

Betty frowned. "Aren't they a bit late? The sheep is gone, and we won't bring in any other animals until we find out what happened to it. Didn't you tell the girl that?"

"I did, and she hightailed it out of the shop."

"Do you think…?" She looked back at the teens, who were working their way methodically around the park. "Do you think they know anything about what happened at the church last night?"

"I don't know what to think," Mary said honestly. "I need to learn more about the group, but I wouldn't put it past a teenager who felt an animal was being exploited to make sure it was taken somewhere safe."

Betty nodded. "Do first and think of the consequences afterward." A hint of a smile tipped her lips. "I remember that time when we were in high school, and we borrowed the car without telling our folks. We never stopped to think that they wouldn't understand that the need for you to have new shoes for the school dance was the only thing on our minds, and we assumed they would know it was one of us."

"Instead they called the police to report the car missing," said Mary, smiling at the memory, "and we got stopped out on Route 6. It took me years to understand why we didn't get punished when we came home with our tails dragging behind us. Only later did I realize that the worst punishment was being brought home by the cops and having everyone see us getting out of the cop's car. It's a story I told my kids when they were growing up, hoping they'd learn from our mistakes."

"Me too." Again Betty glanced at three teens passing out bright green flyers. "Teens can be extremely fervent about their beliefs and oblivious to the consequences."

"Still, I'm puzzled as to why PAP would still be handing out their brochures if they proved their point by halting the living Nativity."

"They may want to make sure that *everyone* knows what they stand for."

Mary nodded. "That's true, but something about them taking Peep and then still handing out the flyers doesn't ring true to me. Why wouldn't they focus on something other than the living Nativity?"

Betty looked at the teens, then shrugged. "I don't have an answer for that."

"Me neither."

"Look, there's Mavis. I think the singing is about to start."

Mary glanced once more at the teens, but didn't see Shelby. Now wasn't the time to ask the teens any questions. After all, she couldn't ask them point-blank if they'd taken Peep. Not when she didn't know much about the group.

She and Betty walked to where they had a good view of Mavis, who stood beside risers that had been brought from the high school and set up in front of the gazebo in the center of the park. As the chorus paraded in and up onto the risers, Mavis watched closely. Not that she needed to worry about mischievousness. The teens were perfectly behaved in front of parents and grandparents and most of the residents of Ivy Bay. Mavis moved to stand in front of them. Her son, Brian, stood at the far end of the upper row, and Mary saw several more young people from Grace Church scattered among the chorus. All the chorus members wore bright red

bow ties. A couple of the kids had put on felt reindeer antlers as well, and one boy sported a white Santa beard.

Yet when they began singing "Angels We Have Heard
on High" in four-part harmony, each face was both serious
and aglow with the joy of the music. The next song, "Silent
Night," was a sing-along with everyone participating. That
set the pattern for the evening. The chorus performed one
song, and then the public would be invited to sing the following one too. Each sing-along carol was a familiar one so
most people would know all the words.

When they paused more than an hour later, Mary couldn't
believe how quickly the time had passed. Her fingers could,
though, because they felt like ten ice cubes. She folded her
arms in front of herself and tucked her gloved hands between them and her body. Funny how she hadn't noticed the
cold because she'd been so caught up in the singing.

She spotted her children talking with people their own
ages, and she guessed they were catching up with summer-
time friends they'd made during their visits to Ivy Bay during
their school years. The grandchildren had joined other kids
playing on the swings and monkey bars and chasing each
other around the trees at the edge of the park.

"How about something warm to drink?" Betty asked.
"Susan has a table set up over there, and she's probably sell-
ing her amazing hot chocolate."

Mary quickly agreed. As they approached the table where
a long line waited, she drew in the luscious scent of hot chocolate, whipped cream, and handmade marshmallows. She

thought about the cookies she had ordered from the bakery for the reading on Christmas Eve afternoon. Her mouth watered as she imagined how good they would smell. By the time she was served, her taste buds were eager for a sip. She took the cup in both hands to warm her fingers, then stepped aside to let others get their cups and waited for the steaming beverage to cool enough so she could drink.

"Mary!"

At the call of her name, Mary turned to discover Dorothy walking toward her. She was bundled up in a lovely light gray coat and a bright blue scarf that matched her jaunty hat and gloves.

"I thought I'd see you here," Dorothy said.

Mary smiled. "Isn't this fun?"

"What have you found out?" *Trust Dorothy to get right to the point.*

"Not much," Mary replied. "I want to find out more about this animal rights group over at the high school. They may know something about the missing sheep."

Dorothy shrugged. "It's your time to waste. I believe in getting answers by asking questions, instead of going on wild sheep chases."

Mary hesitated, then said, "Dorothy, you may want to ask your questions a bit differently."

"Has someone complained?" Her eyes widened. "A person who complains may be our costume thief."

"I know you're as honest as anyone I've ever met," Mary said, "but not everyone is that way. Asking them if they took the costumes or know who did may not be the best way to solve a mystery." As Dorothy drew herself up to retort, Mary went on quickly. "Think about the mystery novels you've read. The sleuths do ask questions, but they never go around asking other characters to list their opinions of 'whodunit.' They also look for clues to lead them to the right people to ask."

"That's true." Dorothy deflated somewhat. "I didn't think it was that difficult to solve mysteries because you keep doing it so easily."

Mary smiled. "That couldn't be further from the truth, because no mystery I've been involved with has been solved easily. I must admit, though, that I enjoy gathering the clues and arranging them and rearranging them and rearranging them again to get to the truth."

"All right. I'll try something else." Dorothy smiled. "I do have a few other tricks up my sleeve. I'll keep my favorite sleuths in mind and strive to solve the mystery as one of them would. You've given me some good advice, so let me give *you* some."

Mary's instinct was to be annoyed, but she bit her tongue. Dorothy was being a bit smug, sure, but Mary tried to let it go. She didn't have anything to prove, even if Dorothy did.

"You do know, don't you," Dorothy continued, "that Mavis put up some more posters last night, and they'd vanished by this morning when the rest of her team went out to hang up more."

Mary shook her head. "I didn't know that."

Dorothy gave her a superior look. "Well, now you do. I'm going to concentrate on persuading Hannah that a lack of costumes isn't any reason to keep from having the living Nativity. Think how many times our children have done pageants wearing sheets and aluminum foil wings!"

"But if the rest of the participants are willing—"

"Nobody wants to hurt Hannah's feelings and other seamstresses' feelings by making it seem like their hard work really doesn't matter."

Mary had to admit that made sense, even though she was sorry that Hannah and her team were holding the living Nativity hostage until the costumes were found. Not that they would think of it like that. They simply were hurt by what had happened, and they weren't willing to showcase anything less than the best of their work. If Hannah would have budged and let the volunteers put together new costumes, the living Nativity could have gone on as planned. Now it had become personal, exactly as Dorothy said.

But maybe she could use Hannah's stubbornness to help Dorothy. She offered a thoughtful look. "That's a good example of why it's important for us to look at clues without any emotion. When we take things too personally, it clouds our vision, and we can miss the truth standing right in front of us."

"How can I do that when my church and my living Nativity have been targeted by thieves and vandals? You were there last night. You saw the disappointment on everyone's faces."

Again, Mary knew Dorothy was right. She'd seen the sadness and dismay last night and again this afternoon when she'd spoken with Ashley and Courtney. The living Nativity meant a lot to everyone involved, especially Betty, who had put so much time and effort into it.

Dorothy wished her good luck on her search, then wandered off.

Mary sipped her hot chocolate while she went to look for her family. The sweet warmth coursed through her. She was halfway back to the risers when a man bumped into her and nearly spilled her cocoa.

He could easily have played Santa if he had a white beard. His hair was snowy, and his round cheeks were apple-red with the cold. He wasn't very tall. His black worsted-wool coat was well-made and looked new, and his shoes shone in the dim light.

"Oh, excuse me." He started to walk away, then paused. "Wait. Are you Mary Fisher, by any chance?"

"Yes." She wondered how he knew her.

He extended his hand to Mary. "I'm Dennis Morton. From Bourne."

"How nice of you to join us tonight, Mr. Morton."

"Make it Dennis." He scanned the crowd. "One of the kids passing out flyers told me to talk to you about the living Nativity that had to be canceled."

"It's actually only been postponed until—"

He didn't let her finish. "Good thing we've got a living Nativity of our own in Bourne. It's going to be on Christmas Eve. By the way, the kid over there told me that you were in charge of the living Nativity."

"Actually my sister is."

"Do you think she'd be willing to talk to me about it?"

"I don't see why not." She motioned for him to come with her as they wove through the crowd.

"Lots of people here tonight," Dennis said. "One thing I've never been able to figure out is why Ivy Bay gets more tourists than Bourne."

"I didn't realize that."

"It's true." His chest puffed out more. "I'm a selectman in Bourne, and it's been a topic of conversation lately at board meetings."

Mary knew several of the towns on Cape Cod were governed by elected Boards of Selectmen. It was each board's job to discuss issues and present them at the twice-yearly town meetings to be voted on by residents.

"Bourne is a beautiful town, the gateway to the rest of the Cape." His voice boomed across the crowd as he went on to list the best attributes of the town that was the farthest west on the Cape. He sounded like a tourist brochure, and she was curious why he felt the need to tell her—and everyone around them—all of that.

Where was Betty? Mary felt a pinch of guilt at wanting to hand off Dennis Morton to her sister. He was clearly in love with the sound of his own voice, and he didn't care who knew that. Heads turned as they passed. He noticed and smiled more broadly as he talked about the super-fabulous events, as he put it, that Bourne had planned for Christmas week.

Suddenly he excused himself and hurried away without further explanation. Mary breathed a deep sigh of relief. Now she didn't have to introduce him to Betty. As upset as her sister was about the cancellation of the living Nativity, she didn't need to have to listen to Dennis's bragging about the one Bourne would have on Christmas Eve.

Mary halted in midstep, and the crowd flowed around her as if she were a boulder in the middle of a stream. Dennis Morton had shown no regret that Grace Church's living Nativity had been postponed. Was Dennis so determined to help his own town that he'd undermine Ivy Bay's Christmas plans? Would he tear down the posters and steal the sheep and costumes to prevent Grace Church's living Nativity, which would have competed with the one in Bourne? Mary couldn't imagine how he would have gotten into the church, but she put him on her short list of suspects. Proving Dennis was involved could be a long shot. Yet she couldn't overlook any possibility, even if it seemed ludicrous now.

The chorus was filing up onto the risers again, and Mary still hadn't found any of her family. She smiled when Rhonda Keaton, the high school principal, waved to her. Rhonda was wearing a letterman's jacket with the words *Ivy Bay High School* circling a tiny ram's head logo on the front. That must be the school mascot.

"Rhonda, how are you tonight?" Mary asked.

"Cold." She wrapped her arms around herself.

Mary laughed. "I agree. Thank heavens for this delicious hot chocolate, which has thawed me out a bit before I turned into a human icicle. Still, I wouldn't have missed the sing-along. The chorus sounded great."

"Mavis works miracles with the kids every year. She challenges them to be better than they think they can be. I wish I had a dozen more teachers like her."

"Can I ask you about a group at school?"

"Sure. Which one?"

"PAP. What can you tell me about them?"

"That group is brand-new," Rhonda said. "Shelby Ellis started it in the fall. So far they only have six or seven members."

"Really? The way Ivy Bay is plastered with their posters, I would have guessed it was four or five times that many."

Rhonda smiled. "A small group of kids with a mission is a force to be reckoned with. These kids really care about protecting animals, especially farm animals and sea birds."

"I've seen that."

"I bet you have." She gave Mary a wry smile. "Grace Church using a live sheep as part of the Nativity gave them a cause to focus on." She shoved her hands into her pockets. "If you have any more questions about PAP or other high school kids, you're always welcome to ask me. I'm in my office for a couple of hours every day after school."

"Thanks." Mary was tempted to ask Rhonda if she thought the members of PAP would take the sheep, but recalled her own advice to Dorothy. She needed facts, not guesses.

"It's a real shame that the living Nativity may have to be canceled," Rhonda said. "The kids in it have been really excited about dressing up, and I was especially pleased that Brian Flanagan was going to be Joseph. Being part of something like that, with his friends as backup, is a good way for a shy kid to come out of his shell."

"It's too bad for the kids. I know the little girls who were playing angels are pretty discouraged too."

"I bet they are."

Emma rushed up and held out her hand. "Grandma, there you are! Come on! They're getting ready to sing more songs."

Taking her granddaughter's hand, Mary said good-bye to Rhonda and went to join the rest of her family, who had gathered to the left side of the risers. She sang "The First Noel" along with everyone else, but her mind was far from silent.

She had several potential suspects. PAP, Dennis Morton, Luis Alvarez, and Abbie Lindstrom. But she could tie each one only to one or two of the pieces of the mystery. None of them seemed to have had the chance to be a suspect in all three. PAP was focused on saving Peep, but why would they need to tear down the posters or steal the costumes? They were plastering their own posters everywhere, and the bright green would catch the eye more than the white and red posters made by Grace Church volunteers. Abbie must have been really upset because she was fired, but would she have taken the sheep and the posters as well as the costumes? Knowing Hannah as well as she must, she would have guessed that the costumes vanishing would be enough to halt the living Nativity. And what about Luis and Dennis?

They might want to keep the living Nativity from conflicting with their events, but to go to the trouble of ripping down dozens of posters and stealing a sheep seemed excessive.

She was still missing something.

But what?

That was what she needed to find out. Right away.

✳ Chapter Seven

The next morning, Mary's first thought upon awakening was that there were only five more days before Christmas Eve and their final chance to present the living Nativity that year. She needed to make use of every minute. While the others were finishing breakfast, she called Abbie Lindstrom. She listened as the machine went through its prerecorded spiel.

When it beeped, she said, "Abbie, this is Mary Fisher. I'm Betty Emerson's sister and a member of Grace Church. Do you have some time when we could get together and talk? I've heard you did a lot of work on the costumes for the church's living Nativity, and I'd really like to chat with you about that. Please give me a call." She left the house's phone number, her cell's, and the bookshop's.

As she hung up the phone, she wondered if she should have left that message. If Abbie had taken the costumes, why would she want to talk to Mary? But Mary wouldn't get anywhere by trying to trick the young woman. Better to be up front right from the beginning and find out if Abbie would call back.

She walked into the kitchen, where Betty was putting the flour canister on the kitchen table.

"Any luck?" Betty turned to get the sugar canister.

"No. She either isn't there or isn't answering the phone."

"I could try calling later, if you'd like. Maybe I'll catch her in."

"Let's give her a chance to call back." Mary laughed. "We don't want her to think we're stalking her."

"Who are you stalking, Grandma?" Daisy asked as she led the grandchildren into the kitchen. Evan's two girls had stayed the night, and the children looked as if they hadn't slept much. From the noise during the night, Mary doubted they had. But they'd had fun.

"I'm stalking our cookie-makers." Mary motioned for the children to hurry into the kitchen.

Laughter rang through the cozy room as the grandchildren discovered that Mary and Betty had set out two prep areas. One was for sugar cookies. The other had the ingredients for making gingerbread. Each child could decide which type of cookies they wanted to make first.

Mary wasn't surprised that, despite the discussion yesterday, Daisy joined Betsy and Allison at the gingerbread end of the table while the others began mixing up sugar cookies. The cousins teased each other and joked as they worked.

Once the dough went into the refrigerator to chill, Betty shooed the children out of the kitchen. Their parents were taking them to visit the Edaville Railroad, about a half hour away on the other side of the Bourne Bridge. Even the older children looked forward to going on the rides set amid cranberry bogs. None of the grandchildren had visited the park before, though Mary and Betty used to take their children there as an annual tradition.

The house became quiet while Mary helped Betty clean up the kitchen. They laughed when they found flour scattered in places they hadn't expected. The children had been enthusiastic about mixing up the cookies.

"I'll try to be back before the kids get home," Mary said as she rinsed the last of the flour out of a dishrag and wrung it out before placing it on the sink. "Do you need anything while I'm out?"

"I think we're good," Betty said. "I asked Evan to pick up more milk on their way back. I guess I've forgotten how much a child can drink. The kids wanted hamburgers for dinner, and I've got the meat and rolls. I'll mix up a green salad once they get home. Nice and simple."

"And we have popcorn for this evening."

"Perfect." Betty took off her apron and folded it on the back of the chair. "I think I'll head over to church and see if there's any place we missed looking for those costumes." She smiled, but shook her head. "I know it's silly, but I've got to do something. It's a shame that everyone put in so much time and was willing to give up even more time to put on the living Nativity, and now it's been cancelled."

"Postponed."

"Call it what you will, but it's not happening." Betty pushed away from the chair and walked to the counter. "I talked to Mavis last night, and she's deeply disappointed. She and her husband are still pleased, though, that Brian was chosen to play Joseph each night."

"Rhonda Keaton, the high principal, mentioned she thought it'd be good for him because he's shy."

"Shy doesn't begin to describe it. The poor kid couldn't even get through leading a responsive reading with his confirmation class a few years ago. He blushed and then lost his place and finally gave up. Since then, the pastor has asked him to do small things behind the scenes, so he's getting some positive feedback."

"Being Joseph would have been good for him."

"Very good. He could have been in front of the public without having to worry about blushing or stuttering or being worried that he'd make a fool of himself." Betty picked up a set of dirty measuring spoons that had been left on the far end of the counter. "Maybe next year."

"Don't give up hope. The costumes may still be found."

Betty sighed. "But in time?"

"I hope so. I keep thinking about Psalm 149: '*For the Lord taketh pleasure in his people: he will beautify the meek with salvation.*' Once Brian realizes that he's never alone when he faces a crowd, he'll find a closer way to walk with God."

"Thank you, Mary." Betty's smile returned. "That is what I needed to hear. I will pray that Brian feels God's presence and comfort within his heart."

Mary hesitated, then asked, "Did Dennis Morton talk to you last night?"

"Who's that?"

She explained about meeting the selectman from Bourne. "He wanted to talk to you about the living Nativity."

"He didn't find me."

Mary glanced at her watch to hide her gratitude that Dennis must have gotten distracted by other people and hadn't bothered her sister. "I'm going to be late if I don't get going. Rebecca's coming in this afternoon, so I'll be home early."

"Great. Maybe we can pop some extra popcorn, and the kids can string it tonight." She laughed. "I don't think they could have come up with different traditions on how to put popcorn on a piece of thread."

"Sounds like a great idea." Mary waved, then went into the hall to get her coat. Pulling it on, she decided to walk to work. It would be quicker than driving the short distance and trying to find a parking place when many shoppers crowded Main Street.

Gus appeared by the front door and looked up at her with an expectant expression. With a smile, she got his carrying case and let him into it.

"Your whole schedule is in a tizzy, isn't it?" she asked as she zipped up the case and her coat. "Too soon everyone will be gone, and you'll be king of the house again."

He mewed, and she laughed. Sometimes, it was almost as if he understood what she was saying.

The morning was even chillier than yesterday. Clouds hung low in the sky, and the ocean had a sallow sheen without the sun to glint off it. Wrapping her scarf even closer to her chin, she walked toward the center of Ivy Bay.

The bright color of the neighbors' Christmas decorations eased the grim day. With no snow, the trees bare, and the grass a wintry brown, the only colors were the red and green and gold of nutcrackers and angels and glittering reindeer and wreaths decorated with cranberries.

In this section of the village, the decorating was more subdued than what she'd seen in the Sea Breezes neighborhood. Some of the houses had lights on their eaves and around porch columns, but nobody had gone overboard.

As she reached the end of the street, Mary paused and stared at Patrick Walker's precious Model A convertible. What had he told her it was called? Some sort of phaeton. The car had a shimmering black finish and a light brown cloth top. Its wheels, including the spare that was set by the passenger-side door, were painted a brilliant red. The chrome had been shined to the point that it would have been impossible to look at on a sunny day.

Glancing around, she didn't see their neighbor. That was odd, because she couldn't remember him ever parking his beloved car in the driveway unless he was washing it with as much care as he would a newborn baby.

Then she noticed a couple other neighbors, who usually parked their cars in their garages, had left their vehicles out too. Plenty of unfamiliar cars and trucks were parked in front of houses, and she looked back at where she and Betty lived. The curb was empty now, but once the kids returned, there would be extra cars there too.

Everyone made changes for their holidays when guests came to stay. It was part of the fun chaos of Christmas.

Mary had to wait for the signal to change before she could cross Route 6A to continue along Main Street. To her left, Jason's garbage truck inched down the highway. He stopped by each trash can and emptied it into the back of the truck.

Several cars passed while she waited to cross the road. She checked again before stepping out and noticed Jason stopping his truck where no trash can waited. He jumped out and went around the front of the truck. Instead of reappearing at the back with garbage to be dumped, he rushed back around the front. He glanced quickly along the street in both directions before he climbed into the truck. Someone must have forgotten to put out their trash last night.

Mary smiled at the memory of how, when she first moved to Ivy Bay, she had a hard time remembering which night they were supposed to put out the trash can. She had been so used to her schedule before the move that her brain kept reminding her on the wrong night.

When Jason drove past her, he waved with a broad smile. She waved back and said another quick prayer for him. He was a nice guy, but he seemed overwhelmed. She added another request for God to guide her to the answers she sought.

Mary hadn't gone more than a few steps before she had to jump out of the way when a man came out of Jimmy's Hardware, carrying a stack of garish blue boxes.

Christmas lights, she realized.

"Hi!" came a somewhat familiar voice from behind the blue boxes. "Don't let me bump into you."

Luis's smile was bright as he stepped past her and went to his truck parked nearby.

Mary hoped her smile didn't look forced. She had so many questions she wanted to ask, starting with whether or not he had taken the costumes and the sheep, but she couldn't exactly put him on the spot when she didn't have anything but circumstantial evidence that he might be the culprit she sought.

When his smile began to waver, she knew she had to say something. She chose the first thing that came to mind that wasn't about the missing items.

"You must have bought every box of Christmas lights in the hardware store," she said.

He laughed, but was she imagining things or was the sound of his laugh as strained as her smile felt? "Here and in Bourne and in Falmouth and in Hyannis." He set the boxes on the open tailgate as he reached into the bed of his truck. He lifted out a sign with his company's name and logo on it and set it between the truck and the curb. He shifted the boxes of lights onto the truck's bed, then lashed them carefully into place and closed the back. "My goal is to make my neighborhood visible from the International

Space Station." He bent toward Gus's carrying case. "Who's your friend?"

"Gus. Actually Augustine, but he answers to Gus. When he feels like it."

Luis chuckled. "That's a cat for you. Ours knows one word. Food. She ignores everything else we say to her." He picked up the sign he'd taken from the back of his truck. Opening the passenger-side door, he put the sign in the truck's cab. "I'd planned to post this by the living Nativity. Your pastor suggested it as a thank-you for my help with the wiring." He shrugged. "Not that it matters now." Closing the door, he asked, "Any sign of the missing costumes? Everyone in Jimmy's Hardware is talking about how they've vanished."

She watched for his reaction when she said, "Nothing so far."

"That's too bad." Nothing but what appeared to be honest dismay showed on his face. "And I'm not saying that just because I could have gotten some nice free publicity." Fishing his keys out of his pocket, he said, "If you've heard people say I started the lighting contest to show off what lighting can do, don't believe them. I simply love Christmas lights."

Mary couldn't help comparing Luis's enthusiasm for the holiday with Jason's lack of pleasure with Christmas. "I'm still praying," she said, "that the costumes will turn up before Christmas."

"That would be wonderful, but it's a good thing I had this lighting contest planned before your church announced its living Nativity. Now people have a place to go."

"They could have done both."

He leaned a casual elbow on his truck as he pulled on his battered work gloves. He'd made a big deal of the fact that he was allergic to lanolin. Such a big deal that…was it possible he was looking for an alibi right from the get-go? He always seemed to have a pair of gloves with him, so he could have taken the sheep without touching it.

His voice was taut and slow as if he was choosing his words carefully. "I checked around town to make sure there wasn't anything competing with the nights of the lighting contest. There wasn't, so I announced the showcase would start on December 22. The award for the house that gets the most votes will be on Christmas Eve. I set it up so people can vote for their favorite house by leaving a nonperishable item in front of that house. Then, after I got everyone fired up about it, your church announced the living Nativity. That was annoying, I have to admit."

"The living Nativity was supposed to run for a week, so people would have had plenty of time to visit both it and the lighting contest."

"Except the living Nativity was having a special choral presentation and procession of animals on Christmas Eve after a candlelight service."

Mary was astonished. "You knew that it would conflict with your lighting contest, and yet you helped Kip with the lighting for the living Nativity?"

"Kip has done me a lot of favors over the years, stepping in to assist on projects so I could get them done on time. When he asked me to help, I couldn't say no, even when he wanted me to work on the living Nativity that was sure to cut into the number of people attending the lighting contest." His brows lowered in a frown. "Speaking of Grace Church, do you know why Dorothy Johnson has been leaving cryptic messages on my answering machine?"

"What sort of cryptic messages?"

He shrugged. "I don't remember word for word, but something about desperately needing to talk to me about an item that I left there. I checked, and I have everything I took to the church. Do you know what she's talking about?"

Mary shook her head. "I really don't." What had Dorothy found?

"If you see her," Luis asked, "would you tell her that I'll get back to her after the holidays? Right now, I'm out straight."

That could be a handy excuse. Or it could be the truth. Mary wasn't sure which.

"I will," she said when she realized he was again waiting for her to answer.

He opened his truck door. As he swung up behind the wheel, he added, "Will I see you at the lighting contest?"

"I'm sure we'll be there."

"Good." He slammed the door and started the truck. He drove away.

Mary watched the truck until it turned a corner at the end of the street, then she continued toward her shop with more questions and no answers.

* * *

The morning at the bookshop was quiet. So quiet that the *drip, drip, drip* of the faucet in the back room could be heard throughout the shop. Only a single customer came in, and he picked up a book that had been ordered the previous week. Mary dusted the shelves, checked to make sure everything was in its proper place, and added a few more copies of books to the holiday table. She went over her to-do list for the upcoming reading in the children's area. Everything seemed to be on schedule.

Deciding they might as well enjoy the peace and quiet, Mary made a cup of tea for herself and opened a can of Gus's favorite food. Currently he preferred salmon, but she knew at any time he would turn up his nose at it and act as if he'd never eaten it without being forced.

She sat where she had a view of the door and relaxed with her fragrant tea. Gus leaped up to sit on her lap while he cleaned each of his whiskers with excruciating precision. When he was finished, he curled into a ball and fell asleep. A soft purr matched his slow breaths.

Petting his head as she sipped, Mary thought about how precious this stray cat had become to her. She frowned down into her cup. The kids in the PAP group took their concerns about animals and animal rights very seriously. Would one of them simply release the sheep from its pen and let it wander away on its own? That didn't seem to fit with their love of animals.

She didn't know enough about the club to be certain about anything they might do. Rhonda had urged her to come over to the high school whenever she needed more information. That sounded like an invitation she should accept today.

The chime over the door made a cheerful sound, and Mary stood. She smiled when Henry Woodrow walked into the shop. Years of plying Cape Cod Bay on his boat, *Misty Horizon*, had left him tanned even in the winter.

"Are you the one who ordered this cold, damp weather?" he asked.

She laughed as she did so often with Henry, who had become such a good friend since her return to Ivy Bay, just as he had been long ago, when they were kids and Mary would visit with her family during the summers.

"Definitely not," she said, "but I did order a plumber to fix the leak in the faucet out back."

He unzipped his dark blue overcoat. "I can look at it now if you'd like, but I'll need to go back to the house to get my tools."

"Don't worry about it now." She held up her cup. "How about a cup of something hot?"

"Coffee, if you've got some."

"It'll take me a minute to brew up some."

"What do you have?" He pointed to Mary's cup.

"Tea."

He grimaced. "No thanks."

She smiled. "I'll make some coffee. It won't take long."

"Good, because the sooner I'm drinking it, the sooner I'll warm up my frozen bones."

Mary kept smiling as she turned on the coffeemaker and fixed him a cup of coffee. Carrying it back to where Henry was petting Gus's head, she heard him talking to the cat as if Gus understood every word he spoke.

Henry took the cup. Drawing in a deep breath of the steam, he said, "Thanks. This will hit the spot."

She motioned toward the chair next to hers, and Henry took it. Gus jumped onto her lap when she sat. Over his purring, she said, "Henry, I'm glad you stopped in. I could use your advice."

"Mine? About what?" Henry looked up from his cup.

"Have you heard about the troubles with the living Nativity at Grace Church?"

He nodded. "Everyone's talking about it. To tell you the truth, that's one of the reasons I stopped in today. I figured by now you'd be on the trail of whoever has tried to ruin the living Nativity."

"I am, but I'm stymied." A quick smile rushed across her lips. "I know I often am when I start trying to solve a mystery, but I really am this time."

"What do you know for sure?"

Mary told Henry what she knew and realized how little she had discovered. Trying not to be discouraged, she finished with, "So what do you think?"

"I think you're barking up the wrong tree. PAP can't be the ones who took the sheep."

"You sound really sure about that."

"I am." He sipped his coffee. "Didn't you say the president of the group is Shelby Ellis?"

"Yes."

"And didn't you say Ken Gomes lent the sheep to the church?"

"Yes."

"Then I don't see how PAP, and most especially Shelby, could be involved in releasing the sheep. Shelby is Ken's niece."

Mary didn't reply straightaway as she added that fact to the few she had already. She recalled how vehement Shelby had been about the sheep being kept in a small pen. That Peep belonged to Shelby's uncle and had gone missing would make a girl who loved animals even more upset.

"Maybe we're looking at this backward," Mary said.

"What do you mean?" Henry asked.

"With Shelby being Ken's niece, isn't it logical to assume that she knows how to tend to sheep?"

"It's possible. If it's true, then Shelby might believe that Peep is safer with her than in a pen at the church."

"That's assuming Shelby and PAP took Peep." Mary drew in a deep breath and let it hiss out between her teeth. "But why wouldn't Shelby return the sheep to her uncle's farm? I think I need to find out more about PAP and talk to Shelby."

"That sounds like a good idea, Mary. Anything I can do to help?"

She considered his question, then nodded. "Keep your ears open. Maybe somebody saw something that they don't realize is important, but added together with what Dorothy and I uncover, it could be the important clue that solves the mystery."

"Dorothy?" His brows arched.

Mary explained how Dorothy was also looking for the answers.

"Now that should be interesting," he said in a slow drawl that made Mary laugh.

She was still smiling several hours later after Henry had left and Rebecca arrived with Ashley, who'd had a half day of school. She wasn't surprised to see Ashley had her halo with her. The little girl obviously intended to keep a close eye on it.

Mary was eager to head to the high school to talk with Shelby and the other members of PAP. She waited until two customers had completed their purchases and left the shop before she said, "Rebecca, I need to run out for an hour or so."

"For some sleuthing?"

"You know me too well." Mary chuckled.

Rebecca did too. "I just recognize that gleam in your eye that tells me you're ready to track down another clue. Go ahead and good luck. Ashley and I'll hold down the fort here."

"Thanks." Maybe she could get some real answers this afternoon.

✳ Chapter Eight

G us didn't want to get into his carrying case, so Mary could take him home before she visited the high school. He was enjoying Ashley's company too much. At last, Ashley convinced him to go into the carrying case by giving him a crumb of her oatmeal cookie from Sweet Susan's Bakery.

Mary thanked her, adding, "What would I do without you, Ashley?"

"I don't know," the little girl said in all seriousness. "You know what?"

"What?"

"I hope we still get to be angels in the Nativity."

"Me too." Mary took her coat off its peg and pulled it on. "There's still time to find the costumes."

Ashley gave a deep sigh. "I wish I'd been smart like Courtney and kept my costume at home."

"Courtney's costume wasn't with the others?" Mary was surprised. She had thought that all the costumes were at the church where Hannah could keep a close eye on them. She wondered if anyone else had held on to their costume.

"Nope."

"Does Mrs. Flanagan know that Courtney has her costume?" Mary had seen Mavis's dismay at the living Nativity's termination.

"Everyone knows."

"Does Brian have his costume at home too?"

"I don't know. Courtney didn't say. She just talked about being glad that she still had hers." Ashley sighed as she gave Gus another cookie crumb. "Now she can dress up like an angel any time she wants. All I have is my halo."

"Have faith, Ashley. It's still a few days before Christmas. The costumes may still be found before then."

The little girl stood. "You're looking for them, aren't you?"

"I am. So are a lot of other people."

Ashley pondered that for a moment, then asked, "Can I help find them?"

"Of course."

"How?"

Mary smiled. "By listening. Sometimes people will say something in front of a kid that they won't say around other adults."

"Yeah." Ashley grimaced knowingly. "Some people think we don't understand anything but video games and cartoons."

"But you must promise me that you will come to me with whatever you hear. Let me ask the questions. Not you, because some adults don't like anyone questioning them." She thought of the reaction to Dorothy's terse questions. "Especially when it's a kid."

"I know." She rolled her eyes.

"Just listen and then you can tell me if you hear anything interesting."

Her eyes widened. "You mean like being a spy?" She giggled. "That'll be fun."

"I hope so." She picked up Gus's cage and carried him out into the blustery afternoon. She doubted that Ashley understood how many things Mary was hoping for, but mostly she was hoping for answers.

*   *   *

Ivy Bay High School had been built as a WPA project during the Depression, but several newer wings had been added since then. The sun had sunk far enough below the clouds to the west that the windows appeared to have been gilded.

Mary pulled down the visor on her car as she pulled into the parking lot. She selected one of the spaces set aside for visitors. Most of the lot was empty. Like Ashley's class, the high school classes must have been let out at noon. More than a dozen cars were in the students' lot, and Mary guessed the teens were still at school for sports practice or participation in one of the clubs.

Mary pushed an intercom button and was let into the school by a hall monitor who checked her driver's license and wrote something on a clipboard. In the distance, Mary could hear the whir of a floor buffer. Muted voices came from one of the nearby classrooms along with the sound of laughter.

The girl by the door asked, "Do you know the way to the office? All visitors need to sign in."

"I think I know, but why don't you give me directions just in case?"

The girl, whose hair was pulled back in a simple pony-tail that sparkled with glitter, motioned toward the end of the hall. "Go down there past the gym. Then turn right and right again. The office will be on your left. You'll see it. It has acrylic walls." She snapped gum that Mary doubted she was supposed to be chewing, though the rules might have changed since Mary's own school days.

"Thanks." She turned to go, then paused. "Do you know if PAP is meeting today?"

"PAP?" The girl looked at her as if Mary had suddenly started speaking Swahili.

"Yes. It's an animal rights group. It's brand-new."

"Oh, *that* club." The girl's disdain made it very clear that she considered PAP way down on the social pecking order at the high school.

Mary didn't react. Things hadn't been that different when she was in high school. Certain groups and students were deemed cool. Others were for artsy types. Then there were the nerds. The terms might not be the same, but the hierarchy was.

"I don't know if they're meeting today or not," the girl went on when Mary didn't say anything. "They'll probably know at the office." She blew a bubble, then popped it with a grin. "That's the biggest one ever."

Mary smiled and thanked the girl. As she went down the hall, the girl returned to her chair and picked up a romance novel to read.

Mary walked along the empty hall. Her footsteps seemed overly resonant on the concrete tiles. She guessed that when the teens gathered between classes around the lockers lining both walls, the noise would be a lot louder.

As she got closer to the gym, she noticed dozens of posters in every size taped to the wall. Each one listed the time for a pep rally tomorrow evening to get everyone fired up for the big game against Ivy Bay's rival, Barnstable. She guessed that the Ivy Bay versus Barnstable matchup must be one of the premier basketball games of the season.

She paused by open doors to the gym. The basketball team was running drills. One boy would race down the court and do a lay-up before running to the back of a line of boys waiting for their turns. Another boy caught the ball and dribbled to the opposite basket to do a lay-up. As a teammate handled the rebound, that boy ran to the back of the other line.

The walls were covered with more posters about the pep rally and big game. On one set of bleachers, some girls were bent over posterboard, making even more signs.

At a sharp whistle from the coach, the boys halted and headed toward the other bleachers. On the lowest seats, water bottles and towels leaned against backpacks. Mary recognized one of the boys.

"Hi, Brian," she said as she walked into the gym. "You looked like you were having a great time out there."

He whirled. "Oh, hi, Mrs. Fisher. Are you looking for Mom?"

"Your principal asked me to stop by." She gave him a wide grin. "Don't worry. I'm not being called to the principal's office because I'm in trouble."

He wore a shy smile, but his eyes didn't meet hers. "I never would have thought that."

"So the big game is coming up?"

"The biggest," said a teen behind him, slapping him on the shoulder. "It's a good thing that Flanagan is on our side. We're going to make Barnstable wish they'd stayed home."

The rest of the team roared with laughter and, grabbing their backpacks and other supplies, jogged off as the coach called for them to hit the showers. Brian lingered behind when Mary asked him if he could answer a question for her.

"I'll try." He still didn't look her in the eyes. His gaze focused on the single backpack left by the bleachers.

"Do you know about PAP?" she asked.

"Mom mentioned she'd seen their posters at the park last night."

"I saw them there too."

"Mom wasn't happy."

"Why?" Mary wondered if she could get more than a few words at a time out of the shy boy.

"The posters she and the other ladies hung up in town yesterday have been torn down again." He stared at the floor.

"Again?" She wondered if Mavis and her prayer circle were wasting their time until whoever was ripping the posters off the poles was identified.

He nodded.

"I'm sorry to hear that."

He grimaced. "Don't know why she bothers. It's obvious the living Nativity isn't going to happen. Everyone needs to accept that." He glanced at her and away quickly.

Mary let her sigh sift out silently. Too many people had been hurt by whoever was trying to stop the living Nativity. Brian did not have to say anything else for her to guess that he was upset because his mother's efforts with the posters had been futile.

"Do you know anything else about PAP?" she asked.

"Nothing much." He again looked at his backpack as if it were the most fascinating item on the planet. "I've been too focused on the big game." He raised his head and grinned. "Are you coming?"

"I think everyone in town will probably be here."

His answer was halted when music blared over the gym's loudspeakers and a group of cheerleaders rushed out to the middle of the floor to begin a complicated routine. Mary held her breath as they formed a human pyramid and jumped back to the floor. Another group of girls danced around them, matching the rhythm by clapping and stamping their feet.

"Wow!" Mary said as she watched the performance. "Those cheerleaders are really brave."

Brian glanced at the middle of the floor. "The ones running around are the pep squad. They work on making sure everyone is excited about the game ahead of time. The girls have been practicing as hard as we have. Most of the time, they've had to practice outside because we're using the gym."

"And they dash in here whenever they have a chance?"

"Guess so."

The coach blew his whistle and waved impatiently to Brian. Mary watched as the teen grabbed his backpack and ran around the cheerleaders and the pep squad to head into the boys' locker room.

She walked out of the gym and toward Rhonda's office. The cheers from inside the gym burst out, barely muted by the walls.

She made the first right turn, and even the girls' shouts disappeared. Again she was wrapped in silence. She fought the temptation to walk on tiptoe so her heels didn't ring on the concrete floor.

Wait a minute...What was that on the floor in front of a door ahead of her? It looked like...It was. Hay!

Someone had moved the bale of hay from Peep's pen in front of the church. Could hay have stuck to that person's clothing? Could it have fallen off here? With the cold December this year, the grass should be frozen, so it was unlikely someone had walked across the school's front yard and tracked it inside.

What was on the other side of the door? Mary didn't expect to open it and discover Peep inside, but she might find out if this dried grass was a real clue or not.

Mary knocked on the door and waited for an answer. She didn't want to interrupt if someone was using the room.

No answer.

She knocked again, and, when she didn't get an answer to that knock, she opened the door and peeked in.

It was a locker room. Rows of lockers were set across from a trio of showers. The combined smells of hot water and perfume and sweat rolled over her. Towels had been dropped on the floor in front of the showers, and some of the lockers were open to reveal backpacks and make-up.

The girls' locker room.

Closing the door, Mary continued along the hall until she reached a trash can. She tossed the dried grass inside and gave an ironic laugh. The perfect clue to point the way to the sheep, except Brian had told her the pep squad and cheerleaders had been practicing outside. With their leaps and tricks, they could have torn out even frozen grass and tracked it into the school.

"No answers come that easily," she reminded herself as she turned the corner toward the office.

She went into the brightly lit office. The secretary asked her to wait until Rhonda finished a phone call, so Mary sat on a bench in the outer office.

A score of thoughts whirled in different directions. The stolen costumes. Peep. The disappearing posters. None of her suspects seemed to have a reason to take all three. Not that she had discerned…yet. If there was no connection between the three incidents, then she might be on a wild goose chase. Making assumptions could lead her to overlook the truth right under her nose.

Now *that* was an uncomfortable thought. She clearly was missing something. A vital clue or point of view that would give her clearer insight into who was behind what she hoped were only pranks. Yet, if more than one person was involved, she needed to be looking for several different people, people who didn't have to have motive and opportunity for the three misdeeds. Any passersby could have had access to Peep or the posters.

She silenced a groan. Everything might have just gotten more complicated.

✳ Chapter Nine

Rhonda ushered Mary into her office. A battered sofa had a bright red, yellow, and green granny square afghan draped over the back. Bookshelves behind a large desk were filled with books, papers, CDs, and magazines. The desk had a blotter in the middle, and a cup with "#1 Principal" printed on it held pens and pencils. The phone had more buttons than a computer, and several were flashing.

"Ignore the phone," Rhonda said with the ease of repetition. "We haven't figured out how to make those lights go out. There aren't any lines connected to those buttons. The kids call those the lines to the school spirit." She laughed. "Not that they need help with the big game coming up tomorrow night."

"I saw the kids practicing in the gym. They're really excited."

"One of the reasons we plan the game for *after* the kids are out on Christmas break. Trying to teach them anything when their minds are focused on the game would be a waste of everyone's time." She motioned for Mary to sit on the sofa. "I didn't expect to see you here on the Friday before Christmas."

Mary sat and sank deep into the cushion. She shifted to keep her feet on the floor. "I was hoping to speak to Shelby Ellis and the other members of PAP. The hall monitor said she didn't have any idea where they're meeting."

Rhonda walked back to the door. A large dry-erase calendar hung there. All the squares had been filled in with notes in multiple colors. "With all the groups the kids have, this is the only way we've been able to figure out how to keep track of when they meet." She ran her finger down the list for Friday, December 20th. "Ah, here they are. They're in the language lab today."

"How do I get there?"

Quickly Rhonda gave her directions that involved going upstairs and down several different intersecting halls. Mary must have looked baffled, because Rhonda laughed and offered to take her there.

"I appreciate that," Mary said. "As long as you don't have other things you need to get done."

"I do." Rhonda opened the door. "But they can wait. I assume you want to talk to PAP about the sheep that went missing from Grace Church."

"I'm hoping they know something about it."

"If we weren't going into Christmas break, I could ask the teachers to keep an ear out for the kids talking about it. That's the first thing any teacher learns: listen to the kids.

With as many as we have here, a secret doesn't stay a secret for long."

Mary put her hand on the banister as they walked up concrete steps. "But you've got to hear a lot of silly rumors too."

"Sometimes even the silliest rumor has a kernel of truth at its core. That's why it's important for the teachers and the staff to listen."

"You haven't heard anything about the missing sheep or the living Nativity?"

"Nothing except some disappointment that it's been postponed. The kids from Grace Church were looking forward to being the center of attention in what they see as a gift to Ivy Bay." Rhonda paused on the landing and smiled. "And I heard several mention an after-party planned for Christmas Eve at one of the kids' houses. They were hoping for snow so they could build a couple of snow forts and have a snowball fight. It's a shame people have been let down."

Mary had no response to that other than to nod. She thought of Betty and Ashley and Hannah and everyone else who had worked hard to prepare for the living Nativity and who had volunteered to take part in it.

The school's upper floor looked a lot like the first floor. Lockers lining the walls, doors that could lead to classrooms or labs, concrete tile floors. Everywhere, posters touted the big game with simple sayings like *Rams Slam the Canalmen* and *Dunk the Canalmen*. There were a few others, but most of the posters had those words. Mary wondered how long it had taken the kids to make enough posters to cover almost every square inch of wall. The posters had hand-drawn pictures of a sheep and a man in a boat. The ram wore an Ivy Bay basketball uniform. It had big muscles and twisting horns while the boatman looked like the scrawny "before" in a body-builder's ad.

Rhonda paused in front of a door. She knocked, then, not waiting for an answer, opened it. Long tables set in three rows were topped by computers. There was one for each seat, and a set of headphones attached to microphones rested in front of the computer. The board at the front was covered with signs in French, Spanish, and what Mary assumed was Mandarin.

Shelby Ellis was the only one in the classroom. She was collecting pages and putting them in a folder. Other folders peeked out of her open backpack. Looking up, she grinned. "Hi, Principal Keaton! Almost done in here." Her smile wavered when she saw Mary.

"Mrs. Fisher hoped to meet the rest of the members of PAP," Rhonda said smoothly. Her voice gave no hint of any incriminations or curiosity.

"Everyone else left to catch the late bus." Shelby picked up the folder and held it to her chest like a shield. "I'm riding home with my brother, so I offered to clean up."

"Shelby's brother plays guard on the basketball team," Rhonda said.

Mary nodded to thank Rhonda for the explanation, which offered a way to try to put Shelby at ease. "I couldn't help noticing the posters. Everyone must be really excited about the big game."

"It's the biggest game of the year." Shelby slid the folder into her bright red backpack. "Is there something I can do for you, Mrs. Fisher? Our next meeting isn't until after Christmas break, but you're welcome to come back then and meet the rest of the members of PAP."

"Who else is in the group?" asked Rhonda, again acting as if she were interested only as the principal.

Shelby listed a half-dozen names, and Mary didn't recognize any of them. None were members of Grace Church or in the living Nativity.

"You've got a good group," Rhonda said. "I'd say the group probably includes the future valedictorians or salutatorians of the next three graduating classes."

"The nerds," Shelby said with a grin. "Go ahead. You can say it. We're proud to be nerds."

Mary laughed along with Rhonda. In recent years, the word that once had been hurtful had become a badge of honor for the smart kids. By co-opting the derogatory term and wearing it with pride, they'd taken the sting out of it.

As their laughter faded, silence settled on the room. Rhonda glanced at Mary and arched her brows. The questions wouldn't get any easier to ask by waiting.

"Shelby...," Mary began.

Rhonda said, "Why don't we sit down?"

The teen's expression became wary, and Mary wished the principal hadn't suggested that. They sat on the brightly colored plastic chairs, and Shelby's feet were pressed against the floor as if she wanted to jump up and flee. Mary couldn't blame her. Rhonda's request made it obvious that the situation was serious.

"Go ahead," Rhonda prompted.

Mary nodded and smiled at Shelby, wanting to put the girl more at ease. "Shelby, I know you love animals, and I know you weren't happy to see a sheep being kept in a pen at Grace Church. That's why I have to ask: Did you or any of the members of PAP take the sheep from its pen?"

"Us? Take the sheep from the pen?" She shook her head, sending her ponytail dancing. "That's not our style, Mrs. Fisher. We want to protect animals. We wouldn't ever use an animal to make a statement or put them front and center to prove a point, especially when the point is that animals should be treated with dignity."

Mary was inclined to believe her, but there were still other questions. "I spoke with your uncle, and he's pretty upset that Peep has gone missing."

Shelby sighed. "Uncle Ken and I don't always agree on how he uses his sheep to teach kids about animals."

"No?"

"Look." Her face eased from its cautious expression and matched the fervor in her voice. "I know kids can't learn about animals without meeting them, but when he goes into petting zoo mode, it bothers me. You can see that the animals aren't comfortable with being surrounded by a bunch of excited elementary school kids." Standing, she zipped up her backpack. "We've agreed to disagree on that."

Mary stood too. She saw no sign on Shelby's face or in her demeanor that she was lying.

"If you hear anything about the missing sheep, you'll let Principal Keaton know right away, won't you?" Mary asked.

"I would have already, but all I've heard is that Peep disappeared when she was left alone out on the church's lawn. She wouldn't be missing if someone had been watching over her properly."

"Shelby," Rhonda said, her tone abruptly stern, "Mrs. Fisher is as anxious for the sheep to be found unhurt as you and the other members of PAP must be. Please don't suggest that she or her friends had any intention to neglect the sheep that your uncle was kind enough to lend to the church."

"Sorry." Her apology sounded sincere. "I'll ask around here at school, and I'll have my brother ask the jocks too. Maybe someone knows something. If so, someone will slip up and the truth will come out."

"Thank you," Mary said.

"I'll call if I hear anything," Shelby said.

"Thank you, Shelby. I really appreciate your help on this." Mary smiled. "At heart, we both have the same goal. Making sure Peep gets home to the rest of the herd, safe and sound."

"I know." She glanced at the clock and pulled on her coat. "I need to go, or my brother will head home without me. All he's thinking about is the game, and he'll forget I'm supposed to ride with him if I'm not in the car before he gets there."

"Go ahead," Rhonda said. "I'll turn off the lights. Merry Christmas, Shelby."

"Merry Christmas, Principal Keaton." She zipped up her coat and swung her backpack over her shoulders. "You, too, Mrs. Fisher."

"Thanks, Shelby, and merry Christmas," Mary said as she stepped aside to let the girl rush out the door.

"Well," Rhonda said, "that wasn't what I expected."

"No?"

"Shelby isn't usually as evasive as she was today. She's more like that old George Burns and Gracie Allen skit that starts with 'How's your brother, Gracie?' Then Gracie speaks for fifteen minutes without stopping, sharing every little detail about her brother. Shelby's like that if you ask her about animals."

"Do you think she's hiding something?"

Mary couldn't keep from thinking that Shelby wouldn't be happy to see Peep returned to Ken Gomes's farm and the petting zoo, which was sure to be busy during the holidays. Would Shelby be willing to mislead them in order to keep the sheep safe? Someone who felt as strongly as Shelby did about animals might have no compunctions about telling what she'd see as a justifiable lie.

Instantly Mary regretted her thoughts. She should not assume that Shelby was intentionally misleading her. Other PAP members could be involved, and Shelby might have no idea.

And, if Mary was wrong about more than only one person being involved in the disappearances, then PAP should come off her list of suspects. None of the members could have had access to costumes inside the fellowship hall at church.

Rhonda pondered Mary's question for a moment, then shrugged. "I don't want to accuse her of hiding something or being dishonest in any manner. I'm just saying that her actions struck me as odd."

Mary considered that, but reminded herself that Shelby would have been put on the defensive by two adults coming into the language lab to ask her a bunch of questions. No wonder she seemed ill at ease, especially when one of the adults was her high school principal.

"What are you going to do next?" asked Rhonda as they went to the door.

"I'm not sure. It's not like I can go and knock on the kids' doors and ask them if they know anything about a missing sheep."

Rhonda switched off the lights and drew the door closed behind them. "I know it's frustrating."

"Very. I can only pray that whoever has Peep knows how to take care of a sheep." She walked along the deserted hall with the principal. "Costumes and posters can be replaced, but I hate to think of Peep's being in a bad situation."

"Whoever took her must have known what they were doing if they managed to sneak her away quickly. *I* certainly wouldn't have the first idea of how to get a sheep out of a pen and away without being seen." Rhonda chuckled. "Even if our team is the Ivy Bay Rams."

Mary started to reply, then closed her mouth as Rhonda's jesting words echoed in her mind.

Our team is the Ivy Bay Rams.

Rams. Sheep. Could that be a clue to the person or persons who'd taken Peep? Could the sheep have been stolen by someone connected with the basketball team?

Excitement rushed through her. She needed to mull this over some more. Shelby had already offered to talk to other students and had assured them that if a student had taken the missing sheep the truth wouldn't stay a secret for long.

She explained her thoughts to Rhonda. The school principal admitted it was possible one of the students was involved, but, like Mary, she needed more facts before she could make any sort of investigation.

"I'll keep my ear to the ground," Rhonda said, "but with school out for Christmas break, I probably won't hear much until after the new year."

"Just let me know if you hear anything."

"I will."

Mary thanked Rhonda and wished her a merry Christmas at the office door. Continuing to the exit closest to the visitors' parking lot, she went out into the darkening afternoon. With the low skies and winter beginning tomorrow, dark came very early on Cape Cod.

She got into her car and turned the key to get it started and warmed up. Folding her hands on the steering wheel, she bowed her head and said a short prayer that Peep was safe and would stay that way. A high school student might not be prepared to take care of a full-grown sheep. Raising her head, she reached for the shifting lever. There was one more stop she needed to make before she headed home.

* * *

The street was brightly lit with streetlamps and Christmas decorations as Mary turned onto it. This street paralleled the shore to the north and west of the village. It was the last street before the Sandwich town line. Past the houses, she could see the shifting darkness of the bay.

She slowed, checking the house numbers. A quick look in the church directory had gotten her Abbie Lindstrom's address. Even so, she almost missed Abbie's house because it was no bigger than a fisherman's cottage. It was tucked between two much larger homes with ornate gingerbread and broad porches. Abbie's house had neither, but in the glow from the streetlight, it appeared to have been freshly painted the color of ripe cranberries. The door was royal blue and was decorated with a Christmas wreath made of grapevines and miniature snowmen, and the shutters had been painted forest green.

Mary parked in front of the house, where a single dim light shone through the sheer curtains in the windows. As she walked up the walk made of broken shells, she noticed the sheers had the silhouettes of tiny Canada geese embroidered on them.

It was a house that should belong to an artist. If Abbie was even half the skilled seamstress Mary had heard she was, she must have an artist's sensibilities. That made the house perfect for her.

A single piece of marble served as the front stoop. Mary stepped up onto it and looked for a doorbell button. She was about to give up and knock when she spied a brass plate that looked like a robin's nest filled with blue eggs. The center one glowed slightly, and she realized it was the doorbell button. As she pressed it, she couldn't help wondering what other quirky surprises Abbie had inside her house.

No answer came to the doorbell. She tried a second time, and again nobody opened the door. Pushing the button a third time, she didn't give in to the temptation to peek through the window.

It was obvious that Abbie wasn't home. The light coming through the window must have been left on for security. No car, other than Mary's, was parked in front of the house or in the driveway.

Maybe she should leave Abbie a note to let her know that she wanted to talk to the young woman. Of course, if Abbie had gone somewhere for the Christmas holidays, then the note would sit until she returned.

But it was worth a try.

Opening her purse, Mary looked for a scrap of paper. She smiled when she found a receipt from her most recent trip to the grocery store. That would do fine. She squatted, so she could write on her knee. The message was simple.

Abbie, will you give me a call when you get this? Mary Fisher, Betty Emerson's sister. She added her cell number and the house number, as well as the phone number at the bookshop, and folded the long strip.

Walking back to the street, she opened the freestanding mailbox that was painted with some design Mary couldn't see in the fading light. Her hopes faltered when she saw how much mail was jammed into it. How long had Abbie been gone? Mary stuffed the note in among the other papers. She closed the mailbox and flinched in surprise when her cell rang.

It was Betty. "Where are you?" she asked over the sounds of children laughing and talking in the background. "The kids are back, and they don't want to start cutting out the cookies until you're here."

"On my way. I'll be right home." Ending the call, Mary looked over her shoulder at the cute house. She would come back whenever she had a chance until she could catch Abbie at home. Then maybe she could discover if Hannah was right or wrong that Abbie had stolen the costumes to get back at the head seamstress. The day had flown past, and there were only four more days until Christmas Eve.

✳ Chapter Ten

Whispers came from beyond Mary's bedroom door, and she opened her eyes. She smiled when she heard her grandchildren hushing each other as they debated who should knock and who should open the door.

She wasn't sure who had the honor of knocking, but when he or she did, Mary sat up and called, "Come in!"

Her three grandchildren came into the room. Luke held a napkin as he walked in with his other hand behind his back, and Emma followed close behind with a pitcher of milk. They both stepped aside to let Daisy carry a wooden tray to the bed.

Mary smiled as her older granddaughter carefully placed the tray's legs on either side of Mary's. "Good morning, Grandma."

"Good morning," echoed Emma.

Luke bounced from one foot to the other in excitement. "Do you like what we made for you, Grandma?"

"Give her a chance to see it." Daisy laughed and lifted the makeshift lids from the tray.

On the larger plate, scrambled eggs were edged by crisp-ly fried bacon. A bowl of oatmeal was topped by brown sugar and honey. Toast dripped with butter and strawberry rhubarb jam, one of Mary's favorites. Orange juice glistened in a small glass, and coffee steamed out of the bright mug with Santa's face on the front.

"We made it all," Luke said. His sister and cousin glanced at him with stern frowns, and he quickly added, "Daisy made the eggs and bacon, and Emma made the toast, but I put the sugar on the oatmeal and poured the juice. Mom watched and kept telling us to be quiet because Great-Aunt Betty is sleeping in today."

Mary swallowed her sigh, sorry to hear that her sister's rheumatoid arthritis must be acting up. Not that she was surprised. Betty had been doing a lot, and the mess with the living Nativity had stressed her out.

Mary smiled, not wanting to ruin her grandchildren's happiness. "It looks wonderful and smells even better." She wished she could give each of them a big hug, but she didn't want to risk tipping over the tray.

"And I brought you these," Luke said. Pulling his hand from behind his back, he held up a gingerbread man and a sugar cookie cut into the shape of a star. A thick layer of green frosting threatened to drip off each point.

"Dessert for breakfast?" Mary asked.

"Why not? We have dessert for lunch and dinner. Why not breakfast?"

Taking the cookies, she thanked him before using the napkin to wipe frosting off her fingers. "I hope the three of you plan to help me eat this. It's enough for an army."

"Or Luke." Daisy laughed as she drew up a chair and sat beside the bed. "Mom says he has a black hole in one of his legs, because he can eat more than the rest of us put together, and that included Uncle Evan, Aunt Mindy, and their girls."

Luke patted his belly. "Dad says I'm a growing boy."

"At the rate you're eating, you're going to be ten feet tall!" Emma said.

Mary picked up a slice of toast and handed it to her grandson. "Good. Once you are ten feet tall, you can help me get down books from the top shelves, and I won't need a ladder anymore."

Her grandchildren giggled, but eagerly accepted toast and some of the bacon. Emma eyed the oatmeal, and Mary, glad not to have to eat everything on the tray, handed it to her younger granddaughter. Sitting on the floor, Emma dug into the bowl with as much zeal as her brother swallowed the toast and then the gingerbread man, some of the eggs, and half the orange juice.

At the same time, they chattered about their lives in Melrose and Chicago. Jack and Christa had invited the younger cousins to come to Chicago once school was out and spend a week or two exploring the Windy City. Already making plans, Luke and Emma seemed determined to see every corner of the city in the short time they'd be visiting. Daisy smiled and let them go on and on.

Mary listened to her grandchildren discuss their adventures in Christmas shopping. Emma and Luke had, for the first time, been allowed to wander together through a Boston store to do their own shopping.

"But Mom wasn't far off," Emma said as if to reassure her grandmother.

"You're growing up fast." Mary shifted the tray and gave each of them a hug. "It's okay if you slow down a bit."

"How?" asked Luke, taking her words literally as only a seven-year-old could.

"Maybe," said Lizzie from the doorway, "by not eating everything in sight."

Everyone laughed as Lizzie had them gather up the dirty dishes and the tray before heading back downstairs to the kitchen. Mary got out of bed and swept the cookie crumbs left by the kids onto her hand. She dropped them into the wastebasket. She'd take them out before Gus found a feast there.

"Thank you," Mary said to her daughter before going into the bathroom to get ready for the day. She quickly brushed her teeth and pulled on a cheerful red sweater over her khakis. Picking up her shoes, she came back into the bedroom and sat on the bed to pull them on. "I know you and Christa probably had to watch them carefully while they prepared breakfast."

"Emma wanted to add half a container of pepper to the eggs." Lizzie sat in the chair Daisy had used. "We tossed those out, and when we stopped sneezing, we started over again.

They wanted to continue the tradition that we started when we were kids."

"And the grandkids made as much food as you and Jack did for your father and me. You must have thought we were part-time lumberjacks."

Lizzie laughed. "Kids have huge appetites, and we assumed because you were bigger, you needed a bigger plate of food."

"Thank goodness, they helped me eat all that breakfast today."

"Exactly as Jack and I did."

"Which your father and I always guessed was the real reason you made so much."

Again Lizzie chuckled. "We never could fool you, Mom."

"Not for long." Standing, Mary smiled.

"And you can't fool me either. You're really upset by what happened at church."

Mary nodded. Putting her arm around her daughter's shoulders, she walked with her to the stairs. "You know me. When I see a mystery, I have to figure out the answer."

"You've always been that way. Even when we were little, you never could stop reading a mystery novel until you figured out whodunit. Now you've got real-life mysteries, and you're just as eager to get to the truth."

That was true, but Mary couldn't allow herself to forget the importance of family time and the reason for the season amidst her search for answers. She must not let solving the puzzles cost her time away from her family.

Rebecca was opening the shop that morning, so Mary had an extra hour before she needed to be there. She spent that time with her children and their spouses. They sat around the dining room table and enjoyed an extra cup of coffee. That way, their voices wouldn't carry to Betty's bedroom, and she could get some rest.

Even though Mary was careful not to speak of it, the topic of conversation quickly turned to the costumes and Peep. She went through the events on Wednesday, detail by detail. She was startled to realize it had only been three days since the living Nativity had to be postponed.

Jack asked, "Is there any chance the living Nativity can still go on?"

"I'd hoped so, and I know your aunt did, too, but some people are being stubborn about not doing the living Nativity without the costumes."

"What can we do to help you and Aunt Betty, Mom?" asked Lizzie.

She thought about what Rhonda had said about the teens at the high school. Just listening was sometimes the best way to discover the truth.

"Right now, I'd like to ask you to keep your ears open. Especially if you're attending an event like the lighting contest out at the Sea Breezes subdivision and any other events in town. Or if you're in a shop and you chance to overhear someone discussing what's happened, listen."

"We can do that," Lizzie said. "If we hear anything, we'll let you know right away."

Chad squeezed Lizzie's hand. "You know you're agreeing to do that simply so you can visit the shops in Ivy Bay."

Laughter raced around the table, and her kids began joking about lurking around corners and in alleyways. The idea of doing such things in sleepy Ivy Bay brought more laughter.

When Mary had to excuse herself to go to work, Lizzie and Jack stood too. She could tell they had something else on their minds, but she didn't ask.

She was pulling on her coat when Jack asked, "How are you doing, Mom? Really doing, I mean."

"Busy, but so is everyone at this time of year."

Her children exchanged a glance, then Lizzie said, "What Jack means to ask is whether or not you're okay. We know this time of year is extra-tough for you now that Dad's gone. Not only Christmas, but your wedding anniversary on the twenty-eighth."

"I miss your dad *every* day of the year, not just at holidays and special occasions, but I know he's in heaven and watching over us." She smiled as she patted her daughter's arm. "And probably getting a big kick out of my investigations."

Jack chuckled, then gave her a hug. "I'm sure he is."

Lizzie reached for her coat. "Do you mind if I come with you to the shop? I'd like to see what you've done since my last visit."

"Of course. I'd be glad to have you there, but I may put you to work."

"I figured that." Lizzie dimpled, suddenly looking as young as her own daughter.

Mary turned to her son. "Could you do me a favor and keep things calm when Evan and Mindy come over with their kids later today? We don't need any spats between the grandchildren to upset your aunt."

"No problem. If they start acting up, we'll figure out a place to take them so they're out of Aunt Betty's hair."

Thanking him, she waited for Lizzie to get her coat. They went outside to find it was raining a cool drizzle, the kind that was as cold as an icicle if a drop slipped down under her collar.

"I wish it would snow," Lizzie said as they walked to Mary's car. "This half-and-half doesn't work for me, especially the week before Christmas."

"Better cold rain than ice."

Her daughter shuddered. "I don't drive when it sleets. Too dangerous, especially on the hills around Boston."

"It's pretty flat out here on the Cape and we don't have far to go, so we should be fine, even if it turns to sleet."

Mary frowned as they drove along the street and past the Walkers' house. "Odd."

"What's odd?" asked Lizzie.

Mary hooked a thumb toward the Model A in the driveway. "I can't believe Patrick's left his car out in the storm. He loves it so much that I would have guessed he'd be more likely to stand in the rain himself than let his car sit outside."

"It's a great car." Lizzie turned as far as her seat belt allowed so she could look more closely at the classic car as they went past. "I'm surprised that Jack and Chad haven't gone over to talk to Mr. Walker about his car every time we come here."

"I doubt they know it even exists. Patrick usually only lets it outside for a parade or an antique car show."

"Maybe there's a Christmas parade somewhere."

"That's possible," Mary said, but she wasn't convinced.

Lizzie must have realized that because she chuckled and said, "You could always send Jack and Chad over to check out the car and also why it's in the driveway."

Mary laughed. "I like how you think."

Finding a parking space on Main Street wasn't easy, because every spot was filled. Mary parked at Grace Church, turned up her collar, and hurried to her bookshop. It wasn't far, but she was shivering by the time she rushed into the bookshop, for once not even tempted by the luscious aromas from Sweet Susan's Bakery.

Lizzie looked around the shop as she took off her coat. After she'd greeted Rebecca and Ashley, who was reading in the bathtub in the children's section, she said, "It looks great, Mom. Betty said something about your having a special event on Christmas Eve."

"We're doing a reading of *A Visit from St. Nicholas*."

"Ah, 'twas the night before Christmas..."

"Actually the reading will be the *afternoon* before Christmas." Mary smiled at her assistant, who was working on the computer. "Rebecca is dressing up as Mrs. Claus and will read the poem. I plan to make hot chocolate, and I've ordered some holiday cookies from Sweet Susan's Bakery next door."

"I'm glad I don't work next door to a bakery." Lizzie patted her stomach and laughed. "I'd be too tempted all the time."

"We are," Rebecca said. "Trust me, we are. Hey, Mary, do you mind if I run a couple of errands? I forgot to pick up some ingredients I need for Christmas pies, and I don't want to wait too long. Otherwise, the mincemeat may be gone. And I need to see if that Mrs. Claus wig I ordered is in yet."

"Go ahead." Mary smiled. "I've got Lizzie and Ashley to help me."

As Rebecca left, Lizzie asked, "Mom, where did you get the idea to put reindeer on strings of garland in the window? Was that Aunt Betty?"

"Ashley." Mary smiled as she motioned for the little girl to come over. "Here's my interior designer, general helper, and reindeer impersonator."

"I'm wearing these for the reading." Ashley set a pair of light brown felt reindeer antlers on her head and grinned. "I haven't decided if I'm going to be Donner or Dasher yet."

"How about Dancer?" Mary asked. "You like to dance, don't you?"

Ashley twirled around, giggling. "Yes, I'm going to be Dancer." She swayed through the low picket gate and back into the children's section.

"I don't know who is more excited about the reading," Mary said. "Rebecca or Ashley."

"Or you, Mom."

"True. It's fun to have children in the shop." Mary started to add more, but paused as the door opened with a bright chime.

Hannah Titus walked in. Without looking in Mary's direction, she headed for the shelves.

Lizzie arched her brows, and Mary gave a quick shake of her head. Instead of asking a question, Lizzie offered to make some tea. She glanced once in Hannah's direction, then went into the back room.

Mary stepped behind the counter as Hannah reappeared from among the shelves.

"I always forget at least one person I need to get a gift for." Hannah put a trio of books on the counter. "I don't forget the person. Just that I haven't gotten them a present. I mean…"

Mary smiled as she picked up the top book. "I know what you mean. To tell you the truth, I've found owning a bookshop has come in handy for last-minute gifts myself. It's a good thing that everyone in my family likes to read."

"Mine too." Hannah opened her purse and pulled out her wallet. "I'm really behind this year. I'd rather sew than go shopping, so now I've got to catch up on everything I put off until after…"

Sympathy rushed through Mary as Hannah's voice trailed away again.

"I know you wanted to have wonderful costumes," Mary said, "but is there any way you and your team of seamstresses can whip up some quick costumes so the living Nativity can go on at least for a few nights before Christmas?"

"I wish we could, but it's not only the sewing time. It's finding the right fabrics. Most of what we used for the first set of costumes was ordered from a specialty shop in New York. There's no way we could get the fabric here and re-make the costumes before Christmas Eve."

"How about if you use some fabrics that we can buy here on the Cape?"

Hannah looked down at the counter. "I know you're just trying to help, but it's not that simple. Doing a slapdash job just seems wrong, especially when the volunteers have do-nated so much of their time already. Now with it being just before Christmas..." She raised her eyes to meet Mary's. "I can't ask that of them. Not more of their time nor to do less than their best work for the church. I know that you're trying to find the costumes, and Dorothy is too. If you want my opinion–" She hesitated and didn't continue.

"I can use all the help I can get."

"I'll tell you what I've already told Dorothy. If you want to find the costumes, go and see Abbie Lindstrom. I think she took them out of spite."

Mary put the books into a bag and set it on the counter. "I wondered if you'd feel that way." She didn't add that she'd considered that herself.

Thinking that way about someone she barely knew bothered her, but what if Abbie had suspected that Hannah would be furious when the costumes went missing? She might have taken the costumes not to hurt the church, but to hurt Hannah.

"I can't imagine anyone else who would have taken them," Hannah said. "Everyone else from the seamstresses to

Pastor Miles to the kids were excited about Grace Church's living Nativity. Dorothy told me that Abbie won't return her calls. Have you called her?"

Mary nodded. She said nothing about the full mailbox at Abbie's house, because there could be plenty of different explanations for it.

"Has she called you back?"

"Not yet."

Hannah's frown drew lines into her cheeks. "See? She's hiding from everyone. What other proof do you need?"

"I'm not convinced she's hiding. She may be busy like the rest of us."

"That's *your* opinion." Hannah grabbed her purse and headed for the door.

"Hannah?" Mary held up the bag of books Hannah had purchased.

Going back to the counter, Hannah took the bag and rushed out.

Mary sat on the stool behind the counter and stared across her shop. She believed what she'd told Hannah, but Hannah held as tightly to her own opinion. If one of them could talk to Abbie, maybe they'd discover who was right.

Reaching for the phone, Mary dialed Abbie's number. It rang once, then twice, and hope plummeted in her.

Then she heard, "Hi."

"Hi," Mary replied quickly. "Is this Abbie?"

"Yes."

"Abbie, this is Mary Fisher. I left you a message."

"I'm sorry I didn't get back to you. I just got home a short time ago, and I haven't even listened to my voice mail yet. Why did you call me, Mrs. Fisher?"

Mary said a silent prayer, then dove in. "It'd be easier if I came over to your house, and we talked face-to-face."

"I'd be glad to talk to you." Abbie didn't sound evasive. Just very subdued. "Can you come over now?"

"I'll be over as soon as I can." She wasn't sure how long it would take Rebecca to finish her errands.

"All right. See you then."

Mary hung up the phone, her fingers lingering on it. She jumped, startled, when Lizzie asked what was up. Mary quickly explained.

"Go ahead, Mom," Lizzie said. "I'll keep an eye on the shop, and Rebecca should be back any minute anyhow."

Thanking her daughter, Mary grabbed her coat and hurried outside. The cold rain had slowed to a drizzle, but she ducked her head as she went along the street. Being out in the lousy weather would be worth it if she was on her way to the answers to these puzzles.

✳ Chapter Eleven

Mary had gone only a few steps toward the church, where she'd left her car, when she heard her name called. She looked up. Henry came across the street, a big grin on his weathered face. He wore a bright yellow mac and a floppy hat, so he resembled the famous fisherman statue in Gloucester.

"You look like a woman with a mission in mind," he said as he reached where she'd stopped.

"Mostly to get out of the rain."

He hooked a thumb toward her shop. "You're going in the wrong direction."

She smiled. It was impossible not to catch Henry's infectious good humor, even on such a cold, damp day. "I can't chat now. I need to get over to...to a friend's house."

She saw his eyes narrow slightly. He asked, "Following more clues?"

She nodded. "And hoping for some answers."

"It sounds like the sleuthing is going pretty slowly."

"More slowly than I'd hoped. I keep thinking about how close Christmas is. If I don't get answers or at least find out where the costumes are before Christmas Eve, there won't be a living Nativity this year. That would be a shame."

"A real shame." His face grew long. "So many people will be disappointed."

"You don't have to remind me of that."

"Sorry." He patted her arm, and she wondered if he had any idea how much his commiseration meant to her. He understood why she wanted to solve the mystery. It meant so much to so many at Grace Church and in Ivy Bay.

Then he smiled. "Before you go off looking for your next clue, Mary, let me give you this."

He held out a wrapped piece of candy that was striped like a peppermint cane. But it wasn't shaped like a shepherd's crook. It had been made to look like a red and white lobster.

"Where did you find something like this?" She turned the peppermint lobster in her hand. Now that she examined it more closely, she saw the claws were hooked like the top of a candy cane so it could be hung on a tree.

"The bay waters are pretty cold. I wasn't surprised that some of the guys pulled up their lobster pots and found frozen lobsters inside."

She laughed. "You can't resist telling a fish tale, can you?"

"Or, in this case, a lobster tale." He grinned. "Do you know there's a big basketball game tonight?"

"I saw the posters covering the walls at the high school. The whole school seems excited about it."

"They should be. This game decides which school gets to claim bragging rights and the old oaken bucket trophy for the next year. Barnstable is desperate to win it back, but Ivy Bay's held on to it for the past three years, ever since that Flanagan boy made the team his freshman year. He's started every game for the past four years, and he'll set a new Ivy Bay record for the most starts when he plays tonight."

"I didn't realize that."

"Well, a couple of colleges do. I hear that there's going to be a scout from one of the top basketball schools at the game tonight to check him out."

"How exciting! Obviously you are going."

"I am. I'd be glad to give you a ride if you aren't going with your kids."

"I definitely want to go and cheer for Brian and the rest of the team. As far as my kids, let me check with them." Then she shook her head. "No, I don't need to. Unless he's changed, Jack will want to go. He loves basketball almost as much as he loves baseball."

"Good. I'll see you there then. Save me a seat if you get there before me. It's going to be a full house tonight."

"I will." She waved as he continued down the street toward Sweet Susan's.

It would be fun to watch the game with her family and with Henry. Maybe by that time, Shelby would have contacted her with information she'd gleaned from other teens about where the sheep might be. And maybe Abbie would have some answers for her too.

*   *   *

Mary parked in front of Abbie's charming house and hurried up the walk. The shells crunched beneath her feet, and thick drops of rain plopped heavily on the rosebushes as well as onto the umbrella she'd found on the back floor in her car.

Lord, give me the right words to persuade Abbie to open up to me. I feel like I'm on a treadmill, hurrying around but getting nowhere. I know I must wait for Your time to be right, so help me be patient too.

This time when Mary pressed the blue egg in the center of the brass robin's nest, the door opened almost at once. Abbie Lindstrom was a slender girl who was even shorter than Mary. She couldn't be even five feet tall. Her blonde hair, which looked natural, was coiled in a bun. She wore a loosely knit green sweater over a shapeless red dress. Scuffed combat boots and thick gray stockings were visible beneath the skirt's long hem. A pair of dark-rimmed glasses gave her tiny face an owl-like appearance.

She squinted through her glasses as she said, "Mrs. Fisher, come in before you end up soaked."

"Horrible weather today, isn't it?" Mary stepped inside and hurried to close her umbrella. Before water ran off it onto the entry's slate floor, she put the umbrella in an earthenware cask where there were already several others.

"My daughter said she'd be glad if it would snow, but I'll take cold rain any day." Mary smiled. "Well, maybe except Christmas."

"Rain or snow. It doesn't matter. Traffic was snarled for miles when I came over the Bourne Bridge. I'm not used to that delay in winter." She motioned toward a wide doorway to the right. "Come in and sit down. I put some tea on after you called. Would you like some?"

"That sounds great."

Abbie led the way into a cozy living room filled with twice as much furniture as it should have had. Every table was covered with paper and fabric and wire coat hangers and bits of plastic. Books towered precariously on top of the other items, and Mary felt like she needed to hold her breath. Even the slightest breeze might make everything tumble to the floor.

"Sorry," Abbie said as she hefted an armful of colored paper from a chair upholstered in bright red leather. "Why don't you sit down, Mrs. Fisher? I'll get the tea and be right back."

Mary sat and looked around the room. The walls, covered in an old-fashioned style of tea rose wallpaper, held art and pictures as eclectic and eccentric as the outside of the house. One ornate frame was empty, showing a section of the wallpaper. Others displayed dried flowers and dour people. Mary wondered if they were Abbie's ancestors or if she'd simply selected the photos to hang in her living room.

Abbie came back with a silver tray that looked as if it belonged in a five-star hotel. She set it, with care, on a low table between Mary and her seat on the dark green wool couch after pushing aside more stacks of paper.

She poured Mary a cup and held it out. "It's raspberry tea. I hope you like it."

"It smells heavenly."

"That's what I like best about it. The scent. It takes me right back to summer when the raspberries are ripe." Filling her own cup, she added, "I listened to my voice mail while waiting for you, Mrs. Fisher. I really appreciate how nice your message was, especially after Dorothy Johnson's message insisted that I call her. 'Right now!'" Her pale skin flushed, and she quickly lowered her eyes. "I know she's a member of our church and I should be more forgiving. It's just..." She sighed. "I'll call her back when I get the time."

Mary couldn't help noting how tired and stressed Abbie looked. Thin lines were drawn around her mouth and threaded her forehead. Was there something more bothering Abbie than the bad traffic coming back onto the Cape?

"How are you?" she asked.

"Busy." Abbie laughed, but it sounded forced. "I guess that's what everyone says around the holidays, huh?"

"Yes, which is why I remind myself every year how important it is to take time to remember why we are rushing around to buy gifts, so we can welcome family and friends and celebrate our Savior's birth."

Abbie's smile looked as strained as her laugh had sounded. "That's good advice, Mrs. Fisher." She took a sip of her tea. "Too bad it's not advice I'll probably be able to follow."

"Me either."

The young woman's face relaxed at Mary's answer, and she leaned back into the camelback sofa that looked like it'd been made in the 1930s. "I know you didn't drop by just to chat, Mrs. Fisher. Your message said you wanted to talk to me about the missing costumes from church."

"You already knew they were missing?"

"Of course. Nothing stays secret in Ivy Bay."

"But if you were out of town..."

Again Abbie flushed, but her voice was now light and carefree. "I have friends who keep me informed of the hottest news in Ivy Bay. But they haven't said anything about if the costumes have been found. Have they?"

"Not yet, but we're still looking anywhere we can think of in the church."

"Good."

"Do you have any ideas where else we can look?" Mary asked the question carefully, not wanting the young woman to think Mary was accusing her of taking them.

"Did you look in the storage rooms at the back of the sanctuary? Choir robes sometimes are kept there."

"I think we've gone over every inch of the church at least twice."

"How about Pastor Miles's house? Someone might have taken them over there and forgotten it. Did you check that out?"

Mary shook her head. "I'm sure he's checked his house, but I'll give him a call."

"If he doesn't find them at his house, I can't imagine where else they could be." Abbie frowned. "I can't imagine why anyone would want to steal a bunch of Christmas costumes. It's not like they could sell them around here, because everyone's probably heard that they are gone."

"Did your friends tell you as well that Hannah has insisted that the living Nativity be canceled unless the costumes are recovered?"

"What?" Abbie sat up quickly, and tea splashed out of her cup. She set it on the tray and used a linen napkin with ducks embroidered on it to dab at the wet spots on her skirt.

"Are you okay?" Mary asked.

"Just baffled."

Mary could relate to that feeling.

"Why," Abbie asked, "would Hannah insist on that?" She rolled her eyes and shook her head. "Why am I even asking that? It couldn't have been a surprise to anyone who worked with her, because she always has to have her way on everything."

"My sister, Betty, told me that you were one of the seamstresses at the beginning."

Abbie's face closed up. "I don't want to talk about that. The whole experience was lousy. Let's leave it at that, okay?"

Mary nodded, though she had many other questions that Abbie might be able to answer. The young woman was exhausted. That was clear, and pushing her wouldn't help. Maybe a different tactic would.

"Did your friends let you know that a sheep lent to the church has gone missing too?"

Abbie nodded. "I think that's horrible. I hope whoever took it is keeping it fed and warm. I'm not fond of sheep myself. Stupid creatures that always look like they need a good bath. But I wouldn't want any animal to be treated badly. Any ideas who might have done it?"

"Not yet, but I've got some feelers out to follow a few clues."

"Good for you." Abbie tried to stifle a yawn and failed. "Sorry. I hate to be rude, but…"

And Mary hated to be pushy, but she needed to ask Abbie about one other thing. She quickly told the young woman how the church's posters had disappeared.

"Really?" asked Abbie, her brows lowering in a puzzled expression. "Who would want to tear down our posters? It sounds like something bored kids might do."

"But if kids tore them down, I think they would have left the flyers to blow away." She thought of the poster she and Betty had picked up in the church's parking lot. It was the only one they'd found.

"True." Abbie put up her hand when another yawn she'd been trying to stifle escaped. Her fingers trembled. With fatigue or something else?

Mary took the hint. Abbie had been very kind to see her when she was clearly longing for a good nap. Standing, Mary thanked Abbie for the tea.

"I'm glad you like it. Let me get you some to take with you." Abbie got up too. She took a single step around the sofa, then gasped. "Ouch!" She winced and rubbed her knee. She grasped futilely for magazines and books that toppled off the table. They hit the wood floor with dull thuds. "I keep thinking about moving that table to the other side of the couch. Maybe with a bruise to remind me, I will."

Picking up the magazines, Mary handed them to her. Abbie set them back on the table while Mary gathered up the scattered books. They were, Mary realized, college catalogs. UMass, Dartmouth, Bridgewater College, and Rhode Island School of Design, which everyone called RIZ-dee. She gave them to Abbie, who put them on top of the magazines in another precarious pile that looked ready to fall at any second.

"Thanks," Abbie said. "Let me get that tea for you." She left the room.

Mary was about to call after her that it wasn't necessary when her eye was caught by a rainbow of color peeking out from beneath the books that hadn't cascaded off the table. From where she stood, the bits of fabric looked identical to the pieces Hannah had shown her at church. The fabric used for the living Nativity costumes, the fabric that Hannah had told her was unique and had been ordered especially for the costumes. The pale blue satin that had been chosen for the Virgin Mary's costume, the shimmering satins in green and white used for the Wise Men, even what looked like a snippet from the plain ecru linen that had been meant for the shepherd's costumes.

Or at least the scraps appeared to match the fabric for the costumes, but she couldn't see much of them because only a small corner of each peeked out. She fought the temptation to lean over and finger the red to find out if it felt as smooth and heavy as the fabric sample from Joseph's robes.

"Here," Abbie said, coming back into the room with a plastic bag holding several tea bags. "I wrote down the Web site where I order it, just in case you wanted to get more."

"Thank you." Mary smiled to hide her confusion.

Abbie had left Mary alone in the living room where she could have poked around. Would someone trying to conceal that she'd taken the costumes be that careless?

But Mary couldn't overlook the fact that the fabric had been hidden until Abbie accidentally bumped into the table. If she hadn't dislodged the magazines and the college catalogs, Mary would never have guessed the scraps were there.

Walking out of the house, Mary opened her umbrella. She slowly went to her car. She couldn't make accusations that might prove to be groundless. For now, she had to uncover more information. She needed to figure out if Abbie had a legitimate reason for taking the scraps of fabric from Grace Church. Maybe she had worked on the costumes at her house.

Betty might know if the seamstresses were allowed to take the work home. She'd ask her sister tonight after she closed the bookshop.

As she turned the key in the ignition, a chill raced through her. What if those hidden scraps were all that remained of the costumes? She wanted to push that thought away. Abbie had seemed genuinely proud of her work on the costumes. To destroy them as well as her friends' work...That didn't seem logical.

Yet Mary realized that she couldn't discount it simply because the thought made her feel uncomfortable.

* Chapter Twelve

Mary finished putting the day's sales figures into the computer, then went to her book distributor's Web site. Some of her most popular holiday titles were almost sold out. Could she have some more copies overnighted so they'd arrive on Monday? Doing that would take a bite out of her profits, but her customers wouldn't forget that she'd made the extra effort. It might be worth it.

Looking at the order deadline, she realized she had only minutes. She raced through the order but double-checked it. She didn't want to order too many by mistake or overlook a really popular book. Satisfied the order was correct, she hit the button to send off the order. Her eyes widened when she saw the shipping cost.

"Christmas comes only once a year," she reminded herself as she pushed back from the counter and went to get her coat.

She paused when she heard a knock on the front door. She'd locked it after her last customer left about fifteen minutes ago, and she'd turned the "Shut" sign to face the street.

Going to the door, she was shocked to see Shelby Ellis and half a dozen other teens crowded together under a trio of umbrellas. She unlocked the door and threw it open.

"Shelby, this is a surprise." That was an understatement.

"We'd like to speak to you, Mrs. Fisher, about the missing sheep."

"Now?" Mary glanced at her watch. "Aren't you going to the pep rally before the basketball game tonight?"

"Just the game, and that doesn't start for an hour or so. Can we come in?"

Mary stepped back to let them enter. Water dripped from their coats, and their sneakers squeaked on every step. They folded the umbrellas and left them outside so they didn't bring even more rain into the shop.

The teens shifted and exchanged eager glances. Mary wondered what they'd discovered. It had to be good news if they looked happy.

"Why don't you take off your coats and sit down?" she asked, gesturing toward the twin chairs on either side of the gas fireplace. She flipped the switch to start a fire, and the kids edged closer to enjoy the heat after being out in the damp evening.

Shelby sat on one of the ivory twill chairs. The rest of the kids dropped to the floor and looked expectantly at Mary. Going around in a circle, they introduced themselves as Jasmine, Nick, Chelsea, Katie, Deon, and Jacob, the total membership of PAP.

Taking the other chair, Mary said, "It's nice to meet you. If I were to judge from your faces, you've got some good tidings to share with me."

"We've been asking around." Shelby glanced at the others, who nodded encouragement. "We think we may know why Peep was taken out of the pen."

"You found that out this quickly?"

Shelby smiled broadly. "It wasn't hard, Mrs. Fisher. We each asked a few people who checked with their friends, and we started getting suggestions pretty quickly. One of the good things about being nerds. We know how to communicate through social media."

Mary laughed. "I'll have to remember that." Leaning her elbows on her knees, she asked, "Why was Peep stolen?"

"We think the pep squad took Peep."

Mary nodded, because Shelby's words confirmed the suspicion that had grown in Mary's mind after seeing the signs supporting the basketball team. "They're different from the cheerleaders, right?"

Jasmine nodded, her red curls bouncing with the motion. "Yes, even though they do pretty much the same thing."

"The cheerleaders lead cheers at the games," said Nick, looking up with a pained expression on his face that suggested he'd rather talk about anyone but the cheerleaders, "and the pep squad is in charge of things like the pep rallies and making sure there are posters around the school to get everyone excited about the games ahead of time. Then there's the color guard, which twirls flags and marches out with the band at half-time. Every girl at school wants to be on one team or the other."

"Not me," Shelby said, and the other three girls echoed her.

"Every *A-list* girl at school does," he said.

Shelby nodded. "That's true."

Mary didn't want the conversation to wander away from the topic of the missing ewe. "What makes you think the pep squad took Peep?"

"The pep squad has been saying since the beginning of the year that our school should have a real mascot instead of someone dressed up in a sheep's costume."

"That sounds like a good motive to take Peep," Mary said, wondering if that was the final piece to fall into place in recovering the missing sheep. "Do you have any idea who actually took her?"

"We think only one or two members of the pep squad are involved in 'sheep-napping.' Any more, and the word would have spread through the school already." Shelby smiled. "Nothing as interesting as having a live mascot at the big game against Barnstable would stay a secret for long at Ivy Bay High."

Again Mary agreed. "But who do you think took Peep?"

"Let's see…" Chelsea tapped her chin. "There's Brittany Rocha and Brittany Delafontaine."

Shelby said when her friend paused, "And there's Alexis Huang and Sierra Gilbert and, of course, there's the pep squad leader, Khloe Walker, and–"

"Walker?" Mary asked. "Is she the daughter of Patrick Walker?"

The kids looked at her, surprised, and nodded.

"Is that important, Mrs. Fisher?" asked Shelby.

"It could be." She thought about her neighbor and how he'd left his precious Model A in the driveway the past few days. Was that because there was something else in the garage? Something like Peep, who must stay out of sight until the pep rally? She quickly explained what she'd observed, and the kids got it right away.

"She'd need a place that's fairly warm and dry for Peep," Shelby said.

"But how could she keep it a secret from her parents?" asked Jacob. "My folks would flip out if they discovered I was keeping farm animals in the garage."

Before the teens could segue into how they'd hide a sheep from their parents, Mary stood. "You've done a great job keeping an ear to the ground."

They beamed at her praise, and Shelby said, "We really care about animals, and we want to help. What do we do now?"

"The next step is to find out if the rumors have any basis in truth, and that means finding out if Khloe really has Peep."

"Great!" Nick jumped to his feet, sweeping his backpack over his shoulders. "Let's go."

"It's not a good idea for all of us to troop over to the Walkers' house," Mary said.

"Yeah," Jasmine said with a giggle. "We'd look like a posse hunting down cattle rustlers." She laughed again. "I mean, sheep rustlers. Not that I wouldn't like to see Khloe's face when she realizes she's been caught. Assuming she really has Peep. Who goes with Mrs. Fisher?"

"I'll go," Shelby said.

The others quickly agreed she was the right choice because not only was she the president of PAP, but the ewe belonged to her uncle.

"Text us," the kids said at the same time, then laughed.

"Text us if you find Peep or if you don't," added Nick, apparently wanting to be precise. "Either way."

"You know I will." Shelby rolled her eyes and glanced at Mary with a shrug.

Mary held back her chuckle. Some things never changed. Teen girls still found teen boys incomprehensible or silly.

Getting her coat and purse, Mary turned off the fireplace. She waited until the teens, except for Shelby, left. She turned off the lights and motioned for Shelby to go out the door first.

"My car is right over there." Mary pointed up the street.

They hurried to get in it before they were drenched, because it was raining even harder than it had earlier. The headlights didn't cut far through the storm, so Mary was glad to be on familiar streets.

As the windshield wipers slapped at their highest speed, Mary said, "I know Khloe's parents, but I doubt I've ever said more than a quick 'hi' to her. She's a member of the pep squad. What else?"

"She's *captain* of the pep squad. Otherwise, I don't know her well. We don't have any friends in common."

Mary understood what Shelby was trying not to say. One aspect of high school never seemed to change. Cliques based on interests or popularity segregated kids. And the cool kids at the top of the pecking order didn't hang out with kids at the bottom, and self-proclaimed nerds were at the bottom.

Pulling the car over to the curb in front of the Walkers' house, Mary saw the Model A still sat in the driveway. Water ran off it in a stream. Why would Patrick leave it outside in a storm?

The answer was simple. He must not know it was out on the driveway. He had to be away. There was no other explanation Mary could imagine for why he'd let his precious car get soaked.

She hurried with Shelby up the walk to the Walkers' front door. Lights glowed in several windows, and the bright colors from a Christmas tree blinked through the picture window on the front of the gray-shingled Victorian.

Climbing up on the porch, Mary shook rain off her umbrella and closed it. Shelby reached for the doorbell, then hesitated, looking back at her.

"There's nothing to be gained by waiting," Mary said with a quick smile.

"Yeah, I know, but..." Shelby pushed the doorbell.

Footsteps sounded inside, and the door opened. A blonde teen girl stood there. Streaks of mascara ran down her face, and traces of eyeshadow were smudged by her eyes.

"Hi, Khloe," Mary said.

Khloe, who was several inches taller than Shelby, gasped. "Mrs. Fisher!" A flurry of emotions rushed across her face. Horror and fear and dismay. "This isn't a good time. My parents aren't home, and…" She stared at Shelby as if she'd never seen the other girl before. Then hope exploded through her eyes. "You're with that animal rights group, aren't you?"

"Yes." Shelby glanced at Mary, then back at the other girl. "Why?"

"Can you help me?"

"With what?"

Instead of answering, Khloe motioned for them to come inside. The entry was as formal as the exterior of the house, and the furnishings were either antiques or high-quality re-productions. Past the entryway with its Williamsburg blue and white striped wallpaper, wide doors displayed an ele-gant dining room on one side and a designer-perfect living room on the other side. A huge artificial Christmas tree sat in a far corner of the living room, decorated with strings of cranberries and swaths of lace as well as ornaments and blinking lights.

Khloe waited until Mary and Shelby were inside the house, then peered out the door toward the main road.

"Are you looking for someone?" Mary asked.

"No…Yes, my dad," Khloe said, hastily closing the door. "He's going to kill me because I moved his car out to the driveway, and now it's raining." She folded her hands and pressed them over her heart. "I need your help. Big-time."

"With what?" Shelby asked.

Mary knew Shelby already had the answer to that question, but she was going to make Khloe admit what she'd done. Saying nothing, Mary waited.

"I've got a-a…an animal in the garage," Khloe said, her facing growing red with a flush. She lowered her eyes. "Okay, you probably know it's the sheep from the church up at the other end of Main Street."

"Thanks for being honest with us." Mary had sympathy for the girl, who clearly had gotten in over her head with an idea that probably had seemed brilliant at the beginning.

"I've got to be honest with someone because that sheep needs to be out of here *now*. It has made a total mess of the garage. When my folks get home tonight, Dad is going to be wicked furious. Not only has his car been out in the rain, but the garage is covered with sheep droppings." Her mouth straightened. "Sierra was supposed to come over and take the sheep to her house. They've got a shed that nobody goes into during the winter."

"Thank heavens she didn't," said Shelby. "Leaving the sheep out in a shed by herself could be dangerous if the weather gets really cold."

Khloe's eyes widened. "How can they get cold? They're covered by wool."

"True, but sheep huddle together when it's really cold. A single sheep is as much at risk as we'd be if we were put in that shed." She folded her arms in front of her. "I'd like to see my uncle's sheep."

The other girl looked surprised, nodded, and led them through a stylish kitchen with the most up-to-date appliances. She went into a mud room and opened a door. She reached in and flipped a light switch.

A sheep raised its head from the bowl of water that was half-frozen. It stared at them as if it had never seen a person before.

Shelby pushed past Khloe. "Peep!"

✳ Chapter Thirteen

Shelby threw her arms around the startled sheep, which tried to back away from her. When she began scratching it behind the ears, though, Peep stopped struggling. It was clear that Shelby knew how to calm a frightened sheep.

Mary couldn't have said for sure that it was the missing ewe. It looked like the sheep that had been at the church, but all the sheep at Ken's farm had looked the same.

When Mary mentioned this, Shelby smiled. "Look at how the sheep's wool has recently been washed." She ran her fingers over the tightly curled wool. "And see her horns?" She traced the horn with a single fingertip. "They've been trimmed exactly as my uncle Ken always does with his sheep. This is Peep." She bent down and smiled. "Peep, my dear Peep, are you ready to go home and see the rest of your flock? I bet you can't wait to see your friends."

Leaving Shelby to her reunion with Peep, Mary turned to Khloe. She picked her way carefully across the dirty floor to where the girl stood by the mud room door.

"I'd like to ask you a few questions," Mary said.

"You don't need to worry. We fed the sheep, and we made sure she had water." Her nose wrinkled. "You can see from the mess on the floor that she hasn't starved."

Mary hid her smile at the difference between Shelby and Khloe. Shelby clearly adored Peep, and Khloe was disgusted with being around a farm animal. Even though Mary wondered why Khloe had agreed to put the sheep in her family's garage, she needed to focus on the other puzzles that must be solved if the living Nativity was going to be held this year.

"I can see you took the best care of Peep that you could," Mary said in the soothing voice she used with children younger than Khloe. "It's just that the night Peep disappeared, so did the costumes for the living Nativity that Grace Church planned for the week before Christmas."

"No! We wouldn't steal anything." Khloe's face turned a brighter scarlet as she stammered, "I-I-I mean we wouldn't s-steal anything that isn't p-part of our half-time prank."

"Khloe, you don't have to–"

"We didn't take anything but the stupid sheep."

Shelby frowned at her classmate, and Khloe quickly muttered an apology.

"I'm not accusing you of stealing the costumes," Mary said. "I was wondering if you or any of the other members of the pep squad might have seen someone with the costumes. Or maybe you heard something at school about the missing costumes or the destruction of the posters that were hung up around town to advertise the living Nativity."

"Honestly, Mrs. Fisher," Khloe replied, "until you mentioned it just now, I didn't even know there was going to be a living Nativity at Grace Church. I know you don't have any reason to believe me because we took your sheep, but I'm telling you the truth."

Mary heard sincerity in the girl's voice. "I'd like to believe that, Khloe."

"You can believe it. I don't know anything about any posters. The only ones I've seen are those ugly green ones hung up by PAP." Her face paled as she glanced at Shelby. "Sorry."

"It's okay," Shelby said, still stroking the sheep. "The color got you to notice the posters, and that is what we wanted."

Khloe looked back at Mary. "All we hoped to do was get everyone excited about the big game. Instead of that ratty costume that's got to be thirty years old, we thought we'd build up big excitement by bringing in a real ram."

"Peep is a ewe." Shelby stood and brushed her hands against her jeans.

"But it has horns."

Mary left Shelby to explain Peep's horns to Khloe while she gave Dorothy a call to let her know that the sheep had been found. The call was surprisingly quick.

"Well," Dorothy said, "you solved one mystery, so congratulations on that. But don't forget we still have two more to solve, including the important one of who took our costumes."

"Have you made any progress with that?"

"None yet, but I expect some soon." Dorothy paused. "Oops. That's my call waiting. Got to go."

Mary clicked off her phone and smiled again. Dorothy never changed.

Shelby came over to her. "I've called Uncle Ken. He should be here in a few minutes to get Peep."

"Good!" Khloe said, then shook her head as she looked around the garage. "What a mess! Dad is going to be furious."

Mary put a calming hand on her arm. From what she knew of Patrick Walker, even though his beloved car was now soaked, he would be stern but fair with his daughter. She suspected that Khloe's parents would insist she leave the pep squad and clean out the garage on her own.

Telling the girls she'd let herself out, Mary went back into the house and out onto the front porch. She didn't bother to open her umbrella. The rain had slowed to a cold drizzle that wasn't quite ice.

One mystery solved, but were the other two related or should she look for two more culprits? Abbie definitely had both motive and opportunity to steal the costumes and tear down the posters. Hannah had treated her poorly, and Abbie had been so hurt that she didn't even want to talk about it.

Luis also had both motive and opportunity. He had been at the church that night, and he lived in town. Lots of people knew him from his electrician business, so maybe nobody would pay attention to his taking down the posters.

Then there was Dennis Morton, who hadn't hidden how eager he was to bring more tourists to Bourne. But how and when could he have gotten into the church? There had been a lot of coming and going that evening, so it was possible he could have slipped in and then slipped out completely unnoticed with the costumes.

Even with one mystery solved, she still had too many questions. She needed to talk to more people. It was the only way she had any chance to discover the clues she needed to solve this convoluted mystery.

The first person she needed to speak with was her sister.

*　　*　　*

A delicious aroma met Mary as she entered her home. "What smells good?" she called toward the kitchen as she took off her coat and hung it up.

"Christa's cinnamon-raisin bread," Betty said from the kitchen. "She spent the last three hours mixing the bread dough, letting it rise, and shaping it." She pointed to the three loaves that sat cooling on racks on the counter. "Then she asked me to bake it because the kids and grandkids went to pick out a tree over at the lot run by the Boy Scouts."

"I hope they make up their minds quickly." Mary looked at her watch. "We don't have long before the basketball game starts."

"It won't matter if we're a little late, will it?"

Mary thought about Henry saving them seats and shook her head. He'd understand how busy things were around the holidays. "What's the plan? Decorate the tree after church tomorrow?"

"After church and before we go skating at the temporary rink that the Chamber of Commerce set up." Betty looked up from the tuna noodle casserole she was sliding out of the oven. "You're late tonight."

"I've got a good reason." Mary shared how she'd found Peep a couple of doors down the street.

"I'm going to call Pastor Miles to share the good news," Betty said. She reached for the phone, then paused. "Would you like me to call Dorothy too? She'll want to know."

"I've already done that."

"How did she take the news?"

Mary smiled at her sister's wry expression. "Very well. She congratulated me, and then reminded me that we still had two mysteries with no answers. She said she might be making some progress with finding the costumes."

"That sounds like Dorothy."

Chuckling, Mary said, "By the way, I talked with Abbie Lindstrom earlier today."

"How is she?" Betty set the phone back on the counter as she faced her sister.

"She looked exhausted and was polite about giving me the bum's rush when she couldn't stop yawning." Mary sat at the table before she added, "Bets, I saw what looked like scraps of fabric from the living Nativity costumes at her house. Can you think of any reason why she'd have them at her house?"

Betty walked over to the table and sat. "I can't, but that doesn't mean there isn't a perfectly good one." She held the phone between her hands. "It puzzles me, though, why Abbie would have that material when she was fired early in the process."

"Me too."

"Did you tell Dorothy about that?"

"No, not yet."

"Don't. She's upsetting people with her questioning."

"I've heard," Mary said, thinking of what Rebecca had told her. "I spoke to her about it, so maybe she's changed her tactics."

"Change? Dorothy?" Betty laughed. "I need to call Pastor Miles."

"Go ahead. I want to get some dry socks on before we go to the high school."

Mary went upstairs and pulled off her wet socks. She wiggled her toes and then pulled on dry socks. She wondered if anything had ever felt as good as soft, dry socks. When she said that out loud, Gus raised his head to look at her. He saw she didn't have a treat for him, so he buried his nose in his paws again.

She laughed and patted his head before heading back to the stairs. As she came down, cold air rushed into the house as the door swung open. She heard jesting shouts while Chad and Jack brought in the Christmas tree. Evan held the door open and struggled to keep the grandkids from rushing in to "help." Mary herded the younger ones aside quickly and smiled as she greeted her children over the kids' eager chatter.

Despite far too many different suggestions, the men managed to get the tree settled into its stand without much ado. Betty joined them in the living room as they admired the Scotch pine that was as fat and round as a Christmas ball.

"I found it first!" Allison said.

"She did." Evan put his arm around his daughter. "That means she gets to put the star on top of the tree."

Luke looked puzzled. "Star? But we always have an angel on the top."

His mother hushed him before urging the children to take off their coats. "If you want something quick to eat before the game, you'd better get out to the kitchen."

With a whoop, Luke ran to the kitchen with the other grandchildren following close behind.

Mary linked her arm with her daughter's. "Lizzie, you know the perfect words to get your son to do what you want him to do."

"When food is involved, it's easy."

They laughed as they joined the rest of the family in the kitchen.

Within minutes, everyone was seated with a serving of tuna noodle casserole and something to drink. Only a little milk splashed, and every plate reached the table without mishap.

As her sister sat between her granddaughters, Mary checked Betty's coloring. She would never caution Betty to take it easy, but her sister needed to be careful not to aggravate her rheumatoid arthritis by doing too much. But her sister didn't look worn out, in spite of the chaos. In fact, she looked more relaxed than Mary had seen her since the debacle with the missing costumes. Betty was enjoying having her family and Mary's at the house.

Mary had to do the same. Solving this mystery was important, but she couldn't let it overshadow the time they had together as a family. And, she promised herself, she wouldn't forget that.

✳　　✳　　✳

The game hadn't started by the time Mary's family entered the high school's gym. The bleachers were filling up fast, and there weren't a lot of seats left. She wondered if they'd be able to sit together. Mary looked around for Henry but didn't see him at first.

Then at the other end of the gym, not far from where the band was playing a catchy tune, he stood up and waved. She herded everyone toward where he had kept a large section empty for them. He greeted everyone as if they were long-lost family and teased the grandchildren until they were giggling while they climbed up to sit on the higher bleacher that Henry had managed to save for them.

"Thanks for saving us seats." Mary sat between Henry and her sister on the next to the lowest bleacher. "It took us longer to find parking than I expected."

"Me too." He chuckled. "I might as well have left the car at home and walked over. But it still looks like it might rain or snow tonight, so I figured I'd be smarter to drive." He laughed again.

Mary laughed along with him. Henry was such fun company. He'd never met a stranger, because everyone took to him right away. Probably because he was as friendly to someone he'd just met as if they'd known each other for years.

Half-turning on the seat, he said, "Here you go." He handed each grandchild one of the lobster-shaped candy canes he'd given Mary earlier. "Save them for our victory dance." He winked at Mary. "Guess we've got a reason already for celebrating. Good job on finding your misplaced lamb."

"I'm glad poor Peep is home and safe with the rest of her flock." She smiled as she thought of Ken Gomes's call before they'd left for the game. He'd thanked her over and over for her efforts and urged her to bring her grandchildren over to the farm before they headed back off the Cape. He offered to give them a personal tour and let them see the sheep. He also generously offered to bring Peep back to Grace Church if the living Nativity took place.

Mary's eyes widened as she asked Henry, "How did you hear of it already?"

"When I was standing in line to buy my ticket, a bunch of kids were talking about it. Even though most of them thought it was 'wicked cool,' as they said over and over, that the pep squad wanted a real sheep for the game, they were glad the sheep was back where it belonged." His eyes twinkled. "A few suggested changing the pep squad's name to the *Peep* squad."

As she laughed along with her family, Mary was glad they were sharing this good time with Henry. It had turned out to be a good day. Peep was home. She was here at the biggest game of the season with her family and Henry, and Christmas was just around the corner.

"One mystery solved," Henry said quietly so no one could hear him but Mary. "How's it going with the others?"

"If you're asking if I've found the answers for them, unfortunately I haven't."

"There was a lot of talk in the ticket line about the lighting contest."

She wasn't surprised. "With the living Nativity postponed and possibly canceled, the lighting contest is *the* biggest event before Christmas."

"I'm sure you've taken that into consideration with your search."

"I have, but I haven't found anything definitive."

"You will. I know you, Mary Fisher. You'll uncover a clue, and then you will get to the bottom of the mystery."

"If Dorothy doesn't first." She held up her hand to halt his retort. "Really, Henry, it doesn't matter which one of us solves these mysteries. All that matters is that they get solved."

"Agreed, though I suspect you would like to get the answer first."

Mary laughed, but as the game began with the boys running onto the court, she forgot about everything else.

Through the first eight-minute quarter, Ivy Bay held the lead, but by the half, Barnstable was up by two baskets. The gym reverberated with support from both teams' fans.

Jack went out to get sodas for everyone, which they needed after shouting for almost twenty minutes.

From behind her, Mary heard, "Mrs. Fisher, are you enjoying the game?"

Mary looked over her shoulder to discover Dennis Morton taking a seat behind her. What was a resident of Bourne doing at a game between Ivy Bay and Barnstable?

As if she'd asked the question out loud, he smiled. "My nephew is playing for Barnstable tonight. Or, more accurately, he's holding down his end of the bench."

She laughed but wondered why Dennis had sought her out. Their conversation at the park had been merely polite. Now he acted as if they were old friends. Then she reminded herself that he served on his town's Board of Selectmen and must be used to talking to everyone while he tried to put them at ease.

"Who knows?" Mary asked. "He may get called in to try to save the game."

"Not likely. He's barely five-foot-five if he stands on his toes." Dennis leaned toward her. "Have you found the missing costumes for your church's living Nativity?" She guessed by the sudden tension in his voice that *this* was what he had come over to find out.

"Not yet."

"That's too bad."

"It is," Henry said, joining the conversation. "A lot of work was put into that living Nativity."

Mary was grateful when Henry introduced himself to Dennis and shifted the conversation to the charter boat business. Why was Dennis so interested in the missing costumes that he'd come over to ask her about them?

She didn't get an answer then, as the cheerleaders hurried out to center court. They formed two lines and waved their pom-poms as Khloe Walker ran out between them. She paused in the center of the court. She glanced once in Mary's direction, then quickly away as she picked up the whistle she wore on a string around her neck.

"I know you've heard the rumors that we're introducing a new mascot tonight, Ivy Bay High School!" she called out while the cheerleaders kept shaking their pom-poms. "You've tweeted and you've texted and you've asked us a ton of questions. Your wait is over."

She blew two sharp blasts on the whistle. The pep squad rushed in, pulling a red wagon behind them. In the wagon, a papier-mâché sheep was painted with the school colors. *Go Rams!* was stenciled on both sides and hung on a sign around its neck.

The Ivy Bay fans leaped to their feet and cheered as the girls pulled the wagon around the center of the floor. The sheep was well-made, so Mary guessed the pep squad hadn't just put it together. Taking Peep must have been a spur-of-the-moment thing, a prank they didn't think through.

Mary snuck a glance at Dennis, who was clapping along with everyone around them. As the cheerleaders began a final cheer before the game resumed, he stood.

"I'd better get back to my side of the court," he said, climbing down between her and Henry. "Don't forget that we're having our own living Nativity in Bourne on Christmas Eve. Why don't you come over and see it? I can guarantee you won't be disappointed."

Mary heard her sister draw in a sharp breath, and she put her hand on Betty's. Surely Dennis didn't mean to sound callous. He might have been simply playing the politician and booster for his town.

Or was he trying to cover his own involvement in halting Ivy Bay's living Nativity by speaking openly of the one in Bourne? Again she wanted to ask him, but she had to have facts, not just circumstantial evidence that didn't add up to much. She kept her mouth closed as she nodded, and he went to the other set of bleachers. She lost sight of him when the teams took to the court again.

Ivy Bay sank four baskets in quick succession. Three of them were made by Brian Flanagan, who seemed to move at warp speed. Wherever the ball was, he was there too. Mary cheered along with everyone else as he went up for another dunk.

Someone near the top of the bleachers began chanting, "Ivy Bay Rams! Ivy Bay Rams! Ivy Bay Rams!" The rest of the hometown fans joined in, and the gym echoed with the shouts. Even though there were nearly as many Barnstable supporters on the opposite bleachers, their voices were drowned out by the chant.

The ref blew his whistle at a foul by one of the Barnstable players. Before the foul shots could be taken, a timeout was called, and the players loped back to their teams' benches to confer with their coaches.

The players looked exhausted but determined. The lead had been regained by Barnstable and then went to Ivy Bay. Through the second half, neither team ever got more than a basket or two ahead.

The clock clicked down to the last minute, and the crowds on both sides of the court grew silent. The *thump* of the ball on the wood floor and the *swish* of it going through the net seemed as loud as thunder.

As the timer went below ten seconds, Barnstable sank a basket to pull ahead by a point. The two teams set up for the ball coming back in for play. A Barnstable player knocked it out of the hands of one of the Ivy Bay players. Before he could dribble, it was stolen back. There were barely three seconds left. He flung the ball toward the Ivy Bay basket, where Brian and another boy were being covered by Barnstable players.

Mary held her breath as the ball flew toward Brian, who ran to it so a Barnstable player couldn't cut it off. He dribbled to the basket and jumped straight up. Instead of dunking the ball as he had before, he passed it to the other Ivy Bay boy, who did a picture-perfect lay-up as the buzzer sounded.

Everyone in the gym looked at the scoreboard. The numbers flickered, then the score for the home team went up by two. The Ivy Bay Rams had won!

The gym erupted into cheers and raucous shouts. The trophy would remain at the Ivy Bay High School. No one celebrated more than Brian and the boy he'd passed the ball to. They flung their arms around each other and bounced up and down in a crazy dance. The rest of the team surrounded them for a group hug that somehow evolved into a conga line that included the team, the cheerleaders, the pep squad, and even the coach and the ram following in its wagon. Everyone in the stands clapped along as the band played a very upbeat version of the school's alma mater, turning it into a victory song.

Mary and Betty and their families hugged, too, drawing Henry in with them as they sang and cheered and celebrated a great game.

Chad wiped his forehead on his sleeve. "Wow! That was exciting! Maybe we should make this an annual event. Coming to cheer for Ivy Bay to keep the old oaken bucket trophy."

Henry laughed and pointed to Brian. "Our chances of keeping it go down when young Flanagan graduates in June."

"He is a superstar," Evan said. "We've been lucky to have him for the past four years."

Mary smiled as Mavis and her husband, Greg, walked toward them on their way to the exit. When Mary congratulated them on Brian's outstanding performance, Mavis beamed, every inch the proud mother.

"He loves basketball," Mavis said, "but he has worked really hard."

"It shows." Mary gave her a quick hug. "I can't imagine how many practices you have taken him to."

"And basketball camps in the summer and clinics in the fall." Mavis laughed. "But what's a mother to do? When your child discovers something that brings him such joy, you do everything you can to nurture his dreams."

"True." Mary plunged ahead with the question she'd been wanting to ask. "Mavis, by any chance, does Brian have his costume for the living Nativity at your house?"

"No." Mavis's forehead ruffled. "Why? Have you found other costumes at the volunteers' homes?"

She didn't want to say that Courtney had mentioned having her angel costume at the Flanagans' house if Mavis didn't already know. She wondered where Courtney was, then saw the little girl running across the court. She must have gone out to speak with her brother. She waved shyly to Mary, pushed up her glasses, then hurried over to her parents.

"Mary?" Mavis prompted.

"No, I haven't found any other costumes at anyone's house." That was the truth. "But if you hear anything–"

"I'll let you know."

Mary edged aside to let others congratulate Brian's proud parents. She turned to make sure her own grandchildren were careful coming down off the bleachers. She didn't need to worry. The crowds were moving so slowly that they had no choice but to walk at the same speed.

She pulled on her coat but didn't zip it. In the aftermath of the game, the gym was as hot as a sauna. She walked with Henry out into the hallway, which was only a degree or two cooler until they got close to the exit doors. The night's frosty breeze was almost welcome.

In the parking lot, Mary thanked Henry for joining them tonight. "I'm taking the kids and the grandkids skating tomorrow. Do you want to come along?"

"At the temporary rink in the park?"

She nodded. "It hasn't been cold enough to form thick enough ice on any of the ponds."

"Been cold enough for me!"

"Then maybe you wouldn't like to join us."

He winked at her, his eyes sparkling. "If I don't come, you won't have a chance to see my double axel."

"You can do a double axel?"

He chuckled. "Only in my imagination, but if I'm skidding out of control across the ice, who knows what I might do?"

Mary laughed as she waved good-bye while he walked to his car. She was glad she'd see Henry again tomorrow. They both had been busy with the countdown to Christmas, and she looked forward to having a nice conversation with him tomorrow. Maybe, if she laid out her clues for him, he'd have some insight she'd overlooked. He was good with that.

Mary took her hope with her back to the house, which quieted after everyone had sought their own rooms. Evan's family was spending the night, so the grandchildren were doubled up. They were tired out from their busy day, and it didn't take them long to go to sleep.

The house settled in the cold night, creaking and protesting the wind off the bay. Mary sat in her bedroom with Gus on her lap as she opened her Bible. Her reading led her to Paul's letter to the Ephesians:

Children, obey your parents in the Lord: for this is right. Honor thy father and mother; which is the first commandment with promise; that it may be well with thee, and thou mayest live long on the earth. And, ye fathers, provoke not your children to wrath: but bring them up in the nurture and admonition of the Lord. Servants, be obedient to them that are your masters according to the flesh, with fear and trembling, in singleness of your heart, as unto Christ; not with eye service, as men pleasers; but as the servants of Christ, doing the will of God from the heart; with good will doing service, as to the Lord, and not to men: knowing that whatsoever good thing any man doeth, the same shall he receive of the Lord . . .

She lowered her Bible to her lap and prayed that she could follow Paul's teachings and be an example to her grandchildren, who had spent the drive home debating whether a star or an angel should be at the top of the tree. Compromise was a lesson that was good to relearn. She hoped God would guide them to the best way to bring hers and Betty's families together as one for the holiday season.

"And I would appreciate a nudge in the right direction to solve these mysteries." She laughed softly. Now she sounded like Dorothy, who entreated God's help as casually as if He were her actual father. At that thought, she added, "And if Dorothy solves them first, help me to be gracious and kind and to remember that the important thing is to get answers, not who gets them."

She smiled as she picked up Gus and transferred him to the foot of the bed before getting in bed herself. Drawing up the covers and trying not to think that she had only three days to recover the costumes before Christmas Eve, she turned off the light and her mind and went to sleep.

✳ Chapter Fourteen

The topic of Pastor Miles's sermon that Sunday morning must have been no surprise to anyone who had been involved in the living Nativity. He chose a passage from 2 Corinthians.

"Let me share with you verses five through eight," he said, before he began reading out loud, "'But if any have caused grief, he hath not grieved me, but in part: that I may not over-charge you all. Sufficient to such a man is this punishment, which was inflicted of many. So that contrariwise ye ought rather to forgive him, and comfort him, lest perhaps such a one should be swallowed up with overmuch sorrow. Wherefore I beseech you that ye would confirm your love toward him.'"

As he paused to let the Scripture sink into their minds, Mary closed her eyes in a silent prayer that she would be able to forgive the person or persons who had taken the costumes and destroyed the posters. Forgiving Khloe Walker had been simple because the girl had readily admitted her mistake and regretted the whole scheme.

Was the person who took the costumes worshiping here with them? If so, she hoped Pastor Miles's words of forgiveness and love reached him or her. It was December 22, so if the costumes were returned today, they could still have the living Nativity for three nights.

Comfort swelled through her. She needed to take her time, even though time was short, and examine the clues she'd uncovered. She'd been rushing from here to there, desperate to get the answers as quickly as possible. Even though she acknowledged that all would unfold in God's time, she had tried to make everything fit *her* time.

She wouldn't do that any longer.

Bowing her head, she prayed, *Thank You, Lord, for having patience with* me. *I will trust that You lead me along the path to solving these mysteries.*

Mary raised her head and glanced toward the beautiful Nativity set atop the board covering the baptismal font. She focused on the angel on the top of the stable. From where she sat, she could clearly see that the angel still didn't have its wings. That surprised her. She'd assumed that Dorothy would have found the broken piece while vacuuming the sanctuary the night the costumes went missing. That was odd, because the wings couldn't have fallen very far when the angel was knocked off the top of the stable.

The choir stood to sing, and Mary opened her hymnal and quickly found the correct song. "O Come, All Ye Faithful" rose in harmony from the choir, and the congregation joined in enthusiastically.

At the end of the service, Mary waited beside her sister in the long line to the door. Theirs weren't the only families with guests for Christmas, so the line moved more slowly than usual as friends greeted friends they hadn't seen in months.

Betty looked at the Nativity set and sighed. "It's a shame about the angel getting broken. The Nativity is old, and it won't be easy to find another angel."

"Maybe someone can make some feathery wings for the angel and glue them on," Mary said.

Betty brightened. "What an excellent idea! I'll talk to Pastor Miles about giving the angel a new set of wings when we set up the Nativity next year."

"Maybe the next time a bell rings…" Mary laughed along with her sister. Watching *It's a Wonderful Life* was a holiday tradition that everyone in their families agreed on, and Mary always ended up dabbing tears from her eyes when Angel Second Class Clarence won his wings for helping George Bailey recognize his blessings.

She took a step forward, then paused to look back at the stable. Odd…

"Is something else wrong?" Betty looked toward the Nativity set. "Has one of the other figurines gotten broken?"

Feeling silly, Mary smiled. "I'm sure it's nothing, Bets, but I thought I left the angel facing the altar. Isn't that the way it's supposed to be?"

"No. We've always had the angel looking at the congregation. When the Nativity was first set up many years ago, our pastor at the time suggested a friendly, angelic face might be just the thing to invite everyone to come to the stable and remember the simple, precious miracle that changed the world."

That made sense, and someone who knew that must have shifted the angel after Mary put it facing the altar. If she started looking for a possible clue in the most commonplace matters, she could easily overlook a real clue.

"It was probably the most exciting game at the high school in a dozen years," she heard someone say.

Heads nodded around them, and smiles burst out. Even those people, like Mary, who seldom attended high school games were excited about the victory last night over Barnstable.

Mavis answered, "I wish Brian had sunk that last basket instead of handing it off. Apparently there was a scout from University of Connecticut in the stands. If Brian had made the winning basket, he'd certainly be guaranteed a scholarship to UConn. Now, who knows?"

Mary was startled by the change in Mavis. Last night, she'd been excited that the team had won and that her son had been a vital part of the victory.

Mary glanced toward Brian, who stood behind his mother, his backpack hanging from one shoulder. She was surprised he'd brought it to the Sunday service, but she seldom saw any teenager without one.

His eyes met Mary's for a second, then he hastily looked away. Color rose up his face, but he kept his head lowered, so she couldn't read his expression. Was he embarrassed by his mother's comments? Or was he upset? She thought of how he had been the first one to congratulate the boy who'd made the basket. Was he angry that his mother didn't see how important it was to the team to work together?

A couple of men congratulated Brian, and he mumbled short answers. The color deepened on his face. Both Rhonda and Betty had told Mary how shy he was. Had Brian handed off the ball so he wouldn't have to be in the limelight alone? No, that was silly. He wouldn't risk losing a game simply to avoid being the center of attention. She smiled at her foolish thought.

Mary continued forward as the parishioners moved toward the door. The Flanagans seemed eager for their children to excel, but what parent wasn't? And a scholarship to a good school was a big deal, so Mavis's frustration was understandable. It was a shame, though, that she spoke of it when her son stood nearby.

When she reached Pastor Miles, Mary thanked him for another excellent sermon.

"I understand you found our vagrant sheep," the pastor said with a smile.

"I had a lot of help, but the important thing is that Peep wasn't hurt. Too bad that the costumes haven't turned up as quickly. We were looking forward to the living Nativity."

He turned to include Betty in the conversation. "Maybe your family would enjoy seeing the living Nativity in Bourne. It's not the same as having one here ourselves, but your grandchildren might enjoy it. Mr. Morton urged me to pass along the word to everyone in Grace Church."

"He came to talk to you?" Mary couldn't hide her astonishment. How much time was Dennis spending in Ivy Bay trying to drum up interest in events in Bourne?

"Yes, he dropped by earlier this week. I guess word of our missing costumes has spread over the Cape. He wanted to make sure we knew about the living Nativity in Bourne, in case anyone wanted to see it." Pastor Miles shook his head. "I didn't say anything from the pulpit because I felt some people would be too upset, but I thought you should know."

"He told me about it already."

"Good, so you can pass the word too. Seeing a living Nativity, even if it isn't ours, will bring hope and joy to our congregation. And he reminded me that everyone attending could make a donation to the food bank exactly as we'd planned for ours."

Mary nodded. Pastor Miles was right. Even though Dennis was on her list of possible suspects, keeping people from seeing the living Nativity in Bourne wouldn't bring back the costumes at Grace Church.

"It sounds as if you've had a busy, busy week," Betty said.

Pastor Miles laughed. "It's always like this during Advent. We've had a regular parade of people in and out of the church. Thank goodness, Mavis has her own key, so she can come in and practice without disturbing anyone. I've come to depend on her to let people in and out when Tricia and I have to be somewhere else."

As she walked out of the church with her sister, Mary's eyes were caught by Dorothy's. She wore a determined expression as she came toward Mary.

"We need to talk," Dorothy said without a greeting.

"Certainly. Now that we know the sheep's disappearance wasn't connected with the costumes, it'd be good to go over the clues we have. I–"

"We shouldn't talk here." Dorothy glanced around as if she expected to find someone eavesdropping in the bushes around the church. "Let's go over to the Chadwick Inn. We can talk over brunch."

Mary hesitated. She didn't want to miss a moment of the time she could have with her family. They were supposed to decorate the Christmas tree back at the house before they went skating.

"I'm sorry, Dorothy. I've got other plans for the afternoon."

"You surely have time for a cup of coffee." She lowered her voice conspiratorially. "I don't want everyone to hear what I've found out."

Telling Dorothy to wait a moment, Mary went to where Betty was waiting with their children and grandchildren. She quickly explained that she'd be home in about a half hour. When Jack promised they wouldn't start decorating the tree without her, she smiled.

"After all," he added, "it'll take at least that long to untangle the lights and get them working."

That brought laughter, and Mary felt better about returning to where Dorothy waited with obvious impatience. True to her word, Dorothy didn't say a word until she and Mary crossed Main Street and went into the Chadwick Inn.

The usual decor was made even more beautiful with the addition of winter greens and candles. Mary could almost believe she was stepping into a private home at the time of the Revolutionary War. The plush carpet softened their footsteps, and the patrons spoke in hushed tones as if caught up in the splendor of their surroundings.

When they were led to a small table in a corner, Dorothy chose the chair that allowed her to survey the whole room. "So nobody can eavesdrop on us."

Mary hid her smile. A waiters' station was on the other side of the half wall, and any of the staff could easily hear everything they said.

Dorothy barely waited for their waitress to take their orders for coffee before she began complaining about Dennis Morton. The Bourne selectman seemed to have talked to everyone he could who was connected to the living Nativity at Grace Church.

"He went on and on about how the one here needs to be officially canceled and how nobody will donate to a non-event." Dorothy sniffed. "A non-event! Could he have been any more insulting?"

Mary doubted Dennis had intended his words as an aspersion, but with everyone involved in Grace Church's living Nativity on edge and looking over their shoulders, people were more sensitive.

"I've met him a couple of times," Mary said when Dorothy asked.

"Was it at the church both times?"

"He's been to Grace Church more than once?"

"At least twice that I know of." She paused as a cup of steaming coffee was placed in front of her. Nodding her thanks to the waitress, she reached for a packet of sugar.

"Pastor Miles said he stopped by recently. When else was he there?"

Dorothy lowered her voice and leaned toward Mary. "I found out he was at the church the day the costumes disappeared."

"Who told you that?"

"Kip Hastings."

"I thought Kip had gone out of town to visit friends for the holidays."

"I spoke to him before he left. He said Dennis Morton was driving past and noticed them working. He came over to talk to him and Luis. Apparently he told them that he was impressed with the stable background they were building and asked if he could take measurements. Don't you find that suspicious?"

Even though Mary wanted to agree with Dorothy, common sense told her that while Dennis's actions sounded odd, it was possible that he had stopped exactly for the reason he said.

"Did he say anything else?"

"Wasn't that enough?"

"Not for me."

"But you don't know the whole story, Mary."

"What else have you found out?"

Pushing back her chair, Dorothy said, "I'm going to get some food, and then we can talk uninterrupted. If we sit here just sipping coffee, *we* will look suspicious."

Mary smiled when Dorothy stood and went to the buffet line. Dorothy intended to draw every bit of drama out of discussing the mysteries with Mary.

Dorothy returned with some eggs and bacon. Setting the plate on the table, she sat and continued as if there hadn't been a break in their conversation. "Dennis Morton asked how Kip and Luis were handling the lighting. How they were getting power and how they were making sure nothing got disconnected and nobody got electrocuted."

"I was curious about that too."

"Listen to this. Luis took Mr. Morton into the church to show him how the wiring was hooked in to the circuit breaker box."

"Okay. That makes sense."

"Mary!" She quickly lowered her voice when heads turned toward them, but the exasperation remained. "Don't you understand? Luis and Mr. Morton went into the church."

"What about Kip?"

"He told me that he had to finish nailing up a board. Once that was done, he went into the church too."

"But did they wait for him to finish so he could go with them, or did they go in on their own?"

Dorothy started to answer, then clamped her lips closed. She stabbed at the scrambled eggs. "I never thought to ask that. After all, what does it matter what Mr. Morton did? He's an irritating, officious man, but you know as well as I do that Luis Alvarez took the costumes so our living Nativity didn't overshadow his lighting contest."

"I'm sorry, Dorothy," Mary said with a sigh, "but I can't say for sure who might have taken the costumes. And there's still the issue of whoever tore down the posters. I know you think you have enough information to point a finger at Luis, but I've found I need to keep an open mind while gathering information and piecing it together."

"I have been keeping an open mind."

"I didn't mean to suggest–"

"I know. I know. But I've also been keeping my ears open, and it's common knowledge that Luis has been bragging that his lighting contest will raise more money for charity than our living Nativity ever could have."

Mary listened as Dorothy repeated conversations she'd had with other people at church and with some of her neighbors. Dorothy already was annoyed that Mary's methods for solving a mystery were different from her own. But Mary knew that often she'd discovered that common knowledge might be common but seldom contained a lot of knowledge.

For her, it came back to the same question: Did Luis have a good reason to want the living Nativity canceled? Yes, because it competed with his lighting contest.

The contest started tonight, and her family planned to go to see the lights switched on. She'd observe the crowd and maybe have a chance to talk to some other people who might have information that she–and Dorothy–didn't.

"One thing I have to admit," Dorothy said after she'd finished her breakfast. "Sleuthing is harder than you've made it look. Even though I've been having fun, it'd be more fun if I had more definitive answers."

Mary simply smiled in response. She wasn't sure how Dorothy would react if Mary told her that she found chasing clues and solving mysteries thrilling—even when the process was frustrating, as it was now. But she had to keep believing that would turn around soon.

✳ Chapter Fifteen

Betty met Mary at their door. She looked annoyed, which surprised Mary. Her sister was usually an even-tempered woman.

"Can I talk to you in the kitchen?" Betty asked.

Mary took one look at the living room, where the tree was draped with lights. Ornaments covered the branches until very little green could be seen, and she felt a twinge. She'd thought they were going to wait for her to help trim the tree. Her eyes narrowed when she noticed the top of the tree was the only bare spot.

"Where is everyone?" she asked.

"I sent them over to the skating rink. I told them we'd join them after you got home. But first I have something I want to talk to you about."

"All right. I hope it isn't as serious as it sounds."

"I hope not too."

Taking off her coat, Mary hung it up and followed her sister into the kitchen. Betty sliced some of the cinnamon-raisin bread left over from breakfast and placed two plates on the table. She offered coffee, but Mary shook her head. She'd already had enough today.

Mary sat and waited for her sister to add a generous portion of milk and sugar to her own mug of coffee. Carrying it to the table, Betty sat and sighed.

"That sounds serious."

Betty gave her a taut smile. "In the greater realm of things, it isn't, but as you can see, the tree isn't finished."

"I saw that."

"I know we were supposed to do only the lights before you got back, but one thing led to another and…"

Mary put her hand gently on her sister's arm. "What is it?"

"Every single thing seems to be up for debate. My family has its traditions, and your kids each have traditions of their own. All the grandchildren want Christmas to be perfect, which, to them, means following their own traditions."

"I hadn't realized how different our traditions have become over the years." Mary smiled when Gus jumped on her lap and nudged at her hand with his head. She patted him and looked back at her sister.

"I'm assuming you noticed that the top of the tree is empty," Betty said.

"Yes."

"Jack and Christa brought a star from Chicago that they bought for Daisy's first Christmas, and it's important for her to have it on the tree. Lizzie and Chad's kids prefer the angel they found in some shop in Vermont several years ago. And

Evan and Mindy's girls want their own angel that is made of shells and came from Chatham."

"Surely there's a good compromise. We could use them all."

"That's what I suggested, but it won't work because each of the angels was made to go on the very top of the tree." She spread butter on her bread. "But that's not the point, Mary. The argument got pretty heated. There were tears. We can't let these petty issues ruin our time together. What we need is to find a tradition we all share."

"Or make a new one."

Betty's eyes widened. "Now that is a good idea. Do you have any idea what we can do?"

"Not off the top of my head, but let me think about it."

"I will too."

Mary set Gus on the floor and reached for her bread. After she took a bite, she said, "Don't take this the wrong way, Betty, but I'm actually glad to have something to think about other than costumes and posters and possible suspects."

"I understand."

Mary took another bite of the delicious bread, then said, "Let's have a good time this afternoon. There's got to be a solution to make sure the grandchildren feel like this Christmas is special. In the meantime, we'll have fun skating."

For the first time, Betty smiled with her usual warmth. "That sounds like a good plan."

* * *

The outdoor ice-skating rink had been put together by the local Chamber of Commerce. Betty's sister-in-law, Eleanor Blakely, had come up with the idea. Eleanor stood at one end of the rink, greeting everyone as if welcoming them into her home. As always, her fashionable clothing looked better suited for New York than Ivy Bay, but she had worked hard to get the rink built. She deserved to be front and center today. Betty congratulated her sister-in-law on getting the ice rink ready in time for school vacation.

"I wish your work at church had paid off as well," Eleanor said, hugging Betty.

Mary left Betty to talk with her sister-in-law and wandered over to where adults and children were sitting on logs specially placed around the rink. Most people were lacing up their skates, but others were simply enjoying the chance to watch their neighbors skate on the rink that was big enough for a hockey game.

She found the person renting ice skates and was glad there still was a pair in her size. The skates looked as if they'd seen better days, their once white leather creased in dark lines. He also gave her a clothespin and explained she could use it to clip her boots together.

Her grandchildren skated over when she sat on the end of a log and pulled off her right boot. Quickly she stuffed her foot into the skate. As she began tightening the laces, she asked the kids how they were enjoying the skating. She and Betty had agreed not to speak of the tree topper discussion.

"This is the best way to spend a chilly winter afternoon!" Emma wobbled a bit on her skates. "C'mon, Grandma. Mom says you're a good skater."

"I haven't skated in more years that I want to admit. Go ahead, and I'll meet up with you when I get my skates on."

With a shout to the other grandchildren, Emma joined her cousins in the line of skaters circling the rink.

Mary removed her left boot, clipped it to her right one with the clothespin, and bent to tie her left skate. A shadow flowed over her. She smiled as she looked up and saw Henry with a pair of skates. He'd lashed the laces together and hung them over his shoulder as they used to when they were kids.

"I'm impressed," she said. "You've got your own skates."

"Don't be. I found them over at the charity shop a couple of months ago. I got talked into buying them, and now I don't have any excuse not to perfect my double axel."

"Can't wait to see it."

"Me either." He chuckled.

She stood on her skates and took a cautious step toward the ice. Her ankles wobbled, but she made it the two steps to the rink. She turned to face Henry, who was struggling to get his foot into his skate. He gave her a silly grin, then shoved harder. She suggested he loosen the laces more. That seemed to do the trick, and he quickly laced them up.

He held out his hands, and she helped him take the few steps to where he could put his blades on the ice.

"All set?" he asked.

Luke skated up and grabbed her hand. "Grandma, skate with me!"

As she stepped away from Henry, she heard a *thump*. She stopped and looked back to see him sitting on the ice.

"I'm fine. I'm fine," he said, waving off offers of help to get back up. Standing, he took a single slide, and his feet went out from under him again.

"Now this looks familiar," Mary said as she skated carefully against the current of other skaters back to him. "You're as good a skater now as you were when we were kids."

"I need to get my land legs under me. An old fisherman like me can dance a jig at sea, but the land trips me up." He chuckled. "Or the ice on the land. Once I'm steady, you'll see how good I've gotten."

"And then you'll do that double axel."

He pushed himself up. "Or die trying."

She laughed. "Maybe you should leave the double axel for another twenty or thirty years then."

"A good idea." He held out his arm. "Why don't you help me around the ice without making it look like I'm holding on to you for dear life?"

Mary agreed, and they slowly inched out to where the kids were skating. Daisy was doing a sit spin in the center of the ice, and the other skaters watched with appreciation.

"That's impressive," Henry said.

"It's what comes from growing up with cold Chicago winters." Mary laughed as he skated alongside her. "She's had a lot of chances to practice."

"It shows." Patti Fernandes took careful steps across the ice, not letting her skates glide. She held her son and daughter's hands tightly. "You must be proud of her."

"I am. She's a great kid." Mary smiled at Patti's children. "Are you having fun?"

They nodded.

"Do you like lobsters?" Henry asked as he fished into his coat pocket and pulled out two more lobster-shaped candy canes. Then he offered a third to Patti, who smiled. Henry's charm worked on everyone, perhaps because he genuinely enjoyed making people happy.

Patti took the candy lobster, then chuckled. "I wouldn't exactly describe our skating as fun, because we're down on the ice as much as we're up on our feet."

"I know the feeling." Henry rubbed his backside and grimaced.

The children giggled.

"Where's Jason?" Mary asked.

"He stayed home to work on putting up lights for the lighting contest." Patti's smile faded. "Not because he's gotten into the Christmas spirit. He wasn't planning on participating until this morning."

"What changed his mind?" Mary asked.

"We found three boxes of lights and everything we needed to make enough luminaria for the front lawn and up the driveway."

"Found? Someone left them?"

Patti nodded. "Isn't that the nicest thing to do?"

"It is. Do you know who left them?"

"No. Lots of people in our neighborhood have been talking about the lighting contest, and several, who didn't have the time or money to get lights, mentioned that they'd found lights on their porches too."

Mary smiled at the wondrous gift of the season to the residents of the Sea Breezes neighborhood. "What a special thing for someone to do."

"It is." Her smile dimmed slightly. "But, Mrs. Fisher, it's frustrating too."

"How?"

"I really would like to thank whoever was so thoughtful. There was a note with the luminaria supplies, but it wasn't signed. All it said was, 'Merry Christmas! Celebrate the Light of the World in This Season.'"

Mary recognized the reference. It was from John 8:12 when Jesus described himself: *"I am the light of the world: he that followeth me shall not walk in the darkness, but shall have the light of life."*

What a perfect gift for the holidays...or any time! She wondered who had brought the message of Jesus's promise to the neighborhood. She hoped that person found blessing in offering such a gift.

"As I told Jason," Patti said, "how could we *not* put them up? Even a Scrooge wouldn't be able to turn his back on such a gift." Her eyes widened. "Not that Jason is a Scrooge. He's just a little burned out this year."

"Mom!" said her son impatiently. "Let's skate."

Mary waved as Patti inched along with the two young children. She and Henry made several circuits of the rink before Jack invited them to join the rest of the family getting some cocoa. Sweet Susan's Bakery had set up a table with cocoa and cupcakes and cookies. The line was long, but the time went quickly as Mary talked and joked with her family and Henry.

"Mrs. Emerson?" asked a young voice to her left. "Do you have a minute?"

Brian Flanagan and Khloe Walker stood there, their expressions uneasy. He was gripping the strap of his backpack like it was a lifeline.

Does he ever go anywhere without it? Mary hid her smile and waited to see what the two teens had to say to Betty.

Khloe held on to Brian's arm with the same death grip he held on the backpack. Behind Khloe, her father had his arms crossed over his chest as his eyes drilled a hole in her back. He glanced toward Mary for a moment, gave a brief nod and a friendly smile, then resumed his pose as the furious dad.

Betty smiled at the teens. "Certainly. Are you having fun ice-skating?"

Khloe took a half step forward, then motioned with her fingertips for Brian to do the same. "Mrs. Emerson," she said, "I wanted to apologize for any trouble the pep squad caused for you and Grace Church by taking Peep the sheep." Khloe's lips twitched on the name, and Brian tried to hide a soft laugh. She quickly became serious again. "We saw it as a prank and never stopped to think that it would cause you or the church any trouble. I'm really sorry. We all are."

"Thank you for telling me that." Betty smiled. "The first step toward forgiveness is an apology. Have you apologized to Pastor Miles?"

"That is where we are going next," Khloe said.

"I'm glad to hear that." She gave the teens a kind smile. "He will appreciate it."

"Do you forgive us?" Khloe glanced over her shoulder toward where her father was watching with a stern expression.

"Certainly. Now that the sheep is home safe and sound, everything is all right."

"Thank you. Thank you. Thank you." Khloe's breath of relief was audible.

Brian stared at the tips of his boots as if they were the most interesting things on the planet. Was he suffering from his usual shyness, or was he embarrassed over what had been done at his own church? Even though the basketball team hadn't been involved in taking Peep, Mary guessed that they'd heard rumors that something was up. As Khloe looked back at her father to make sure he'd heard every word, Mary shifted her attention to the boy by her side.

She began, "Brian—"

"Got to go," he said as he grabbed Khloe's hand.

Mary watched him hurry so he and Khloe could catch up with some other teens. His shoulders were hunched, and each step was as heavy as it had been when she'd seen him in church. Poor kid! He was under a lot of pressure to get a scholarship and make his parents proud. He couldn't even relax when he was out with his friends.

"That was nice," Betty said. "Even though Patrick probably insisted that she apologize, it was good of Khloe to do so."

"What did you always say, Mom?" Evan asked. "That kids have to accept the consequences of their actions? I hope the apologies went more than word-deep and that those kids learned a not-too-terribly tough lesson."

"Look who's talking! I seem to recall my son getting in trouble for trying to hijack another school's mascot costume when he was around the same age as these kids." Betty laughed as her son's ears turned red when his daughters giggled and asked for details.

They were still jesting with him by the time they got their hot chocolate and found a couple of empty logs close together so they could sip it as they talked and watched the other skaters. The sun poked through the clouds a few times, causing the ice to glitter like tinsel.

Mary took a few more laps around the rink with her grandchildren while the others finished their drinks. She'd taken off her skates and was putting on her boots when she saw an unexpected person walking toward where Betty was again talking with Eleanor.

Dennis Morton! She should have guessed he'd turn up sooner or later at the skating rink. He was in Ivy Bay more than he was in his own hometown. He gave Eleanor a broad smile as he shook her hand.

"This is a brilliant idea," he said, and Eleanor beamed. "I hope you don't mind if I borrow it and share it with the other selectmen in Bourne. I would, most certainly, tell them that the idea was originally yours."

"Of course, I don't mind, Mr. Morton."

"Dennis," he insisted as he had to Mary. "Be sure to come over to Bourne for our living Nativity. It's a short drive, and we're having a special night out for the last-minute shoppers. All the shops will be open until eleven every night between now and Christmas." He laughed as if he'd made the world's funniest joke. "What's not to love about that?"

Mary kept her head down. She didn't want to be drawn into another conversation with Dennis. Not until she could confirm what Dorothy had told her about Dennis being inside the church on the very day the costumes vanished. He had moved to the top of her list of suspects, but she had to talk with Kip and discover if Dennis was ever alone in the cellar of the church. Luis and Abbie remained on her list of suspects too. All three of them had access to the costumes, and any of them could have easily torn down the posters. All she needed to do was figure out a way to whittle down her list of suspects, so she could identify the real culprit. She intended to start at the lighting contest tonight.

✳ Chapter Sixteen

M ary looked out the window as Jack turned the big van he'd rented into the Sea Breezes neighborhood. Through the trees, she could see dozens of cars already parked along the street that led into the subdivision. Large boulders were scattered between the scrub pine and maples, and the first house was still out of sight around a slow curve.

Her hands quivered in her lap. She took a deep breath to try to calm herself. She had high hopes for tonight, but if she made this evening the be-all and end-all of her sleuthing on this Christmas mystery, she could get discouraged if she didn't find that vital clue.

In the passenger-side mirror, she could see Evan's car following them. He'd lit the Christmas tree at the house before leaving for the start of the lighting contest but never said a word about the tree's bare top. Nobody had spoken of it, in silent accord that there had been enough disagreements about different traditions.

But if she and Betty could devise a new tradition that everyone could embrace...That sounded great, but what should it be?

Jack tapped the brake as the road ahead filled with people walking into the subdivision. He pulled to the side of the road and parked between two cars.

"I don't think we're going to find anything closer," Jack said as he shifted into park and turned the key. "Hope you don't mind walking from here."

The sound of seat belts being unhooked was his answer. He grinned at Mary, and she smiled back. His grin, so much like her late husband's, touched her heart with joy mixed with lingering grief.

Mary held Luke's hand and looped her arm through Daisy's as soon as they got out of the van. Emma grasped her brother's other hand, and she swung a bag of groceries for their donation-votes as they walked along the road leading into the subdivision. Strains of Christmas carols wafted through the trees, and excited voices rose from the other people walking toward the houses.

Suddenly the trees edging either side of the road cleared, and the houses came into view. Half of the streetlights were off, and not a single bulb was lit on any house. Mary assumed that the neighbors had decided to wait until the contest started to show off their light displays.

Luis stood in the center of the dimly lit street, greeting people and handing out flyers that explained how to vote by depositing a nonperishable can or box of food into the box in front of each person's favorite house. He grinned broadly, and Mary guessed he was enjoying his role as host and ringmaster for the event. Behind him, a dark box about three feet high had several wires running out of it. Was it something for the lighting contest?

"Brilliant idea, Alvarez," a man said, slapping Luis on the shoulder. "This should get your company's name out everywhere."

Luis smiled. "It's not my name I want to get out everywhere, but our Lord's. How better than to hold a big party for His birthday with all the decorations?"

Mary bit her lower lip. That comment didn't sound like one that would be made by a man who had undermined Grace Church's plans for the living Nativity.

He held out a flyer to her and smiled. "Mrs. Fisher, I'm glad you came." He added a hello to her grandchildren and offered them a flyer as well. "I think you're going to be wowed!" He reached past her to hand out other flyers as people passed by.

"You must be excited to see this getting underway," she said.

"More than you can guess." He kept giving the flyers away, and his smile grew broader with each person who took one.

"Must have been a huge job."

"I could have used Kip's help with some of my neighbors who have never swung a hammer before. With his close attention to detail, he would have come in handy."

Mary wished she could see Luis's face more clearly so she could judge if he was being honest or not. She needed to talk to Kip, so he could confirm what Luis had told her. She wondered when he'd be back. Maybe not before Christmas.

Her grandchildren tugged her hands, and she went with them along the street to where the rest of the family had gathered. They'd have a good view in both directions along the curving street. Chad swung Luke up on his shoulders so he could see over the crowd, and Evan did the same for his younger daughter.

The few remaining streetlights faded to orange and then went out, one by one, along the street as if blown out like a row of candles. Emma gripped her hand more tightly, and Mary squeezed it to reassure her. Around them, the crowd buzzed in anticipation.

Luis stepped back to the center of the street, carrying a single flashlight that seemed as bright as a lighthouse's beacon. He walked to the box she'd noticed before.

She waited along with everyone else for him to speak. This was his chance to be in the spotlight, to speak of how his knowledge as an electrician gave him the idea for the contest.

He raised the flashlight and shined it at the box. He touched the side of the box, and a large button rose up to glitter in the light. The crowd drew in its collective breath as he reached out and pressed the button.

No lights came on, and she heard a murmur of disappointment around her.

"What's wrong?" Emma whispered.

Before Mary could answer, a single luminaria flickered by the curb. The electric candle set within a brown paper bag gained strength. At the same time, another luminaria about a foot from it came to life. More luminaria awoke to glow, one after another, until a river of light marked the street's gentle curve.

The street was silent, and Mary realized she was holding her breath too.

Luis raised his flashlight again, drawing attention back to him. He pushed the button a second time.

Light erupted from houses on both sides of the street. Music swelled as "Joy to the World" surrounded them. Slowly turning to take it in, Mary wasn't surprised when spontaneous applause broke out.

Each house was brighter than its neighbor. Animated reindeer and blow-up figures were draped with even more lights. On roofs, Santa sat in his sleigh or stood beside it with a pack of gifts flung over his shoulder. It was garish and glorious.

Then she noticed one house had only a single string of lights along its eaves. Through its front window a beautiful Christmas tree glowed.

As people wandered along the street, admiring the houses and voting with canned goods for their favorites, Mary's eyes kept being drawn back to the house with the one string of lights. She asked one of the neighbors whose house it was.

"The Alvarezes live there," was the answer.

She was puzzled. Luis had been carrying that huge stack of boxes of lights when she saw him outside the hardware store on Main Street. What had he done with the lights? A suspicion tickled the edge of her mind, but she needed to confirm it. She waved to Patti and Jason, who stood on their front porch. It was almost completely covered with lights that blinked in time with the music. She walked over to congratulate them on how great their house looked.

As she came closer, she saw Jason try to hide a yawn. "Jason, you've done an amazing job," Mary said. "You've obviously worked overtime to get this put together this quickly."

"Thanks. I hadn't planned on participating, but when the kids found the boxes of lights out here, I got dragged in."

Patti gave his arm a playful slap. "Can't you stop playing Scrooge for one night, Jason?"

"If you'd put in the hours that I have this week, and next week will be all those Christmas trees…" He halted himself and gave Mary a guilty look. "Sorry."

"It's okay," Mary said. "I know too much about long hours of work before Christmas. Any chance you still have the boxes for the lights you found?"

"They're in the garage." His brows lowered. "Why?"

"I'd like to see one. Patti told me about your secret Santa, and I was curious."

"Let me see if I can find one. Luis wants us to keep our regular house lights off as much as possible, so it may take a few minutes."

"Thanks." She started to add more, but halted as a familiar voice caught her ear.

Kip Hastings! He was in the next yard talking to a man and a woman.

Telling Jason that he'd find her next door, Mary walked over to where Kip and the man were discussing what looked like artificial snow coming from under the house's eaves.

Kip smiled as she approached. "Pretty spectacular, huh? A white Christmas is guaranteed here."

"It's wonderful," Mary said, congratulating the homeowner on his ingenuity. "Kip, could we talk for a moment?"

"Sure thing." He walked with her to a spot between the houses. "What's up?"

"I'm glad to see you here. I thought you might be out of town until after Christmas."

"Heather wanted to visit some friends up in New Hampshire, so we went for a few days." He smiled, his love obvious as he spoke his wife's name. "Neither of us would want to miss Christmas in Ivy Bay." He waved his hand toward the houses across the street. "I'm glad we got back in time to see this. Luis worked his tail feathers off to put this together."

Mary sent up a silent prayer of thanks for Kip bringing the conversation around to Luis. "I need to ask you something about Luis working with you at Grace Church."

"Is this about the missing costumes? Dorothy left about a dozen messages on our phone asking us to call her right away, but the one time I called, her line was busy."

"It *is* about the missing costumes. We're still trying to figure out who might have had a chance to take them. I don't want to accuse anyone, but–"

"You think Luis might have taken them? Impossible. Even if he was the kind of guy to steal the costumes—and he isn't—Luis never went into the church without me. I trust him completely, but if anything happened, I didn't want fingers pointing at him." He grimaced. "Is this what Dorothy wants to talk to me about?"

Mary nodded. "I'm glad to hear that you've got so much trust in Luis."

She was glad that Kip had given her reassurance that Luis hadn't taken the costumes. That was one name off her list, leaving only Abbie and Dennis.

"What do you think of Dennis Morton?" she asked. "Did you ever see him go into the church by himself?"

"Who?"

Mary described Dennis, but before Kip could say anything, Jason walked up and held a box out to Mary.

"Here's what you wanted to see, Mrs. Fisher," he said.

Mary took it and tilted it to see it more clearly in the lights from the nearby house. She wasn't surprised to see it was bright blue. It looked like the same color and the same size as the boxes Luis had carried out of the hardware store a few days ago.

"Thank you, Jason," she said, handing it back to him.

"Sure." He looked confused, but didn't ask the questions visible on his face.

"And, Kip," she began, then realized he'd been drawn into another conversation and was walking with another man down the street. She'd ask him later about Dennis

Morton. For now, she would satisfy her curiosity about the lights.

It didn't take her long to find Luis, who still stood by the box with the button that had activated the lights. Her grandson ran over to join her, chattering about the decorations he'd seen and how he planned to vote for his favorite.

Luis was encircled by his neighbors, so Mary waited for her chance to speak with him. Person after person thanked Luis for coming up with the idea for the lighting contest. Some also thanked him for teaching them about luminaria.

"I'm glad you've had so much fun," he said over and over. "It's been great getting everyone involved." He smiled in Mary's direction. "You aren't leaving yet, are you, Mrs. Fisher?"

"No, not yet." She looked down at Luke. "This is my grandson, Luke. Luke, this is Mr. Alvarez. He's the guy behind these beautiful lights."

"Wow!" The glow from the lights reflected in her grandson's wide eyes. "This is cool."

"You know what?" Luis asked.

"What?"

"I think it's cool too." He laughed along with Luke. "How about you, Mrs. Fisher? What do you think?"

"I think you've done a wonderful thing by making sure everyone in the neighborhood could participate by ensuring that everyone had lights to decorate with."

He lowered his voice and leaned toward her. "How did you guess?"

"I saw you with those boxes of lights, remember?"

Laughing loudly, he said, "I remember, and I should have guessed you'd figure it out pretty quickly. Do me a favor and don't tell everyone. It's been a lot of fun playing one of Santa's elves. I may want to do it again next year."

"My lips are sealed, but maybe you could do me a favor too?"

"Sure. Anything."

His quick response told Mary that Kip was right about Luis being a nice man. She explained that she was trying to find out more about Dennis Morton's visits to Grace Church.

"He only stopped by once when I was there. He hung around for about ten or fifteen minutes." Luis grimaced. "I don't like working with someone looking over my shoulder, so I tried to pretend he wasn't there. Finally, one time, I looked up, and he'd gone."

"So, you don't know if he went into the church on his own?"

"No." His smile faltered. "Do you think he's involved with the missing costumes and the other troubles?"

"I don't know, but I certainly don't want to accuse any-one unfairly." She didn't add that she'd had Luis himself on her list of suspects until moments ago. Thank heavens Kip had been able to confirm for her that Luis couldn't be guilty. Anyone who loved Christmas and his neighbors as Luis did had no place on her suspects list.

"That's good of you. Some people aren't like that."

She didn't ask him to explain, but she remembered that he'd been upset about Dorothy's calls. She'd talk to Dorothy as soon as she had a chance and urge her to change her tactics and not to keep calling people and insisting they talk to her. Dorothy wasn't going to be happy to hear her primary suspect–Luis–had been cleared by Kip. It wouldn't be an easy conversation, and Mary would have to choose her words with care, so she didn't hurt Dorothy's feelings.

As Luis was called away to talk to a reporter from the Hyannis newspaper, Mary walked with Luke to look for the rest of the family. They found them in front of a house with *Adeste Fideles* spelled out in lights.

Jack asked, "Has everyone seen everything? Are you ready to vote?"

Eager yeses came from the grandchildren. He gave each child a soup can and a box of crackers. Parents and grandmothers and the grandkids broke into groups to vote. They agreed to meet up back where they'd parked.

Luke grasped Mary's hand again and grinned. "Let's go, Grandma."

"Who are you going to vote for?" she asked.

"The one with the dogs with reindeer antlers."

"I missed that one."

He tugged on her hand. "Let me show you, Grandma."

Mary walked along with him, admiring the lights as he led her to the far end of the subdivision.

"This is nothing in comparison with what you'll see in Bourne." Dennis Morton's voice rose over other spectators' on the street.

Mary ducked her head and hurried Luke past the Bourne selectman. As much as Dennis was constantly underfoot, talking about how people should come over to Bourne, she wondered how much time he spent in his own hometown. She could still hear him expounding on the wonders of Christmastime in Bourne when Luke stopped in front of a house and ran forward to drop the can and crackers into the cardboard box on the house's front steps.

As her grandson grinned and pointed to the two stone dogs wearing felt reindeer antlers, Mary nodded and gave him an automatic smile. Her thoughts whirled. It seemed more and more likely that Dennis had played a part in trying to ruin Grace Church's living Nativity in order to draw people to Bourne. She needed proof of that, and neither Kip nor Luis had it. She had to figure out a way to get it.

But not now. Now she wanted to enjoy the lights and her grandson's company.

Beside her, Luke kept a steady commentary on what he liked and didn't like about every house they passed. Mary walked with him toward the van. She made a point of listening to him and gave him a genuine smile. She greeted friends and neighbors and let the Christmas cheer ease her disquiet.

"Hey, Mrs. Fisher, how are you doing?" asked a young woman Mary recognized as Ginnie, a member of Grace Church.

"We're doing great. What do you think of the lights, Ginnie?"

"They're nice, aren't they?" She sighed. "But they remind me that we should have had our living Nativity tonight."

"It's a shame that the costumes haven't been found. I've talked to a bunch of people, but so far, no luck."

"We worked hard on those costumes, and it's too bad nobody's going to see them."

"You were one of the seamstresses too?"

Ginnie nodded. "Including Abbie and Hannah, there were six of us who volunteered to sew. Not that we would have if we'd known the drama ahead of us."

"You mean with Abbie and Hannah?"

Ginnie drew Mary to the side of the road, so the stream of people admiring the lights could pass by them. Luke asked if he could continue to where Daisy and his sister stood a couple of houses away. Mary agreed but reminded him to stay with them.

Lowering her voice, though there was no need because dozens of conversations rolled over them, Ginnie said, "If you want my opinion, Abbie finally got tired of Hannah ordering us around. None of us wanted to complain, but now it really doesn't matter, does it?"

Mary said nothing, waiting for the young woman to go on.

She did. "Hannah is overbearing and exacting. There's no nicer way to say it. She made almost impossible demands of us. Abbie wasn't the only one upset about it. We all were. When Abbie stood up to Hannah on our behalf, she did it because she wanted Hannah to see the situation from our points of view."

"That was good of her."

"Very good, but Hannah considered it a personal attack. She refused to listen to Abbie. I'm ashamed to say that the rest of us backed down reluctantly because we wanted to make sure the costumes were ready on time. Abbie cared about that, too, as much as any of us. But when Abbie kept pressing, Hannah kicked her off the team."

"Yes, I know. I asked Abbie about that, but she was too upset to discuss it."

"We were upset too. We really needed Abbie's artistic ability. She's absolutely amazing." Ginnie smiled again. "Have you ever noticed the cloth and wire sculpture in the library? The one that's supposed to represent a sea bird flying out over the waves?"

Mary nodded. The sculpture was set between two windows near the rear of the library. "Of course. It's beautiful."

"Abbie made that when she was in high school. It won some sort of national contest, and she donated it to the library. Her skills were really needed when we started the costumes. But I understood why she took as much as she could carry that night and left. She got tired of being bullied all the time."

"What do you mean that she took what she could carry?"

"A whole bagful of stuff." Ginnie shrugged. "Don't ask me what, because I don't exactly know. We made do with what she left behind."

"Do you know why she took it?"

Again Ginnie shrugged. "I don't have any idea, and I didn't ask because Hannah was furious. I didn't want her to turn that anger on me. I was there to help the church by sewing, not to get caught up in a diva war."

"I don't blame you." Mary wished Ginnie a merry Christmas and continued toward where the others must be waiting.

She was more puzzled than before. Why would Abbie, who cared enough about her friends that she'd made a stand to help them, try to sabotage the living Nativity by first taking the fabric and then stealing the costumes? If the plan was to get revenge on Hannah for her high-handed tactics, it didn't make any sense for Abbie to take the fabric.

There must be a clue that would connect everything. She had to keep looking and have faith that she'd find the answer before Christmas.

✳ Chapter Seventeen

....

Too bad it wasn't possible to be in a half dozen places at the same time. Mary would have found that helpful on Monday morning, especially because each of the places she needed to be were right in her very busy bookshop.

The shop buzzed with last-minute shoppers as well as people who'd come back home to Ivy Bay for the holidays. They wanted a nostalgic walk beneath the retro Christmas decorations on Main Street as they recalled past holidays in the small town. Customers stood in clumps, greeting new-comers as they renewed old acquaintances. Passersby on the street waved to people in the shop, then came in to wish friends a merry Christmas.

Each time the door opened with a cheerful chime, the aromas from the bakery next door billowed in on the icy air. Mary's stomach growled, even though she'd stopped for a hearty sandwich at lunchtime.

She didn't have a chance to enjoy the cheerful chaos. She assisted customers while Rebecca gathered the last few items needed for reading *A Visit from St. Nicholas* tomorrow. Her costume was set, and Ashley couldn't wait for the chance to help out and wear her antlers.

Thinking about the mysteries was an exercise in futility. Each time Mary thought she might have a minute to consider her clues and suspects and how she might arrange them into a useful pattern, she was interrupted by a question or a greeting or someone wanting to check out.

She finally realized that the next to the last shopping day before Christmas wasn't a good time to try to concentrate on anything but her bookshop and its patrons. Once she did that, she enjoyed talking with her customers and those who came in simply to look around or to get out of the cold.

Ashley came to sit on the stool behind the counter. She swung her feet and smiled as she asked, "Did you go to see the lights last night?"

"We did. Are you going?"

"Tonight," said Rebecca as she came around the counter with an unopened box of books. She held out the packing slip she'd ripped off the top. "Are these ones you want me to put out now or wait until after the holiday? Joe dropped them off earlier, and he said to tell you merry Christmas."

Mary smiled as she realized the box held the books she'd put on rush order. She was glad the UPS man had delivered them already but sorry she hadn't had a chance to wish him a happy holiday. "Please put them on the holiday stories table. It looks as if they arrived just in time. This morning, I sold the last Hercule Poirot Christmas mystery. Now we've got a few extras if someone else wants one."

"Great."

"Everything set for tomorrow afternoon?"

Rebecca nodded, then smiled at her daughter. "But you'd better ask the head reindeer." She went to the table to set out the new books.

Ashley giggled and began chattering about the costume she'd be wearing. It was a light brown sweatshirt over a pair of khakis, but it would be perfect with her fake antlers. "I wanted a red nose, but I'm Dancer. He didn't have a red nose. Rudolph did, and he's not in *A Visit from St. Nicholas.*"

"That's true," Mary said. "What if I bring along a red cotton ball in case you change your mind which deer you want to be?"

"Are you going to bring Gus?"

"He likes the shop better when it's quieter."

"But he has to come tomorrow. I've told the kids he'll be here."

Mary leaned an elbow on the counter. "You aren't thinking of dressing him up like a reindeer, too, are you?"

"Maybe..."

"Gus wouldn't want to dress up. Cats are very vain, and they like how they look exactly the way they are. I think he'd be better off at home until after Christmas. Don't you think so?"

Ashley considered it seriously, nodded, then jumped back down and went to talk to a friend who'd come in with his parents. They were soon giggling together in the children's section.

By the time the shop closed at six, Mary was ready for a nice cup of something warm and a chance to put up her feet. She was glad that Lizzie and Christa had volunteered to make supper tonight.

The cold air almost took her breath away as she left the shop. The street was surprisingly deserted after the day's crowds. She understood why when a gust of wind screamed between the buildings. Huddling into her coat, she hurried to her car and turned the heat and fan up on high. Warmth was just beginning to come out of the vents when she stopped in front of the house. Evan's car was parked there too. She hoped nobody had any big plans for tonight. She'd prefer a quiet evening of enjoying each other's company because she didn't have energy for anything more.

"Only one more shopping day before Christmas," she reminded herself with an exhausted laugh as she got out of the car and went to the front door.

But that meant only one day left to find the costumes, or Christmas Eve would pass without a single performance of the Grace Church living Nativity.

Voices burst through the door even before she opened it. She went in, and hopes of a peaceful evening vanished. The families were gathered in the doorway to the living room, their backs to her. Everyone was talking at once, and nobody had noticed she'd come in until the cold air hit them.

As one, they turned. Each face displayed dismay and irritation. She looked past them and gasped. The Christmas tree lay on its side in a pool of water. Ornaments were scattered on the floor. Several of the glass balls had shattered.

"What happened?" she asked.

As everyone spoke at once, it took Mary a moment to figure out that Daisy had come into the living room to ask her younger cousins to set the table. She'd discovered Gus had climbed up into the tree. She had let out a shriek, frightening him. He jumped out of the tree, tipping it over.

Mary searched the room. Beneath one of the chairs, two bright yellow-green eyes peered at her. She got down on her hands and knees to coax the cat out. It took several tries, but when he edged toward her, clearly scared out of one of his lives, she scooped him up. His claws clamped onto her arm, and she was glad she still wore her coat.

Petting him, she held him close. He nuzzled his head up under her chin in an apology.

"Let me put him upstairs," she said, not looking at her sister. Betty must be furious that Gus had tipped over the tree and made such a mess of the living room. "I'll be right back to help clean up."

Hurrying up the stairs, she put Gus in her room. She made sure he had water and litter, then went to the door. Looking back, she saw him watching her. She sighed and stroked his head. He hadn't intended to cause any damage. He'd acted like a cat, fleeing out of the tree because he was terrified.

Mary heard the debate when she came back downstairs. Everyone had a different idea of what to do. The grandkids wanted to try to save the tree and set it up again, but Jack shook his head.

"Half of the branches are broken," he said. "Even if we got it back up, we couldn't hang anything on those branches." He knelt by the downed tree. "And it looks like a lot of the needles have come off, so our tree may look pretty weird."

He contorted his face into a strange grimace, and the grandkids began laughing.

"Betty," Mary said, "I'm sorry for what happened."

Betty waved away her words. "It's all right. Gus can't be blamed for this. I sent the younger children out of the kitchen so Lizzie and Christa could get started on supper. From what I heard, they were playing in here, and the cat got spooked. That might have been what sent him up the tree in the first place."

"Grandma?"

Mary and Betty looked at Betsy, Emma, who held her younger brother's hand, and Allison. The quartet stood in the doorway, and they each wore a hangdog expression.

"Grandma, it's our fault," Emma said.

"Our fault," Allison echoed.

"Is that so?" asked Betty, giving Mary a quick glance.

"We were goofing around," Emma said, "and someone threw a pillow. Then we all did." The kids exchanged a guilty look, but no one volunteered who had thrown the first pillow.

Mary guessed they didn't actually know because they'd been in the midst of their fun.

"Gus raced up the tree to get away from the pillows. Then..." Luke looked at Daisy.

"Then I came in and was shocked to see poor Gus in the tree. I frightened him." Daisy smiled sadly. "He should be down here, and we should be the ones shut in upstairs."

"That's true," Betty said sternly. "I think you owe poor Gus an apology."

"And maybe a special can of cat food?" Betsy asked.

Mary put her hand on Betty's granddaughter's shoulder and smiled. "That's a nice thought."

"And a catnip mouse!" Luke added.

"Another nice thought."

Luke whirled to his father. "Can we go out and get some catnip for Gus?"

Chad smiled. "Maybe after supper. For now, your mothers have worked too hard making tonight's meal to let it get ruined."

"My rolls!" gasped Christa and pushed past them to run into the kitchen.

The other women followed, leaving the guys and the kids to clean up the mess in the living room. Mary offered to stay to help, but her son sent her with the other women so, "you won't be in the way while we men do men's work."

That remark rid the house of the last of the bad mood. Daisy was sent upstairs to let Gus out, but Mary didn't see him while the final preparations were made for dinner. The scents of herbs and garlic and tomatoes filled the kitchen, and the children and their fathers came quickly when Betty called that the meal was ready.

They sat around the dining room table, quieting only when Evan said grace. The clatter of plates and silverware followed as pasta was topped with spaghetti sauce. Bowls of salad and plates of homemade garlic rolls were passed around the table.

Mary was only partway through her meal when Luke asked, "Can I have some more spaghetti and gravy, Mom?"

"Gravy?" asked Daisy, confused. "What gravy?"

He pointed with his fork to the marinara sauce. "*That* gravy."

"That's spaghetti sauce," Allison said, "not gravy."

Luke opened his mouth to retort, but his mother put a hand on his arm. With a smile, Lizzie said, "A lot of people of Italian descent live in Melrose, and they call marinara sauce gravy. Luke's picked it up from friends there."

"Gravy?" Betsy wrinkled her nose. "That's crazy."

"Why?" asked Emma, coming to her brother's defense. "Brown gravy goes on potatoes. Red gravy goes on pasta."

"She's got you there," Jack said with a laugh that rippled around the table. He winked at Mary and changed the subject to whether they thought it would snow before Christmas.

✳   ✳   ✳

Mary and Betty were alone in the house after the kids and grandchildren went to the pet store. At first, it was just going to be one or two people going, but then everyone decided to join in, especially Luke when he heard there might be snakes for sale at the store. Mary suspected he wanted a chance to scare his sister and cousins.

Finally the last of the dishes were in the dishwasher, and Mary switched it on. The kitchen smelled of more freshly baked raisin bread in addition to the garlic rolls and spaghetti sauce. Mary put on the coffeepot while Betty got two mugs from the cupboard.

They sat at the kitchen table and leaned back at the same time.

"I didn't know that spaghetti sauce was called gravy," Betty said as she stirred more sugar into her coffee. "Did you?"

"I first heard 'gravy' used for marinara sauce in the North End of Boston," Mary said, "and I had no idea what everyone was talking about. Our children and their children have been lucky to experience different sorts of people and places that they can share with each other."

"Maybe so. Maybe not."

"What do you mean?"

"You know, nobody ever was willing to compromise on what to put on top of the tree."

"Probably a good thing, because those special ornaments might have gotten broken when the tree fell over."

"True. Mary, it's okay when they can learn something fun from each other, but I still wish we had a common tradition we could share. It'd give us a connection when we're far apart."

"I know." Mary sipped her coffee, then put her cup down as an idea occurred to her. "You know, the tree tumbling down could be a blessing in disguise."

"How so?"

Mary quickly outlined her idea. "What do you think? We still have a tree, but it's like no other tree anyone in this family has ever had."

"And it'll be a new tradition that everyone can share when they come here for Christmas."

Mary smiled. "Exactly. But it needs to be a surprise. If everyone begins talking about it before Christmas Day, then we won't have the special moment I hope it will be."

Betty agreed. Both of them waited for their families to return. Sitting their children and grandchildren down, they explained what Mary had proposed.

"But you've got to keep it a surprise," Mary said.

"No peeking," Betty added with a smile.

As the grandchildren began talking excitedly, Betty's words played over and over again in Mary's head.

No peeking.

No peeking.

But maybe a bit of peeking would be the way to find out, one way or the other, if Dennis Morton was so determined to draw people away from Ivy Bay to Bourne that he'd taken both the costumes and the posters. She knew the perfect way.

✳ Chapter Eighteen

Jack tore another strip of tape off the roll and hung the poster announcing the living Nativity tomorrow night on the outside of the bookshop window. Then he tacked another poster onto the light pole on the sidewalk. He glanced back at the shop, arched his brows, then smiled when Mary gave him a thumbs-up.

He came back into the shop and shrugged off his coat. "I shouldn't have glanced in the windows next door. That list of goodies for sale is almost cruel to a man who has already eaten too many cookies and other sweets for his own good." He patted his stomach. "I foresee many long sessions on the treadmill once I'm back in Chicago."

Mary smiled, but her expression became serious as she looked from the poster on the glass to the one on the pole. She edged to the side of the shop opposite the counter and sat on a bench that wouldn't be noticed by the casual passerby. She still had a good view of the posters.

It was a simple plan, and there were more ways it could fail than she wanted to think about. The posters were a trap she expected to be sprung by Dennis Morton. She'd made sure the posters had a lot of glitter and big letters on them so nobody could fail to notice them.

"I hope this works," she said as she returned to the counter.

"Have faith. That's what Dad would say."

She nodded. "I know. I hear his voice in my mind when I get frustrated about a puzzle, and I know that he wouldn't have given up."

"I'm glad you're here with Aunt Betty in Ivy Bay. With all the miles between you and us, it's good to know that you two are looking out for each other." Jack grinned. "I'm not sure how Lizzie and I would do if we ended up living together again. We used to get on each other's nerves all the time."

"That's what siblings do when they're kids. It's not the same once you're an adult. Then you're more accepting of the differences between you and you're more likely to compromise."

He arched his brows. "Really? We couldn't even get an agreement on whether to put a star or an angel on the tree."

"We would have. You know that." She wagged a finger at him. "If I didn't know better, I'd guess that you and Chad and Evan were egging the kids on."

"Us?" He tried to look innocent, but couldn't. Laughing, he said, "Okay, you caught us. We should have known better than to try to pull the wool over the eyes of Mary Fisher, Master Sleuth."

She chuckled. "What was your plan? I can't believe you intended to have a tree with nothing on top for Christmas Eve."

"We found this wooden lobster with a Santa hat in a shop on our way back from the Edaville Railroad. The gals and the kids were looking somewhere else in the store, so we decided we needed to have a special tree topper when we were together on Cape Cod for Christmas."

Warmth seeped through Mary's heart. She should have known that she and Betty weren't the only ones who had realized that the families needed a new tradition they could share. She was grateful for the love and connection they had, even though they were not together as often as she wished.

Pushing back from the counter, she said, "Might as well get this show on the road." She reached for her coat and pulled it on.

Jack did the same as she went to switch off the lights. Darkness clamped down on them, because clouds were low in the sky, obscuring any moonlight or stars. She hoped that anyone who had noticed the lights on thought she was working late to prepare for shoppers and the reading on Christmas Eve afternoon. She waited for Jack to go out, then drew the door shut.

"This is really weird," he murmured as she turned the key.

"I know." She began walking toward home as if it were any other evening.

Neither of them spoke as they went around the rear of the block's buildings and turned back toward the bookshop.

If anyone had been watching, it would have appeared that they turned the corner and kept walking. But they didn't see anyone else while they moved faster and faster to get back inside out of the cold.

"Careful," Jack warned in a whisper. He put his hand on her elbow as they picked their way around dumpsters and air-conditioning units.

Mary nodded, then guided him through the garden behind the bookshop.

"It's beautiful in the summer," she said. "Your aunt Betty has created an astounding garden. My regulars love looking out the window to see the parade of flowers from snowdrops and daffodils in the spring to mums in the fall."

"Maybe we can get back next summer and see it."

"I'd love that."

She patted his arm then pulled her keys out of her coat pocket. The *click* when she unlocked the back door seemed as loud as an explosion. She knew that was silly. She was on edge, and every little sound was magnified.

Going inside and hearing the steady drip of the faucet, Mary automatically reached for the light switch, then yanked her hand back. After sneaking around, she couldn't make such a silly mistake. She gave her eyes a chance to adjust, and slowly she could make out the bookshelves and the chairs at the back of the shop. Closer to the window, light came from the streetlight and glistened on the register on the counter.

Using only whispers, because she wasn't sure how far their voices would carry out of the shop when the street was empty, she led her son around the furniture. They slipped out of their coats and took their seats on the bench that would give them the best view of the street.

As time passed and they finished the coffee Jack had brought in a thermos, it wasn't easy to stay awake. Mary had to fight to keep from nodding off as the night wore on. But it would be worth it if Dennis sprung their little trap, and she could name him as the poster bandit. And if he had the costumes, too, it would still be possible to have the living Nativity after Grace Church's candlelight service tomorrow evening.

* * *

Mary roused at the sound of ripping paper. It took her a second to realize she was in her bookshop. She hadn't fallen asleep, but she'd been close. The deep gray light of the hour before dawn poured into the bookshop.

Jack put his hand on her arm, and she touched it gently, not daring even to breathe as she heard paper rip again. Someone was outside. Tearing down the posters.

She glanced at Jack. He motioned toward himself and then the front door. She gave a slight nod.

"Wait until I'm at the door, then flip on the lights," he whispered as he inched past her.

Mary held her breath. *Protect him, Father.*

The chime sounded as he ran out the door. There was a motion. Jack shouted something. She couldn't discern much in the twilight and through the glass.

Then the door reopened.

"I caught him." Jack had a man by the arm as they came into the shop.

Mary's eyes widened in disbelief. The man holding the torn poster wasn't Dennis Morton.

He was Jason Fernandes!

✳ Chapter Nineteen

In one hand, Jason had the big poster. In the other, several crumpled-up posters squeezed out between his fingers. Torn bits of paper fell to the floor like discolored snow.

His eyes shifted away from her, and he glanced at her son.

Jack frowned.

Still not looking at her, Jason mumbled, "I'm sorry, Mrs. Fisher."

Mary walked over to him and drew him away from her son, who watched with concern when she led Jason to the bench where they'd spent the night. She asked Jack to turn on the lights. As he did, she blinked in the sudden brightness.

"Sit down, Jason," she said quietly. She wasn't sure she could speak louder.

Not once had she imagined that their simple trap would catch the local garbage man. Jason Fernandes was a nice guy with a lovely family, and he was respected in Ivy Bay. Why would he resort to vandalism?

He sat, and Jack murmured that he was going to get some coffee started. Mary nodded, glad that her son understood that what they needed now was to talk calmly and without condemnation. There had to be some compelling reason that would bring Jason to this point.

Jack stood in the door to the back room as Mary drew up a chair and sat facing Jason. She wasn't sure how to begin, and she added a silent prayer for the right words along with her gratitude that her son wasn't hurt in apprehending the poster thief. The only sounds in the shop were the wind rattling against the windows and door along with the steady drip in the sink and the hiss of the coffee coming through the filter.

"I'm sorry," Jason said again as if he couldn't bear the quiet a moment longer. "You believe that, don't you?"

"I do," she said, "and I hope you believe that I forgive you. But I have to ask. Why did you rip down our posters?"

His shoulders sagged, and he leaned forward, his hands clasped between his knees. "It's not that I have anything against you or your church. I really admire you, Mrs. Fisher, and you've always been nice to me. Patti tells me how she enjoys talking to you and how kind you and your friends and family have been to the kids."

"Then why?"

"It's this season." He shook his head and let his breath sift out through his teeth. "All the chaos surrounding Christmas. It gets to be too much. You saw it yourself. Patti really,

really, *really* loves the season. Almost like an obsession. She doesn't want to miss a single opportunity to celebrate it. She is obsessed with every book ever published with a Christmas scene in it. Not that she has time to read any of them because she's busy with lights and buying more presents for everyone than I can afford to pay for. Then I saw these posters..." He looked down at the torn one on the floor in front of him.

Mary patted her son's hand as he sat beside her and handed her a cup of coffee. Jack said nothing when he offered another mug to Jason, and she appreciated his knowing that Jason needed to explain without them peppering him with questions.

"Once I saw the signs," Jason said after taking a quick sip of the coffee, "I was sure it was one more thing that Patti would insist that we go to this week. I understand that, by the end of the day, she's eager to get out of the house after being home all day with the kids. I really do. What she doesn't seem to understand is that I work hard, and I'm exhausted after a long day's work. The idea of going to one more event this week was more than I could bear. I wanted to make sure Patti didn't see the signs and insist we go to the living Nativity. I know that sounds stupid because she was sure to find out anyway." He took another sip, then raised his head to meet Mary's gaze for the first time. "I drive around town with the garbage truck, and nobody notices me. I figured I could rip down the signs and nobody would notice that either."

A memory burst into Mary's head from the morning she'd seen Jason stop his truck at a spot where there wasn't a trash can. He'd gotten out, gone around to the far side of the truck, then gotten back in. At the time, she'd thought his actions were peculiar, but she hadn't connected them with the missing posters. Probably because that morning she'd believed that the sheep and the costumes had been taken by the same person who'd torn down the posters.

When she didn't answer, Jason hurried on, "Look, I've known from the beginning that it was silly to think I could halt the living Nativity just by taking down the signs. But all I could think of was keeping Patti from seeing them and wanting to go. At the beginning, that is. Then I realized how good it felt to tear them down, like I had some control over my own life again. Maybe that's why I kept ripping them down. Like I could stop the hectic pace of our lives and have some peace and quiet time during the holiday season with my wife and kids…just for a few minutes. It probably doesn't make any sense to you. I'm not sure it does to me either, but taking down those posters became my way of saying that the Christmas craziness needs to stop." He shook his head again. "Clearly I haven't been thinking straight lately."

"That happens when we're tired," Mary said. "A lot of us are feeling stressed this week with all we have to do, and, if you can't find any joy in the season, it adds to your burden."

"I used to love this time of year." His tone begged her to forgive him, and she wished he would believe she already had.

"What did you love about it?"

"I loved the times when I would lie on the floor and stare up at our Christmas tree and just…just be part of the quiet happiness I felt around me."

She watched a genuine smile warm his face. Poor Jason. He'd lost himself amid the hustle and bustle of the season. She would pray that he could regain that inner peace that had been smothered by his responsibilities.

But there was a question she had to ask. "Did you take the costumes for the living Nativity from the cellar at Grace Church?"

He shook his head. "No! Of course not. How could you think that I–?" He paused and puffed out his breath in exasperation at himself and the situation he'd gotten into by making a single poor decision. "You have every right to ask me that. I tried one way to stop the living Nativity, so why not another? But I didn't take them, Mrs. Fisher. I may tear down posters, but I'm not a thief."

"I'm glad to hear that." She really hadn't thought he was the person who'd taken the costumes. He hadn't had access to the church. But she'd had to ask.

"I guess you'll have to tell your pastor about this," Jason said.

"It would be better if you did."

He rubbed his fingers beneath his chin. "I don't know. It's been a long time since I've talked to a minister."

"Then Pastor Miles is a good one to start with. He'll listen, Jason, and he may even have some advice for you." She smiled gently. "He knows what it's like to have a demanding job and a family."

"I don't know if…" He hung his head. "I don't want my kids to find out what a fool I've been."

"The only way they'll find out is if you tell them." Mary reached out and put her hand on his tightly clasped ones. "Jack and I aren't going to say anything, and Pastor Miles certainly won't."

"You are really kind, Mrs. Fisher." Tears filled Jason's eyes. "I'm sorry for what I did. I can understand if you can't ever forgive me."

"You haven't been listening, Jason. I have already forgiven you."

He stared at her, astounded. "Really?"

"Yes."

His mouth trembled, then he lowered his head so neither she nor Jack could see his expression. He stared at the floor for a long minute while nobody spoke.

In a cracking voice, Jason whispered, "Thank you. I appreciate that more than I can say. If I can ever return the favor—"

Mary glanced again at her son, then said, "Return it by forgiving yourself for a few unwise decisions. Only when you can forgive yourself can you come to understand the full breadth of God's love which is the real reason for celebrating this time of year."

"You make it sound easy. I wouldn't know where to start."

Jack said quietly, "Jason, I don't know you, but I do know that you sound like a drowning man who's about to go down for the third time."

"I've felt that way sometimes," he replied.

Mary looked from one young man to the other. They were of a similar age, and they had similar obligations. Maybe the wisest thing she could do would be to let them talk it out.

"So have I." Jack balanced his coffee cup on his knee. "When I have an emergency call at the same time I'm supposed to be doing something with my wife and daughter, I'm torn. I want to give them everything that will make them happy, but sometimes I can't. Then I feel awful."

"Like a failure."

Her son nodded. "Exactly. But then I remind myself that I don't need to give them everything as long as they know I love them and am doing the best I can. The rest is in God's hands."

Jason nodded, then looked back at Mary. "I'll think about what you've both said, Mrs. Fisher."

"Good." Mary stood and went to the counter. Opening one of the drawers at the back, she pulled out a notepad. She jotted down the phone number for Pastor Miles's office. Handing it to Jason, she said, "Call him when you're ready."

"I'll call him later today. I've got to think about what I'll say."

"Tell him the truth and express your regret as you have to us." She laid her hand on his shoulder. "He'll understand."

While Jack walked Jason to the door, Mary sent up a quick prayer of gratitude to God that He had offered her a chance to help Jason find peace within himself again. A conversation with Pastor Miles might be the next best step.

251 * THE LOST NOEL

She looked down into her untasted coffee. Dennis hadn't been the one taking down the posters. Yet, the Bourne selectman was determined to build up the tourist business in Bourne. Was he willing to do so by stealing Grace Church's costumes in order to halt the living Nativity?

And where did Abbie fit into this?

Maybe it was time to compare notes with Dorothy again, but Mary wasn't sure when she'd have the time. It was Christmas Eve, and the Christmas reading of *A Visit from St. Nicholas* was set for that afternoon.

She stifled a yawn as she reminded herself that she must find time to chase down the answer. Today. Tonight was the last chance to hold the living Nativity this year. If she didn't find the answer today, it no longer mattered.

✳ Chapter Twenty

Another yawn escaped Mary as she unlocked the bookshop door later that morning. She'd gotten a grand total of two hours of sleep. Though her body was heavy with fatigue, her mind tried to devise ideas of how she might find the answer to where the costumes might be.

Gus gave an insistent *mew* from inside his carrier, and she went inside. She hadn't planned to bring him with her today, but she didn't want to have another incident with the Christmas tree.

She switched on the lights. A torn poster had been left on the floor. Picking it up, she stuffed into a trash can in the backroom where nobody would see it. She didn't want to say anything about Jason tearing down the posters until he had a chance to talk with Pastor Miles. Their pastor would know the best way to make the truth known, and she would follow his lead.

She quickly took off and hung up her coat, scarf, hat, and gloves. The day was raw and cold with clouds scudding near the horizon, so the warm welcome of the shop seemed even nicer than usual. As Gus scampered out of his carrier and to one of his favorite spots where he could enjoy a catnap, she reheated some coffee from the pot Jack had made earlier. It was strong, but she added extra milk and sugar. She took a sip and wondered how many more cups she'd need to get through the day and the candlelight service.

Her family planned to arrive in time for the Christmas poem reading at 3:00 PM. For now, they were busy with the project she and Betty had suggested. When she'd announced she was bringing Gus to the shop with her, she had seen the relief on her sister's face. The tree was definitely flat on one side, but they'd turned that section against the wall. Nobody wanted to take a chance that Gus might climb the tree again and knock it over. Not that Mary thought he would. He was too smart to make a mistake like that a second time, but better safe than sorry.

Turning the open sign in the door, Mary double-checked that everything was set for the reading. It was, and she'd known it would be. Rebecca was good at taking care of such details, and Ashley was too excited to let any aspect get overlooked. Cookies would be delivered from next door a half hour before the event began, so they'd have time to make some hot chocolate and get everything set up for their young guests.

The door opened with its friendly chime. Mary smiled when she saw Kip Hastings come in. He was carrying his battered tool box.

"Sure looks like snow," he said.

"It'd be nice to have snow for Christmas."

"And gone the day after."

She laughed. "Things seldom work out that neatly."

"Okay if I look at that drip now?"

"Your timing is perfect. I'm sure Rebecca will be glad that drip isn't going to be in the background when she's reading about Santa coming down the chimney."

He grinned and followed her into the backroom, pausing only to pat Gus's head. The cat barely opened one eye in acknowledgment.

"That cat never hides his feelings, does he?" Kip asked with a chuckle.

"Not often." Mary stepped back as Kip bent to examine the sink.

He turned the faucet on and then off and then repeated it. Watching the water slow to the continuous drip, he said, "It may just need a new washer." He reached to unscrew a round piece of metal at the end of the faucet. It didn't want to move, so he opened his tool box and pulled out a wrench. "That's usually the problem with a slow, steady drip like this. If you want, I can show you how to change it, so when it happens again, you won't need to wait for me or Henry to come over."

"That would be great." She smiled. "Of course, by the time it needs changing again, I'll probably have forgotten."

"Not you. You don't ever seem to forget any small detail." He grinned over his shoulder. "That's how you solve those mysteries and make it look so easy."

She smiled as she thought of how Dorothy had thought that following a set of clues, even while being distracted by red herrings, was simple. It certainly was fun and frustrating and exhilarating when she pieced together the puzzle. But easy? No, she'd never describe it that way.

Kip replaced the washer. He pulled a stained cloth out of his back pocket and wiped his hands. He turned on the hot water and then the cold and let them run for a moment. Then he shut them both off. No drip began.

"There. Good as new." He put his wrench back in the tool box. "If you need anything else, let me know." He held up a finger to halt her answer. "Listen. Is that your toilet dripping too?"

Mary heard of the soft *plop* of water. "I guess we didn't hear it when the faucet was dripping."

"I might as well fix it while I'm here." He lifted the top of the tank and placed it on the floor. "Let's hope it's as simple as the faucet."

"Can I ask you something, Kip?"

"Sure."

"I was wondering what you could tell me about Dennis Morton."

"Dennis Morton?" he asked, peering into the toilet tank and tapping something inside it.

"The selectman from Bourne who's been attending events here in Ivy Bay for the past week."

"Oh yeah. That guy. What about him?"

"We started talking about him at the lighting contest, then got interrupted."

"It was a zoo there, and I don't think I got to finish a single conversation that night."

"I know what you mean." She rested a hand on the sink. "Dorothy said that you'd told her that Dennis went into the church."

"He did. He stopped by and talked to Luis and me about the living Nativity scene."

"And you took him into the church…"

He wiggled something inside, and water started and quickly stopped. "He was interested in how we got power out to the stable, so we showed him the electrical setup. After that, we went back to work, and he left."

"Did you ever see him go in alone?"

Kip straightened and faced her. "No. The only time he went inside was with us." His eyes narrowed. "Are you trying to find out if he took the costumes?"

"I was, but now I don't see how he could have, Kip. If the only time he was in the church was with you and Luis, and the three of you were together all the time…?"

"We were, and the costumes were in the fellowship hall which is several doors beyond where the circuit breaker box is. He couldn't have slipped past us and snatched the costumes." He picked up a screwdriver and reached into the tank. "Morton was pretty annoying, but unless he can make himself invisible, there's no way he could have taken the costumes."

Mary nodded and said, "Well, that's good to know."

But it wasn't. Her only other suspect was Abbie Lindstrom, and Mary had hoped the young woman hadn't decided to repay Hannah's high-handed behavior by stealing the costumes.

"And while Luis and I were working that afternoon," Kip said as he wiggled something inside the toilet tank again, "nobody else went into the church until everyone gathered for the living Nativity practice. Not even Abbie."

"Not even Abbie?" Mary's stomach tightened. "What do you mean?"

He smiled as Gus slipped in front of him to rub his head against Kip's arm. Greeting the cat, Kip then said, "I don't mean anything, really. When we were there, Abbie was always in and out of the church. I saw her go in a bunch of times almost every day I was working on the stable."

"Why didn't you tell me that when I first asked you if you saw anyone else at the church?"

"Abbie's a member of the church, and she comes and goes a lot. Just like Mavis Flanagan and Dorothy Johnson. They're always busy with something or other."

"True."

But Abbie hadn't been busy with anything at church after Hannah fired her. Again Mary's stomach cramped.

Abbie could have taken the costumes easily, because nobody would suspect anything if they saw her going into the church and coming back out. She must have believed she had a good reason for taking them after Hannah kicked her off the team of volunteers. Abbie was a nice young woman, but she might have reacted in anger. If she regretted it now, as Khloe Walker had rued taking the sheep, she might be too embarrassed to return the costumes to the church. Perhaps she would be willing to hand them over to Mary, who could then bring them to the church without naming the person who'd stolen them.

"Rebecca will be here any time," she said. "Kip, do you mind if I slip out for a few minutes?"

"Go ahead. This is going to take a little longer than I'd hoped." He grimaced. "I say that about most jobs."

She rushed to grab her coat. She snatched up her hat and gloves, too, as she went to the front door and into the cold slap of the winter morning. If she was right and Abbie had taken the costumes to get back at Hannah, she didn't want to delay recovering them. The living Nativity still might be able to go on tonight after all.

*　　*　　*

Abbie answered the door before the sound of the doorbell faded. Instead of the exhausted woman Mary had seen before, Abbie appeared happy and relaxed. She was dressed in a quirky sweater with animals shaped into the words *Merry Christmas* and she wore a welcoming smile. She didn't look like a woman with a guilty conscience.

"Come in. Come in," Abbie said. "It's damp outside. I wish it'd snow and get it over with."

"I think everyone feels the same way." Mary slipped off her coat when Abbie held out her hands.

The young woman hung Mary's coat on a peg shaped like a crooked finger. Mary wondered why she hadn't noticed that before, then realized it was because Abbie's house was crowded with artistic, eccentric items. It was impossible to take them all in at once.

"Have the costumes been found?" Abbie asked.

"Not yet." Mary didn't mention that Courtney Flanagan had her angel costume because she'd taken it home.

"But today's Christmas Eve." Abbie sighed. "I heard Hannah threw a hissy fit and refused to make other costumes on short notice. She shouldn't stand in the way if everyone else wants to put on the living Nativity without costumes."

"I don't think most of the participants' hearts are in it if they're standing out there in contemporary clothes."

"But with a bit of imagination..."

Mary smiled. "Abbie, you've got to remember that few people have as much imagination as you do."

Abbie gave her a shy grin as she led the way into the cluttered living room. "Can I get you something to drink?"

"No, thanks. I really can't stay long. We've got a Christmas Eve event over at the bookshop this afternoon, and I need to get back to it."

"Not even some tea and Christmas cookies? They're from Sweet Susan's." Abbie scooped up some wire and cloth and yarn from the couch and motioned with her elbow for Mary to sit. Putting the materials on top of some others in a corner, she added, "I haven't had a chance to make any homemade goodies because I've been busy with my college sophomore portfolio review project." Her eyes widened, and she looked quickly away, clearly upset that she'd said something she hadn't planned.

Sitting, Mary thought about the college catalogs she'd seen when she visited before. "So you're going to college?"

For the space of a half-dozen heartbeats, she thought Abbie was going to refuse to answer. Emotions fled across the young woman's face. Frustration. Dismay. Irritation. Finally the faint hint of a smile.

"Mrs. Fisher, I'm not crazy, though it probably seems like I'm acting that way." She dropped to a chair facing Mary. "Yes, I'm going to college, but I don't talk about it. In fact, I've been trying to keep the fact that I'm going to college a secret."

"But why?"

Abbie's mouth twisted. "I know what people say. They say I never stick with anything. Since I graduated from high school, I've bounced between college courses and jobs. Lots of them." Her gaze swept the room. "My parents insisted that I study something useful." She counted on her fingers. "I tried nursing, but the sight of blood makes me sick. I tried secretarial work, but as you can see, I'm not a very organized person. I tried studying education, but I have to admit, while I love spending time with kids one-on-one, I don't enjoy standing at the front of a classroom. And that's only the start of what I've tried and quit because each of them made me miserable."

Mary folded her hands on her lap. "From the looks of your house, Abbie, I can tell you probably weren't cut out to be a nurse or a secretary."

"I wish my parents could accept that. It was only after my grandfather died and left me this house that I took the time to think about what *I* wanted to do instead of what my parents wanted me to do. What I want to be when I grow up." Her expression softened. "I'm over thirty, but I decided to go back to college and study art at the Rhode Island School of Design."

"RISD is one of the best art schools in the country."

"And they let me be me. I love studying there, even though it's not a quick or easy drive from here to Rhode Island, especially at rush hour when I need to be there for evening classes. Shortly after I started, I met some friends who invited me to stay over at their place in Providence. That's great, especially with the winter roads. I'm often gone for several days at a time, which saves me the drive back to Ivy Bay. Even on a good day, it's at least an hour each way."

Mary thought of Abbie's mailbox stuffed with mail. A college student who wasn't sure when she'd be home couldn't put a stop on the mail and plan to restart it on a specific date. "Now I understand why you didn't get around to answering the messages I left on your machine."

"Sorry about that. Often I don't even know I'm going to have to stay over until it's time to head back. I just keep an overnight bag in the back of my car, so I can stay over whenever I need to."

Abbie sat up straighter. "But, Mrs. Fisher, please don't tell anyone that I'm studying at RISD. I don't want to deal with those who think I'm going to drop out of this program too.

They may not say anything to my face, but I see the looks and I hear the whispers."

"Of course. I won't say anything."

Abbie relaxed against the chair, draping her wrists over the chair's arm. "Thanks. I'm going stick with this program until I get my degree, and I don't want to have to explain myself all the time. Right now, I'm grateful for Christmas break and the chance to get some balance in my life. I hope to get more involved with church again. I miss the Bible discussion group I belonged to."

At the mention of Grace Church, Mary knew she couldn't put off getting some answers to her questions. "Abbie, I need to ask you something difficult."

The smile vanished from her face. "I think I may know what you want to know. I guess someone saw me sneaking in and out of the church."

"Yes."

"I wasn't doing anything I shouldn't." A mischievous smile suddenly tilted her lips. "Well, actually I guess I was doing something I shouldn't have been doing."

Mary arched her brows in a silent question.

"Up until a week ago, when the living Nativity was supposed to start and the costumes vanished, I've been sneaking into the church whenever I had a chance to work on the costumes."

"But Hannah fired you."

"Yes, she did, and she may have been right or wrong. Eventually we'll work it out." There was no hint of rancor in

Abbie's voice. "That wasn't what mattered. The project was important to the whole church and especially to the other volunteers. I realized the costumes wouldn't be done on time if I didn't continue to help when I could."

Mary was amazed. "Didn't anyone notice the costumes were further along than they'd been the last time someone worked on them?"

Shaking her head, Abbie smiled. "Everyone was working on different aspects of the costumes, so they must have believed that one of the other gals did the work. The only one who should have noticed was Hannah, and she apparently never did."

"I saw some fabric scraps here when I came over last time."

Abbie got up and went over to the pile of materials she had taken off the couch. She pulled out some small squares of fabric. "You mean these?"

"Yes."

"I guess Hannah never mentioned to you that I donated a large quantity of fabric for the costumes. I was able to get a good price on it at the vintage shops in Providence and through contacts I had at RISD for more vintage stores in New York City. I took the old clothing apart and provided the material for the living Nativity."

Mary sighed. She couldn't fault Hannah for not revealing that Abbie had donated most of the fabric. Mary hadn't asked. She'd assumed when Hannah said the material for the costumes came from New York that the head seamstress had ordered it herself.

"When Hannah fired me," Abbie continued, "the costumes had already been cut out. I took the material that was left over and brought it home. I plan to make some quilts for homeless shelters with what's left." She chuckled. "When I can find the time."

Mary's shoulders relaxed as she realized it was exactly as Ginnie, the volunteer seamstress she'd talked to at the lighting contest, said. Abbie had taken as much as she could carry when she left after Hannah banished her from the team, but she'd taken what the church couldn't use. Now she planned to put it to good use. Local homeless shelters would be delighted to accept her donation of warm quilts.

"Do you remember the last time you went over to Grace Church before the costumes vanished?" Mary asked.

"That was last Tuesday or Wednesday, wasn't it?" Abbie rolled her eyes. "Sorry. I lose track of time when I'm cramming for finals and worrying about my portfolio review."

"I understand. The costumes disappeared last Wednesday."

"The last time I was down in the fellowship hall must have been the week before that. This past Wednesday, I was taking a final. I left on Monday to stay with my friends, and I didn't come back until my tests were over." She smiled sadly. "That's why I can't help you with anything about the day when the costumes disappeared. I wish I could."

"I wish you could too." Mary sighed as she stood. "But I don't give up easily when there's a puzzle to be solved, and I want to find out who took the costumes."

Abbie got up, too, and walked with Mary to the door. "I hope you figure it out before tonight. After the work we did, it'd be a shame if the whole thing got cancelled completely."

"I'm not giving up. Even if it takes me until after Christmas, I want answers." Mary pulled on her coat and gave Abbie the best smile she could. "After all, we can always debut the living Nativity next year."

Abbie nodded and wished her a merry Christmas.

Wishing the young woman the same, as well as a happy new year, Mary walked out into the day that was as dreary as her low spirits. She had to be happy that Abbie hadn't taken the costumes, but that left one question.

Who had?

✳ Chapter Twenty-One

Mary shivered as she opened the door to her bookshop. She hadn't guessed that the cold day could grow damper and still have a storm start. Inside, as she shrugged off her coat, she heard Rebecca talking to a customer. The topic, as it had been for the past few days, was whether it would snow before Christmas.

Before she could speak with Rebecca, another customer asked Mary a question about a book on the holiday titles table. Then another customer was looking for a suggestion for a last-minute gift.

It didn't let up all morning. The bell over the door seemed to ring continuously as people came and went. Mary didn't have time to be tired or even to think about what she'd do next, now that she'd discovered Abbie was innocent. She was too busy helping her customers. She always enjoyed a day like this when she could talk books with people who loved them as much as she did. Days like this were what she'd imagined when she first thought about opening Mary's Mystery Bookshop.

Rebecca came behind the counter while Mary was ringing up a sale. When the books were in the bag and the customer happily on her way, she asked, "Mary, are you okay?"

"Yes. Why do you ask?"

"You look strange, as if you're happy and unhappy at the same time."

Mary laughed in spite of herself. "Rebecca, you nailed it. I *am* both happy and not happy." She didn't elaborate because a customer asked if Mary could help her find a particular book.

Mary was relieved she didn't have to explain how she was glad that Abbie hadn't been the costume thief, but how she was unsure now where to turn. Her list of suspects had dwindled to two, then one, and now to zero. She couldn't remember the last time all her suspects turned out to be innocent. There usually was one person on her list, maybe not from the beginning, who turned out to be the culprit. Each time, that person had been right in front of her all along.

And he or she probably was this time too. She only had to figure out who it was.

Maybe Dorothy had found something that pointed to a suspect that Mary had overlooked. It took almost a half hour before she had a break long enough that she could call Dorothy.

As she reached for the phone, the door opened. She lowered the phone with a sigh. Her eyes widened when Dennis walked in. He pulled off a bright red knit cap, and his white hair spiked in every direction. Shoving his hat in his coat pocket, he strode over to where she stood by the counter.

"Good morning," he said. Without giving her time to reply, he went on, "I wanted to stop by and thank you for answering questions for me about what makes Ivy Bay special. I know you probably got tired of seeing me pop up everywhere."

"We're always happy to have visitors in Ivy Bay." Mary laughed. For once, she, rather than Dennis, sounded like she was reading from a chamber of commerce brochure. "As I guess you've observed for yourself."

He smiled. "That much is obvious. You've been very hospitable, which is why I wanted to give you this."

Mary took the envelope he held out. When he motioned for her to open it, she drew out a gift certificate for dinner for two at a restaurant. In Bourne. She wasn't surprised. Dennis was Bourne's premier promoter.

"This is kind of you," Mary said.

"I wanted to give you a chance to enjoy *our* hospitality. Someone told me that your church is having a candlelight service tonight, so I guess you won't be attending our living Nativity."

"I'm afraid I won't be able to, but I hope you have a successful living Nativity."

"There's always next year, right?" He pushed back from the counter. "Merry Christmas, Mrs. Fisher."

"Merry Christmas, Dennis, and a wonderful and blessed new year for you and your family."

He nodded, pulled his knit hat down over his ears, and went out.

269 * THE LOST NOEL

Mary couldn't hold her laughter back any longer. Dennis was consistent, that was for sure, but it was clear that his heart was in the right place. He loved his hometown, and he wanted everyone else to love it too. She could appreciate that, because she loved living in Ivy Bay.

Rebecca sidled up to her behind the counter. "Should I get the hot chocolate started?" Rebecca asked. "Russell is dropping Ashley off soon, and I know she'll be glad to make sure it tastes right."

"That sounds great. I've got to make a quick call, so why don't you get changed into your Mrs. Claus outfit after you start the hot chocolate?"

Rebecca vanished into the back room, and Mary reached for the phone again. She quickly scanned the shop. There were several customers, but none of them seemed to need her help at the moment.

Dorothy answered on the second ring. "Oh, Mary. I didn't expect to hear from you today, especially with you having a reading this afternoon."

"I've got a few free moments, so I thought I'd give you a quick update on what I've found out." Mary quickly listed how she had found proof that the person who took the costumes couldn't be Abbie Lindstrom or Dennis Morton or Luis Alvarez. She paused, waiting for Dorothy's response.

All Dorothy said was, "Uh-huh. I see."

"I know you thought Luis might be involved and so did I for a while, but he wasn't."

"I guess I was wrong."

Mary was so shocked she couldn't answer. Dorothy Johnson hated admitting that she was mistaken, and Mary couldn't remember her ever doing so with such indifference. She understood better when Dorothy continued.

"I guess this is one mystery that won't be solved," Dorothy said.

"What do you mean?"

"Do you have any other suspects?"

"No," Mary had to say. "I was hoping you did."

She could almost see Dorothy's shrug. "I don't, and what's the point of chasing down the costumes now? It's Christmas Eve."

"If they were found today, the living Nativity could be held tonight."

"Maybe, but I really don't have time to think about that. It's Christmas, and I'd rather think about enjoying Christmas with my family and friends than chasing after some missing costumes. You should do the same."

Mary gave her a noncommittal answer, wished Dorothy a merry Christmas, and said good-bye. She couldn't take Dorothy's advice, even though Dorothy was right that solving the mystery was distracting Mary from spending time with her family. But she could not keep from imagining Betty and Ashley's disappointment if the living Nativity had to be canceled completely. And not only them. Everyone involved in the living Nativity, both openly and behind the scenes. She thought of Abbie sneaking into the church whenever she could steal time from her studies to work in secret on the costumes like a character from "The Elves and the Shoemaker" fairy tale.

Someone had taken the costumes. Someone who had both the opportunity to sneak into the church unseen and who had a reason to steal them.

But who?

Who?

Who?

The word echoed in her head as if an owl had taken up residency there.

It had to be someone whose presence at the church wouldn't draw anyone's attention. She sighed. That meant it must be someone connected to the church. She couldn't imagine a single member of their congregation who had a reason to take the costumes. It wasn't as if they could be used or displayed. In a small town like Ivy Bay, someone would see them and the word would get back to Grace Church faster than summer lightning.

She was missing some fact, the very fact that would compel everything to make sense. But what was the fact that both she and Dorothy had overlooked?

Mary didn't have time to muse on that question. It seemed as if everyone for miles around had suddenly discovered they needed gifts for the next day. Mary did her best to help Rebecca with preparations, but she was interrupted over and over by customers who still hoped to find the perfect gift for someone dear. The books on the special holiday table seemed to fly out the door, and Mary was glad she'd ordered extras.

As soon as Ashley arrived, she offered to take over replenishing the books on the table. She decided that Gus should be her assistant. The cat, who was standoffish with many people, acquiesced to her plans with the enthusiasm of a puppy. Only when she tried to convince him to wear a miniature pair of fake antlers like the ones she donned did he protest. He crawled under a shelf in the children's section, his pride pricked by Ashley's assumption that he would wear something that ridiculous.

Ashley simply shrugged and put on her halo along with her reindeer antlers. She wore both while she helped Mary and her mother set out the cookies that had been delivered from Sweet Susan's Bakery. Mary urged her to take one as a thanks for helping, and Ashley chose a gingerbread reindeer that was almost the exact color of her fake antlers. She went into the back room to eat it along with a cup of hot chocolate. Once the reading began, she wouldn't have time, as the other children would, to eat or sip the cocoa.

About fifteen minutes before the reading of *A Visit from St. Nicholas* was scheduled to start, families began to arrive, including her own. She asked her children to make sure everyone had a place to sit. Some of the mothers or fathers dropped off their children so they could run last-minute errands along Main Street. Other children were brought by an older sister or brother. A few parents stayed, sitting next to their children on the floor. The number of people overflowed the children's section, but nobody seemed to mind. Everyone was smiling and savoring the aura of holiday spirit.

"Courtney!" Ashley's voice rose over the increasing commotion of voices in the shop.

As Ashley rushed to the door to greet her friend, who wore a backpack that was a smaller version of her brother's, Rebecca peeked out of the back room. Her mob cap sat atop a white wig, and she adjusted gold-rimmed glasses.

"You'd think they hadn't seen each other in a year," she said as the two girls began chattering like squirrels.

"Hi, Mrs. Fisher!" Courtney called as she pulled off her backpack and pushed up her glasses. "Do you have any other antlers I can wear?"

"Sorry," Mary said, "I don't."

"I got them over at the dollar store," Ashley said. "I thought you were going to have your mother take you over to get some too."

"I had an extra violin lesson because school's out, so we didn't have time." Courtney spoke with frustration. "One of these days, Mom is going to learn that school break means a break from lessons."

Ashley laughed. "You know you enjoy the lessons."

"I do, but…" She glanced at Mary. "I wish I had antlers like yours, Ashley."

"There are the antlers you got for Gus," Mary said.

That suggestion set girls to giggling as they scurried to find a place where they could sit together on the floor. Ashley pulled out the small antlers, and Courtney put them on her wrist, making them dance until both girls were laughing so hard they had to lean against each other to keep from falling over.

The door opened again, and Courtney's older brother, Brian, walked in. His shoulders still slouched, and Mary realized the only time she'd seen him standing up straight was on the basketball court. He scanned the shop, then shouted, "Courtney!"

Every head turned toward him, and he put his head down as he rushed over to where his sister sat. In a softer voice, he said, "I asked you to wait for me at the store."

"You knew where I was going."

"Yes, but…Don't run off like that again." He shrugged and walked out of the children's area.

"Are you staying for the reading, Brian?" Mary asked as she offered him a cookie. She wanted to commiserate with him about having a child wander away without letting anyone know where he was going, but the incident with Jack in Jordan Marsh's large department store had been enough years ago that Brian would consider it ancient history. He probably didn't even remember the name Jordan Marsh in Downtown Crossing in Boston.

He took an oatmeal-raisin cookie instead of one of the decorated ones. "I guess so. Mom is over at the church. She said she's got to practice for the candlelight service tonight." He grimaced. "I don't know why. She plays the same songs every year."

"I'm sure she wants to make sure she's familiar with the music."

"Yeah, that's my mother. The perfectionist."

Mary hoped that wasn't anything other than normal adolescent irritation she heard in his voice. She couldn't forget how his face had fallen when his mother suggested at church that he should have taken the shot himself instead of letting a teammate win the glory of sinking the winning basket. The Flanagans wanted to give their children every opportunity, and the kids would come to appreciate that eventually. Or so she hoped.

Brian wandered over to sit near the holiday table with the other teens who'd come with their younger siblings. He set his backpack on the floor between his feet. As he listened to the others chatter with as much excitement as Ashley and Courtney, the drawn lines on his face eased.

Mary was glad to see that. He must have been terrified to find his sister had left without telling him. Mary had been when she discovered Jack had slipped away in order to ride up and down on the escalators. Even many years later, her heart still beat a bit faster at the memory.

She looked back at the children and saw Gus had found the perfect seat on Ashley's lap. She had her arms around him, and Mary guessed he was purring loudly. The nearby children gave him an occasional pat, but Ashley made sure he wasn't overwhelmed. Beside her, Courtney was admiring the small antlers on her wrist as she folded her arms over her backpack. She leaned over to whisper in Ashley's ear, and both girls giggled.

Rebecca's signal that she was ready to start caught Mary's eye.

Picking her way carefully through the crowd so she didn't step on any little fingers, Mary said, "Welcome to

Mary's Mystery Bookshop's Christmas Eve party. How about a big round of applause for Ivy Bay's Mrs. Santa Claus?" She clapped loudly, and the children and their parents and siblings joined in.

The children's faces glowed with excitement and anticipation and the wonder of the season as Rebecca emerged from the back room in her costume. Her full red skirt was held out by crinolines that rustled when she walked. A starched apron was decorated with appliqued candy canes and gingerbread men. Lace trimmed her crinolines, the hems of her sleeves, and the high collar that closed with buttons that looked like silver gum drops. It was a beautiful costume, and Mary wondered where Rebecca had gotten it. Not from a store shelf, she guessed. It fit too perfectly to be anything other than handmade.

Every eye was focused on Rebecca as she sat in the rocking chair and opened the book that had been waiting on the table beside it. She began to read, and the familiar words brought smiles throughout the shop. Not just from the children, but from everyone. Sudden tears filled Mary's eyes as she remembered her dear late John once saying that adults became children again at Christmastime because they found it easier to believe in miracles.

Rebecca read:

The moon on the breast of the new-fallen snow
Gave the luster of mid-day to objects below,
When, what to my wondering eyes should appear,
But a miniature sleigh, and eight tiny reindeer,

With a little old driver, so lively and quick,
I knew in a moment it must be St. Nick.

Bells jingled merrily in Courtney's hands. The listeners loved it.

Except for Gus.

At the strange sound, he sprang out of Ashley's arms. With a yowl, he sped across the room.

Everyone burst into laughter at the same time. Gus tried to slow, but skidded into Brian's backpack. It toppled over, and the top gaped open.

Mary rushed to pick up Gus so she could calm him down. At the same time, Brian grabbed for his backpack, shutting the top, but not quickly enough. As Mary bent to scoop up her cat, light sparkled off something in Brian's backpack.

Something arched and white and gold. Something that looked like porcelain wings that were the right size for the angel in Grace Church's beautiful Nativity set. The angel who had lost her wings.

✳ Chapter Twenty-Two

Brian didn't met Mary's eyes as she lifted Gus into her arms. Did he think she'd point out that he had the angel's wings *now*? When the shop was filled with children and their families and Rebecca was in the middle of reading the Christmas poem?

Mary walked back to the counter and set Gus on it as Rebecca said with a smile, "I guess we have one creature stirring here."

More laughter filled the shop, and Gus protested by trying to squirm out of Mary's arms.

Rebecca went back to reading the poem. She smiled at Mary and winked over the youngsters' heads.

Mary smiled back as she held Gus on the counter. She didn't let him scamper away, and he slowly grew still as she petted him.

"Good boy," she whispered softly enough so her voice wouldn't intrude on Rebecca's spirited reading.

Anyone who chanced to hear Mary wouldn't guess that her words were not meant only to console. She was grateful

279 ✶ THE LOST NOEL

to Gus for helping her discover a clue. She wasn't quite sure what having the angel's wings in his backpack meant yet, but she suspected Brian Flanagan might know more about the missing costumes than he'd let on.

He'd been at Grace Church the night the costumes vanished. He had been even quieter than usual then and at the Sunday service. He hadn't let that backpack out of his sight any time she'd seen him since Wednesday. She needed to be patient, though. Now wasn't the time to speak to him about the angel's wings.

As soon as Rebecca finished the poem to grateful applause, she urged their guests to enjoy the cookies and hot chocolate. The kids jumped up, eager to do so. The teens did as well and hurried to where the cookies and hot chocolate waited on the counter.

Except Brian. He went to his sister and grabbed her arm. "C'mon. We have to go," he said as Mary walked closer with a plate of cookies.

"But I want a cookie and some hot chocolate," Courtney said. "They've got mini-marshmallows."

He glanced at his watch. "You know Mom will be done in ten minutes."

"I could drive you over," Mary said as she held out the plate to Courtney, who took a cookie, and to Brian, who didn't. "That way, you can enjoy some hot chocolate and still get there on time. And not get wet." She glanced at the window where rain ran down the glass.

"See? Thanks, Mrs. Fisher." Courtney hurried over to get a cup of hot chocolate from Rebecca before she went to sit beside Ashley, who was feeding small pieces of a sugar cookie to Gus.

Brian went back to sit with the teens. He didn't talk to them, and he didn't look at anyone. He was the picture of misery...as he had been all week except when he was on the basketball court.

Mary was determined to get the answer on the way over to Grace Church. She knew she'd have a very short time because it would take only minutes for her to drive over there and park. She needed to make every minute count.

* * *

"We're hanging up stockings tonight," Courtney said from the back seat of Mary's car. "Before we come to the candlelight service. Then when we get home, I'm going to put out some of the cookies I made yesterday for Santa. Do you think he likes coconut cookies or date nut bars better?"

Mary didn't have a chance to answer as Courtney continued on, chattering like a magpie. The little girl was excited about Christmas, and she couldn't sit still, in spite of her seatbelt.

In the passenger seat, Brian said nothing. He stared out the window. As soon as they reached the Grace Church parking lot, he unsnapped his seatbelt.

"C'mon, Court," he said, opening his door as Mary put the car in park. "Tell Mrs. Fisher thanks." He jumped out. "Merry Christmas."

Mary unlatched her own seatbelt and got out of the car. She opened the back door and offered her hand to Courtney.

"That's okay," Brian said. "I'll take her inside."

"That's okay," Mary said without a hint of emotion in her voice. "I need to go inside."

She could see the teen struggling not to ask her why she had to go into the church. His mouth pursed, and she guessed he longed for a polite way to tell her to get lost. Then his shoulders sagged, and he seemed to shrink in on himself.

He said nothing as they walked into the sanctuary where Mavis was arranging her music by the organ. She must have heard their footsteps because she turned. Her eyes grew round when they met Mary's.

"Mary! What are you doing here?" She eyed her kids. "I hope they didn't pester you for a ride over here."

"No, I offered. They wanted to stay for refreshments after the reading, but they didn't want to keep you waiting." She kept her smile in place, but her eyes cut to Brian who had walked to the front of the church. Mavis's smile faded as she looked from Mary to Brian and back. "Is something wrong?"

"Brian?" Mary prompted.

He hung his head even lower.

"Brian, please answer Mrs. Fisher," Mavis said. "If you've gotten into some sort of trouble at the bookshop, tell me. You know how important it is for you to keep your nose clean if you want to get that scholarship."

Mary held up her hands. "Mavis, it's nothing like that. Brian hasn't done anything wrong at my shop." She looked at the boy. "Brian, why don't you show us what you've got hidden in your backpack?"

No one spoke for a long minute, then Brian dropped to sit on a front pew. He stared at the Nativity set on the baptismal font.

"Brian, it's going to be all right," Mary said.

He didn't answer.

Courtney ran to stand beside him, her eyes wide. "What's in your backpack? Is it a surprise?"

He groaned and hid his face in his hands.

Mavis asked, "What's going on, Mary? What's wrong?"

Instead of answering her, Mary walked to where Brian sat. He was a good kid, and what he'd done must have been eating him up inside. She made sure her voice held no hint of any emotion but kindness as she asked, "Brian, you've been holding on to this secret for almost a week, haven't you?"

"Yes," he said in barely more than a whisper.

"And that secret has been making you miserable."

"Yes, and I don't want to keep this a secret any longer." He raised his head, pain filling his eyes.

"You don't have to." Mary kept her voice calm. "If you want to share it now, what better place than here in our church with your mother and sister who love you, no matter what."

"No matter what," Courtney echoed.

He looked at his sister, ruffled her hair, then stood. "Okay."

He put his backpack on a pew and unzipped the top compartment. He lifted out the broken angel's wings and placed them in Mary's hand.

"I'm sorry." His voice cracked on the two words. He drew in a deep breath, then words exploded out of him as swiftly as Courtney had talked in the car. "Not just for breaking the angel. That was a mistake, and I feel awful about it. But I'm sorry, too, that I took the costumes."

Mavis drew in a sharp breath.

"Actually I didn't take them," he said, rubbing his hands together nervously. "I hid them."

As Mavis asked him where, Mary recalled the trail of glitter that had led right up the center aisle to the baptismal font. That night, she had assumed that Ashley's halo had been shedding its glitter, but that had been impossible. Ashley hadn't been in that part of the sanctuary until they heard Dorothy using the vacuum.

"You hid them under the board holding the Nativity set, didn't you?" Mary asked, astounded how close she and Ashley had been to the costumes right from the beginning!

That day, she'd noticed many clues that the costumes had never left the church. Nobody who could have taken them and snuck away while everyone was looking for them. Kip and Luis had been working both outside and inside, so nobody could have slipped past them. Neither Dennis nor Luis had been inside alone without Kip. Abbie had been in Rhode Island. Instead of looking at the facts right in front of her, she'd let herself get sidetracked by the assumption that a single culprit took the sheep, the costumes, and the posters.

"Yes," Brian said.

His mother made a small moan, and he held out his hand to her. Mavis came forward and took it.

Brian took a deep breath, then said, "I put them in the baptismal font because it was the only thing big enough to hold them." Mary could see the burden come off his shoulders as he owned up to the truth. "How did you know?"

She motioned for him and his mother to sit in the pews. Once they were seated, she said, "Once I saw the broken wings in your backpack and you tried to hide them, I suspected that the angel must have been broken when you moved the board holding the Nativity. You found the wings, but not the angel which somehow ended up *inside* the stable behind the manger."

"I didn't look there," he said.

"But by then other people were arriving, so you hid the wings in your backpack."

"I planned to glue them back on, but I never had a chance." He shifted his gaze to his mother. "There's always someone in the church on the days leading up to Christmas. The one time I used your key, Mom, and got in here alone, I only had time before someone else arrived to straighten up the Nativity in the hope that nobody would notice it'd been moved."

"That's when you moved the angel that I'd left looking at the altar?" Mary asked.

He nodded. "I was really scared that someone would notice the angel wasn't in the right position. Then they might have poked around and found the costumes."

"We should have found them that night," Mary said. She didn't add that she had been so caught up in the drama that she hadn't stopped to realize that Ashley had, by that time, been only in the two storage rooms.

Mavis's face grew paler with each word, and Courtney's eyes got wider as she looked in disbelief at her older brother.

"I can't believe this." Mavis moaned. "These are our friends and our church family. I can't believe you'd do this, Brian."

"Will my brother go to jail?" asked Courtney with sudden tears welling up in her eyes as she looked at the big brother she adored.

"No," Mary said gently. "He did something wrong, but he's admitted what he did and said he was sorry. Actually, Courtney, you are the person who offered me the first clue, even though I didn't realize it then, that Brian might have taken the costumes."

"Me?" She dashed away tears with the back of her hand.

"Did Brian help you sneak your costume out of the church the day before the others went missing?"

She nodded, and more tears fell as she looked at Brian. "I didn't mean to tell, Brian. I only told Ashley because she was upset that her costume was gone. I thought maybe she could come over and wear my costume sometimes. I wanted to make her feel better."

"I know." He ruffled her hair, and she grimaced. "I love you, squirt."

She flung her arms around him, and he gave her a big hug as she said, "I love you, too, bigfoot."

Mavis stood. Anger sparked in her eyes as she said, "You haven't answered my questions, Brian. How could you do such a thing? How could you ruin everything so many people had worked hard for?"

"I don't think," Mary said, rising and putting a hand on Mavis's arm, "that Brian intended to hurt anyone. I think he was simply desperate to halt the living Nativity."

"But why?"

Brian got up, his shoulders straight and his gaze steady as he looked from his mother to Mary. "Simple, Mom. I didn't want to get dressed up in that costume and play Joseph. Not one night, not two nights, not any night."

"But you could have told me."

"I tried, Mom. I tried over and over, but you didn't hear me. You know I hate being in the spotlight. Even when I play basketball, I don't like to be the center of attention. I put up with it then, but it's tough." Taking a step toward his mother, he held out his hands palm up to her. "I know how proud you and Dad have been that I was chosen to play Joseph. I know you thought that the living Nativity would be the perfect thing to add to my list of activities for college applications, but I..." He blinked back tears. "I tried, but..."

No one spoke as he fought for the right words.

"I freaked out," Brian finally said. "There's no other way to say it. I freaked out. All I could think of was doing what I had to keep the living Nativity from happening. I didn't want to damage anything, so I took the costumes. It wasn't a good decision, and I know now that I hurt a bunch of people.

I'm really sorry." He looked at Mary. "I'm really, really sorry. Please tell Mrs. Emerson that I didn't mean to cause her any distress. It's just that I— I— I couldn't stand up there, night after night, having people staring at me."

"I could tell her, Brian," Mary said, "but it'd be better if you did."

"I'll call her as soon as I get home." He glanced at his mother. "If I still have phone privileges."

Mavis's mouth was taut. "*That* we will discuss at home, but Mary, he will call Betty and apologize." She shook her head. "I wish I could understand why you'd do this, Brian."

"You'd understand if you'd listen to me, Mom. Really listen. When I tell you that I don't feel comfortable doing something, it'd be great if you'd listen. Just once, I'd like you and Dad to appreciate what I do without pushing me to do more."

"Me too!" Courtney added.

"I love basketball, but I hate the idea of standing out on the church lawn and having everyone look at me."

"I love the violin," his sister said, "but I don't like playing the organ. I'm sorry, Mom. You love playing the organ, but I don't."

"And if you could stop mentioning a scholarship with every other breath—"

"Or the Cape Cod Youth Orchestra." Courtney smiled up at her brother. "I want to join it, but can't it be okay if I'm not the first chair? At least to begin with?"

"If you could be proud of me–of us." Brian corrected himself as he put his arm around his sister's shoulders. "If you could be proud of us without pushing us to do things we aren't interested in, that would be the best Christmas present ever."

Mavis paused. Then she held out her arms and drew her children to her. As she hugged them, she said, "Of course. You know that your father and I only want the very best for you."

"And for us to be happy," he said.

"And for all of us to be happy." She smiled as Brian and Courtney grinned at her. "I'll do my best, my dears, but I've only ever wanted the best for you."

"We know that," Brian said, hugging her again before he went to the baptismal font.

His long arms easily allowed him to grasp each side of the board beneath the Nativity set and lift it off the baptismal font. He placed the board on the floor before reaching in to lift out the costumes, one by one. They were wrinkled from being stuffed into the font.

He handed the top one to Mary. She shook it out and draped it over the front of the first pew. As he drew out each one, either Mary or Mavis would take it and repeat the motion until the front of the pew was a rainbow of vivid colors.

"They don't look too much the worse for wear," Mary said.

"Then there's no reason not to have the living Nativity tonight, is there?" Mavis asked, looking at her son.

Mary said, "If we can get in touch with everyone, we should be able to pull it together. We've got three or four hours, and I know my son or son-in-law will step in to play Joseph."

"That won't be necessary," Brian said as he squared his shoulders. "I will hate every minute of it, but the best way I can show everyone I'm sorry for what I've done is to stand up and be Joseph."

Mary smiled broadly as Mavis gazed at her son with more pride than when he sank basket after basket at the game on Saturday night. Mary wasn't sure how long they would have stood there, grinning at each other, if Courtney hadn't spoken up.

"Mom, can I call Ashley and tell her we're both going to be angels tonight?" the little girl asked.

Brian pulled out his cell phone and handed it to her. "That's a good first call."

Mary heard Courtney giggling with Ashley as she went to get her own phone out of her purse. She sent up a prayer to God, thanking Him for how He had done more than help her find the costumes today. He had healed the hearts of a family who needed it the most.

* * *

Mary stood with her grandchildren on the sidewalk in front of Grace Church. They held their breath as Luis flipped the switch to light the living Nativity. Bright lights illuminated Kip's stable, and a fake star blinked overhead. The real stars were hidden by the low clouds, but at least the rain had stopped.

Gasps and applause came from the spectators who had come from both the candlelight service and the lighting contest in the Sea Breezes neighborhood.

The living Nativity had come together so quickly that Mary had sensed God's help in reaching the cast members as well as Luis. He'd agreed to leave the final night of the lighting contest and delay the announcement of which house had collected the most "votes" so he could come to the church to make sure that the lighting for the scene was perfect.

In the center of the stable, Brian Flanagan stood behind the manger. He gazed down at the doll that served as the stand-in for Baby Jesus. He had apologized to the other volunteers, and they had forgiven him. The night was too cold for any real infant to be placed on the hay. The girl playing the Virgin Mary gazed at the doll with adoration.

On the far side of the living Nativity, standing out of the glow where they would be invisible unless someone looked closely, the members of PAP kept a close eye on the sheep, two chickens, and a cow. The animals were penned securely, so they couldn't escape and wander out into the parade of cars inching past the church.

Luis kept to the shadows as he walked to where Mary stood. "Who would have guessed the living Nativity would ever happen?" he asked.

"I had to have faith it would."

"Faith is a powerful tool."

She smiled. "That it is. Thank you for coming over tonight."

"It's my pleasure. Isn't it lovely? My lighting contest brings the light to a cold winter night, but this scene reminds us of the true reason for the holiday season, the true source of the light within each of us."

She smiled. "Do you want me to call you when we're ready to shut down for the night?"

"Not necessary. I showed Kip and Pastor Miles how to turn the whole shebang off with one switch." He stuck his hands in his coat pocket. "I'd better get out of here and back to the lighting contest." He grimaced. "And away from that sheep. It poked its head out of the pen like it knew I'd back away because I'm allergic to it."

She laughed. "Sheep aren't that smart, or so Ken Gomes tells me."

"Maybe this one is the exception. Oh, by the way, I thought you'd like to know who's in the lead–by a wide margin–to collect the most canned goods and win the lighting contest."

"Who's that?"

"Jason and Patti Fernandes. I don't know what's gotten into Jason, but he left notes taped to the trash cans he picked up today and asked people to make a donation to the food bank and come to see the lights."

Mary smiled. God had already reached out to touch Jason's heart and help him enjoy the holiday. Whether it was through Pastor Miles or another way, God's gifts of love and grace were wondrous.

After Luis left, Mary looked for her sister. She walked along the sidewalk and saw Dorothy coming purposefully toward her.

"Hi, Dorothy," Mary said. "It's a lovely Christmas Eve, isn't it?"

"If it would snow, it'd be perfect. And it *is* Christmas, so…" Dorothy smiled broadly. "I must concede that—this time—you beat me in solving the mystery. Well done, Mary."

"Thank you. I appreciated your insights into this puzzle."

"You did?"

"Of course. Sometimes I find the best thing I can do is talk over a mystery with someone else who looks at the clues in a different way than I do."

"Then I really did help?"

Mary hesitated. She didn't want to say that Dorothy's insights had led her in the wrong direction more often than not. That would hurt Dorothy's feelings.

"Everyone I talk to helps me in solving mysteries." It was a diplomatic answer, and she hoped Dorothy would hear the words that way.

She needn't have worried, because Dorothy's smile grew even wider. "I'm glad to hear that. Maybe next time, I'll beat you to the punch and solve the mystery first."

"Maybe you will."

With another "Merry Christmas," Mary continued her search for her sister. She found her on the cross street, watching the cars drive slowly past the living Nativity.

"You did good, Bets."

"It might be for only one night, but it was worth the work," Betty said with a broad smile.

"There must already be several cases of food to be donated to the self-help cupboard in the boxes by the church door."

Betty lowered her voice and asked, "How did you solve this mystery, Mary? How did you figure out that Brian had hidden the costumes?"

"You can thank Gus."

"Gus?"

Mary started to explain, then simply smiled. "God works through all of us, whether we have two legs or four."

Epilogue

O n Christmas morning, Mary woke to the beauty of gently falling snow. She looked out her window to discover that almost half a foot of snow had accumulated overnight.

The village of Ivy Bay could have been posing for a Currier and Ives picture with the roofs topped by fresh snow, and the trees outlined in white. The pines looked as if angels had sprinkled them with confectioner's sugar. Even the marsh wore a light mantle of snow on the reeds.

Dressing quickly, she rushed down the stairs. She followed the scents of coffee and toasted raisin bread to the kitchen. She could hear her children and their families making plans to go outside and play in the snow later. Snow wasn't unusual in Chicago on Christmas, but it was in Massachusetts, so they intended to enjoy it before it melted away.

A chorus of "Merry Christmas!" greeted her when she walked into the kitchen. She shared kisses and hugs and thanked God for the most perfect present: having her family together for Christmas.

She poured a cup of coffee but had time only for a sip before the front door opened. She looked out into the hallway to see Evan stamping snow off his boots before he followed his family into the house.

"Mom, where's your shovel?" he called. "I'll get your walk cleared."

"Later," Betty said, holding out her hands for his coat. "Now that everyone is here, the snow can wait. Not much sense in shoveling until the snow is done falling."

"And we want to look at the tree!" Luke was almost jumping up and down in his excitement. "Wait till you see my…" He clamped his hands over his mouth, but his eyes twinkled like twin stars.

Mary took his hand and walked into the living room. Someone had already come in and turned on the tree's lights. That emphasized how the tree had been flattened on one side, but she didn't pay any attention to that. Instead she looked at the top of the tree where a wooden lobster in a Santa hat brought smiles to each of them. Then she admired the ornaments that had been hung for each member of their families. The ornaments had been made in secret yesterday and given to either Mary or Betty to place on the tree.

Each ornament symbolized a special blessing in the past year that the person making it was grateful for. Mary and Betty hadn't asked what each ornament was intended to mean. They placed them on the tree, being careful not to disturb the presents underneath the branches.

The families gathered around the tree and decided that they would go from youngest to oldest with the ornaments before they opened a single gift.

"That means I'm first!" Luke stood and plucked his ornament off the tree. It was shaped like a soccer ball, which surprised nobody. "What do you think it means?" he asked. "I'm not telling. Right, Grandma?"

Mary smiled and hugged her grandson. "That's right."

"But you have to tell us when we guess right," Daisy said, laughing. "We aren't like Grandma who can sort through clues and come up with the right answer every time."

"Not every time," Mary said. "Trust me. I've chased a lot of red herrings this past week."

"Still, you got to the right answer in the end."

"She sure did," Betty said. "Just in time too."

Mary's smile grew wider with each ornament taken off the tree and displayed for everyone to guess. Some were simple like Luke's soccer finals, but others weren't as easy. Chad's almost stumped everyone until Lizzie guessed it was supposed to represent the new gas grill he'd gotten in the summer and had used with the youth group at their church.

Eventually, after Betty's turn, a single ornament was left. No one claimed it, so Mary took it off the tree.

"It's a Christmas tree that's flat on one side." Mary laughed. "This must be Gus's ornament. Who made it for him?"

Everyone looked at everyone else, but nobody answered.

"C'mon," Allison said. "Someone made it."

"Maybe Gus did." Emma's eyes were wide.

"I can't imagine him using scissors and glue."

"He's got claws," Emma said. "He could have used those."

Everyone laughed, and Mary glanced at her sister. She guessed Betty had made the simple ornament because she considered Gus a part of their family now. Mary wanted to give her sister a hug, but that might reveal her suspicions to the others. Instead, she smiled at Betty, who had opened her home to both Mary and a stray cat.

"But how is that a blessing?" Luke asked.

"He's blessed that we forgave him." Betty's stern tone was contradicted by her sparkling eyes.

"And he brought us the blessing of this new tradition." Mary gazed around the room, so glad that they could be together on Christmas morning. She hoped it would happen again soon. "Anyone want coffee?"

"Me," said Jack. "I'm still short a night's sleep after setting a trap with Mom."

"Me too," Lizzie said. "Not the trap part, but the coffee part."

Luke jumped to his feet and stared at them as if they'd lost their minds. "Aren't we going to open our presents first?"

Everyone laughed, and Chad grabbed his son and tickled him until they were both weak with laughter. Only then did they start handing out gifts. They took turns opening the gifts, so each person could see how the recipient of their gift reacted.

"Here's one for Aunt Betty and another for Mom that are both the same size. And they're from each other." Jack held them out. "Why don't you each open them together?"

"Why not?" said Mary. "Shall we go at the same time?"

"On the count of three," Betty said. "One, two…"

"Three!" shouted the grandchildren.

Paper ripped, and Mary and Betty looked at what they held and then at each other. Both broke out into laughter as they raised their gifts so the whole family could see them.

They each held the same book, which they'd both been eager to read.

More laughter filled the room along with Christmas joy when the torn paper on the floor rustled, and Gus peeked out to give them a big meow.

"That's his way of saying merry Christmas!" Mary said.

"Merry Christmas, Gus," everyone replied in unison.

Sign up for the

Guideposts Fiction Newsletter

and stay up-to-date on the Guideposts fiction you love!

You'll get sneak peeks of new releases, hear from
authors of your favorite books, and even
receive special offers just for you.

And it's free!

Just go to

Guideposts.org/newsletters

today to sign up.

A Note from the Editors

. . . .

We hope you enjoy Merry Mysteries, created by the Books and Inspirational Media Division of Guideposts, a nonprofit organization that touches millions of lives every day through products and services that inspire, encourage, help you grow in your faith, and celebrate God's love in every aspect of your daily life.

Thank you for making a difference with your purchase of this book, which helps fund our many outreach programs to military personnel, prisons, hospitals, nursing homes, and educational institutions. To learn more, visit GuidepostsFoundation.org.

We also maintain many useful and uplifting online resources. Visit Guideposts.org to read true stories of hope and inspiration, access OurPrayer network, sign up for free newsletters, download free e-books, join our Facebook community, and follow our stimulating blogs.

To learn about other Guideposts publications, including the best-selling devotional *Daily Guideposts*, go to ShopGuideposts.org, call (800) 932-2145, or write to Guideposts, PO Box 5815, Harlan, Iowa 51593.